HIS WIFE'S SISTER

AJ WILLS

PROLOGUE

July 2000

I'M SO SCARED I can hardly breathe. I want to yell at the top of my lungs. But I can't. I'm frozen, cowering in the corner with my head in my hands, the floor cold and gritty. The man, I don't know his name, smells like he's been working all day in the sun and needs a shower. I can still smell him now, the lingering stink of his hand over my mouth as he pulled me from my sleeping bag, stuck in my throat.

I don't understand what's happening, but I know it's not good. I want to go home to be with Mum and Dad.

He's whistling to a tune I don't recognise on the radio, his thick, curly black hair bobbing up and down in time to the beat.

'All right back there?' he asks cheerily.

A lump forms in my throat like I've swallowed a marble. I want to go home, for this nightmare to end.

I didn't know I could miss my parents so much. What if I never see them again? I sniff back the snot running from my nose and try to think happy thoughts.

The van finally comes to a stop, and as he kills the engine, a chill runs down my spine. He gets out. I hear the crunch of his footsteps. The rear doors fly open, and as he snatches my ankle, I finally scream. But it's too late. There's nothing around us but trees. We're in the middle of nowhere where nobody can hear me, and there's no one to see.

He stands me on my bare feet and grabs a handful of my hair, pulling me towards the shadow of a dark building. I stumble along, watching the ground race under my feet. Up four steps. Along a narrow path. In through a door. Lights flash on, blinding me.

He pulls me into a room with a red, floral carpet that's soft on my soles. His hand is rough on the back of my neck as he pushes me down a flight of wooden steps into the dark.

I'm falling, losing balance, and hit the cold ground hard. I cry out in pain. He lands on top of me, rolling me onto a thin mattress, his body pressing against mine. I beg him to let me go, but he doesn't even look at me. His hand wraps around my wrists, and he yanks my arms above my head as I hear the sound of a heavy chain and feel cold metal against my skin.

It's clear now he plans to leave me here, in this dark pit with my hands chained to the wall, my shoulders aching from the awkward position he's put me in.

As much as I hate him, I don't want him to go.

'Please,' I cry, hot tears running down my cheeks, soaking into my pyjama top. 'Don't leave me.'

But he's already lumbering up the steps. He drops a hatch into place, and I'm plunged into total darkness.

I hold my breath as furniture scrapes across the floor above my head, and I listen to his footsteps pad across the floor. And then there is only silence and the galloping beat of my heart.

I know then that I am utterly alone. Nobody knows I'm here. The thought makes me shiver. I take a deep breath and scream until my throat is raw.

1

Damian stood squinting into the sun, his hand shading his eyes, seeking out April's yellow t-shirt or a glimpse of her long, russet hair amongst the hordes of excited children. He took a step to his right to see past the slide, ignoring the faint pangs of panic simmering in his chest. There were kids everywhere, running, jumping, climbing, chasing, screaming. But none of them were April.

'Stop kicking that ball,' he shouted at Dylan, every thud against the metal railings sending his irritation levels soaring.

Dylan stared at his father with a sulky pout. He scooped up his football and ran off to the other side of the playground.

Damian sighed. He loved his kids, but the school holidays were a trial. The thought of another five long weeks of full-time childcare, while he tried to run the business, filled him with dread. And it was only the beginning of the second week of the break.

The last time he'd seen April, she'd been on the roundabout squealing with delight as two older boys spun her faster. He'd only taken his eye off her for a second to check his emails on his phone. She couldn't have gone far. Christ, he'd drilled it into her not to wander off.

'April?' he shouted, trying not to sound anxious.

A group of young mothers sipping iced lattes looked up. He shot them a humourless smile, pushing away the dark thoughts. He was over-reacting. Nothing had happened to her.

'Dad...' Dylan's voice whined.

His son was trailing across the playground empty-handed, his bottom lip stuck out.

'Where's your ball?'

He pointed to a bushy horse chestnut tree, its leaves rustling in the gentle breeze. 'It's stuck.'

'Well, it's probably lost.' Even the tree's lowest branches were well out of Damian's reach.

Dylan's face crumpled.

'It's okay, we'll get you a new one.' Damian couldn't bear the thought of those disgusted looks he knew they'd attract from the self-righteous stay-at-home mums chatting around the edge of the play-ground with their fresh-from-the-salon haircuts and perfect teeth if Dylan had a full meltdown in public.

'I don't want a new one.'

Damian placed a fatherly arm around his shoulder. 'And maybe a new pair of football boots?' Lucia would kill him if she could hear him now. But what the hell, she wasn't here.

Dylan sniffed and wiped his sleeve across his nose. 'The silver ones?'

'Sure,' Damian said, hoping he didn't mean the expensive ones they'd admired in the window of the sports shop in town a few weeks ago. Money had been tight since he'd gone freelance, and Lucia had returned to her marketing job in London. They couldn't afford new football boots this month, especially as it meant they'd have to treat April as well.

'Really?' Dylan's face lit up.

He'd grown up so much in such a short time. It didn't seem long ago that they'd brought him home from the hospital strapped into his car seat, lost inside an enormous sleepsuit, feeling totally bewildered by the experience of bringing a new life into the world. The first few days they'd spent marvelling at his tiny fingers and toes, his wrinkly, pink skin and his minuscule fingernails that left nasty scratches across his face, wondering what they were supposed to do with him. Dylan was older now, but parenthood was still a trial.

'Can we go and buy them now?'

'Let's get an ice cream first.'

'Dad, please?' Dylan dragged out the syllables in a pitiful whine.

'Ice cream first, then we'll see. Have you seen your sister?'

'Nah,' Dylan said, kicking a stone.

'April!' Damian shouted again, scanning a meandering path that ran through the park adjacent to the kids' playground. It was conceivable that April had gone chasing a squirrel or a dog. She loved animals, maybe more than people. It would have only taken a big pair of round eyes and a furry coat to lure her away.

Damian's stomach flipped. Oh God, what if she'd been taken? He swallowed hard, his throat dry. Should he call the police? No, they'd think he was over-reacting, although with their family history perhaps they wouldn't be surprised. Come on, lightning doesn't strike twice, he told himself.

When his phone buzzed in his hand, his thumb automatically moved towards the little red symbol planning to dump the call, until he noticed it was Lucia. She always phoned around four; usually the last of several calls during the day checking up on him. He didn't think she entirely trusted him to look after the kids while she was at work.

'Hi, love,' he said, a tremor in his voice. 'How's your afternoon?' He forced a smile, even though she couldn't see his face.

Out of the corner of his eye, he saw Dylan's ball drop out of the tree and roll away. At least that would save them a trip into town for new boots.

'We're just at the park,' he continued. 'It's such a nice afternoon I thought I'd get the kids out of the house for a few hours.'

He was gabbling.

When Lucia didn't say anything, he kept talking. 'Dylan lost his ball in a tree, but he's got it back now, and April's been making new friends on the roundabout. I was just about to take them for an ice cream. It's the only way I'm going to get them out of here.' He laughed, but it sounded hollow.

Come on, April.

'Are you okay?' he asked, sensing something, but not sure what. 'Has Helen said something again?'

Helen Flannerty, one of the senior account managers at Lucia's firm, was always quick with a put-down or sarcastic comment. It wouldn't have been the first time she'd reduced Lucia to tears.

'No.' Lucia's voice was husky with emotion. Had she been crying?

April burst out of a red, plastic tunnel, screaming, her eyes screwed tightly shut, and her face flushed red.

'It's April. She's hurt herself. I'll call you right back,' Damian said, about to hang up.

The three mothers with iced lattes turned to Damian, looking horrified, watching to see what he would do.

'They've found her.' Lucia's voice was barely a whisper. 'I've just heard from the police.'

Two of the mums trotted towards April. They crouched down to her level as she lifted a leg to show them the blood dripping from a nasty graze to her knee.

'Found who?' Damian asked, filtering out the shrill noise in the playground to focus on his wife's voice.

'Mara.'

Even though Damian had been anticipating this moment for nearly twenty years, it still caught him off guard.

'Lucia, I'm so sorry,' he said, tripping out his practised platitudes.

It was a miracle she hadn't been found before, and he'd started to wonder if they would ever find her body.

'You don't understand,' Lucia said.

April had stopped crying, seemingly revelling in the attention of the women who'd run to her aid.

'Mara's not dead. They've found her alive.'

2

Damian had so many questions racing through his head as he pulled up outside the station opposite a snake of queuing taxis, but most of all, he wondered what Mara looked like after all these years. He thought he had a vague recollection of her from school, but couldn't be sure he'd not superimposed phantom memories from Lucia's photos onto fragments of his own.

He remembered her as a goofy-looking kid with blonde bunches and a crooked smile. Nothing extraordinary. But he was only fourteen when he'd last seen her alive, just another face among the new intake of year sevens. He hardly even knew Lucia at the time, and she was in his class. That was until the day Mara went missing, and the whole town went crazy.

All the photos of Mara had given him the mistaken impression he knew her better than he did. He'd seen her as a baby and as a snotty-nosed toddler, playing on the beach on holiday and dressed in a frumpy-looking grey pinafore dress on her first day at school. He'd seen pictures of her at Christmas and at birthday parties, wearing fancy dress costumes and blowing out candles. But it was an image taken at school in front of a mottled screen, where Mara's tie was slightly askew, and her over-sized blazer swamped her like a hand-me-down, that was most familiar to him. It had been the poster image in the 'Find Mara' campaign in the weeks and months after she went missing, and the one used widely in the press, even though it wasn't the most flattering picture of her. Her attention seemed to have been caught by something going on behind the photographer. You could see her fixed grin starting to slide and her eyes shifting away from the camera.

She would be thirty by now. Damian had no idea how she'd changed, whether she was tall, short, fat, thin, with long hair or short. The only clue to how her appearance might have altered had come nine years ago. On the tenth anniversary of Mara's disappearance, they'd commissioned a specialist company to age her image using advanced computer software in the hope it might throw up some new clues about her whereabouts. They'd elongated her face, thinned her nose and added some creases around her eyes. With a few mouse clicks, they'd transformed her from a girl into a young woman. The effect was startling. It was like looking at a stranger and reminded them both that the old Mara was lost forever. And although the enhanced image had been featured by several news outlets and shared widely on social media, it yielded no fresh leads, only a handful of crank calls and messages.

Lucia emerged from the station into the late afternoon sunshine among a herd of weary-looking passengers. She spotted Damian parked on double yellows and skittered across the road with the Gucci handbag he'd bought her for Christmas slung over her shoulder.

He snatched a kiss as she slid into the car. Her hands were clammy. 'Are you okay?'

'Yeah.' A lump rose and fell in her throat as she swallowed. A single tear rolled down her cheek. 'I'm sorry,' she said.

'You should be happy.'

'They're happy tears,' she sobbed, flapping a hand in front of her face as if she was trying to fan them away. 'I'm just worried I'm going to wake up and none of this is real.'

'What did the police say?'

'Only that a woman found her wandering lost in the woods.

They're going to tell me more at the station. They want me to make a formal identification.'

Damian hadn't considered the possibility that the woman who'd been found might not be Mara, that it could be a cruel hoax or even a case of mistaken identity.

'Maybe you shouldn't get your hopes up until we're certain it's her,' he said. 'I don't want you to be disappointed.'

'Just drive, will you.'

Damian put the car into gear and pulled out into the rush hour traffic, crawling slowly through the town until they hit the dual carriageway.

'Where are the kids?'

'I've left them with Rose.'

Lucia relaxed a little. 'What did you tell them?'

'That we had to go and sort out something important.'

'Were they upset?'

April had thrown a minor tantrum when Damian told her he was leaving them with Rose, but there was no point upsetting Lucia. She'd felt enough guilt about returning to work and leaving the childcare to Damian. 'No, they were fine,' he lied.

'I'd better call them.' Lucia reached into her bag.

'Leave them. Rose'll think you're checking up on her.'

'I am.'

'Lucia, don't.'

'Oh my God, Damian, did you leave an Epipen?'

'Of course, I did,' he said, trying to recall if he'd remembered to tell Rose about the two auto-injectors in the drawer in the kitchen.

'Did you show her how to use them?'

'I've shown her before. Relax, nothing's going to happen. And besides, April knows what to do. She's been practising on her dolls.'

'April's five years old. You can't trust Dylan's life to his younger sister.' She sighed and cupped her forehead in her hand.

'Stop worrying. Everything's going to be fine.'

THE POLICE STATION was a grim-looking red brick building off the ring road. Damian had barely pulled up outside and yanked on the handbrake before Lucia had flung open the door and rushed towards the entrance. He caught up with her as she bounded breathlessly into a reception area.

'My name's Lucia Sitwell. You've found my sister, Mara,' she said, reverting inexplicably to her maiden name.

The receptionist smiled, made them fill in their details in a book on the counter and gave them visitor passes to hang around their necks.

Two minutes later, they were being ushered along a corridor and into a simple office where a middle-aged officer in uniform and a younger woman in civilian clothes and with long, jet black hair were waiting.

'Please, sit down, Mrs Caslocke,' the officer said.

'Can I see her?'

He glanced at the other woman, who was sitting with a welcoming smile plastered across her face. She looked like she was used to dealing with difficult situations and putting people at their ease.

'Yes, shortly,' said the officer. He introduced himself as Superintendent David Drake and told them he was leading the reopened inquiry into Mara's disappearance. 'This is Helen Barratt. She's a psychologist who's helping Mara come to terms with everything. She'll also be able to guide you through what to expect when you see your sister again.'

'Obviously, we'll have to take things slowly to start with,' Barratt added, her tone warm and treacly.

'I'd like to see her.'

'Of course,' Drake said 'but first, we'd like you to make a formal identification, to make certain this is your sister.'

A frisson of excitement bubbled in Damian's stomach. A few hours ago he'd had no doubt Mara was dead, but now everything had changed, and it was all happening so quickly. It didn't seem real. After nineteen lost years, it would be extraordinary to witness the sisters being reunited. And of course, the kids would be wild with excitement to find out they had an aunt they never knew existed. Lucia had always thought they were too young to understand, so had never mentioned she had a sister.

'Where was she found?' Damian asked.

Drake looked at him as if noticing him for the first time. 'In woodland near the house where we believe she'd been held all this time.'

'And how is she?'

'Undernourished and she has some superficial injuries, but on the whole, she's doing remarkably well.'

Damian sensed Lucia getting impatient, as her knee jogged up and down on the spot.

'All right, let's get the formalities sorted,' Drake said, reaching for a cardboard file on the desk. 'Would you please take a look at this photo.'

Barratt leaned forwards and looked Lucia square in the eye. 'You might be a little shocked by her appearance. We understand this woman, if it is Mara, has been incarcerated for a considerable length of time. She's had limited access to the outdoors, and her food has been restricted. She's thin and pale, but don't be alarmed. It's nothing a few months of rest and recovery can't fix.'

A few months? Damian didn't know what he was expecting, but he hadn't even considered Mara might need a long period of rehabilitation.

'Let me see.' Lucia took the file and opened it on her lap.

'And remember, it might not even be her,' Barratt added.

Over Lucia's shoulder, Damian saw a photograph of a woman looking straight at the camera, her hair shorn close to her scalp and her eyes sunken into their sockets. Lucia stroked the picture with her finger, but from the angle he was sitting he couldn't read her expression.

After a few moments, she closed the file and handed it back to Drake.

'Mrs Caslocke, to the best of your knowledge, is that your sister, Mara Sitwell?'

Lucia crossed her legs and pursed her lips. She'd stopped jiggling her leg and was strangely calm.

'Lucia,' Damian prompted, reaching for her hand.

'No,' she said. 'I'm sorry, it's not her.'

3

'Are you absolutely sure?' Damian asked, taking the file from Drake. 'Have another look.'

An awkward silence filled the room.

'It's not her,' Lucia said.

Damian opened the file. The woman in the photograph was curled up on a chair wearing a green surgical gown, her feet tucked under her body. Her face was gaunt and painted with sadness, and there was something about her sallow cheeks, prominent skull bones and milky skin, tinged green, which made him recoil. If this was someone faking it, they'd gone to extraordinary lengths.

'Please,' Damian pleaded. 'You need to be one hundred per cent sure.'

Lucia continued to stare ahead, beyond the police officer, her gaze fixed on nothing in particular.

'Look at her eyes.' Damian slid the photo under Lucia's nose. 'And the way she's holding her head. I've seen you do that exact same thing a million times when you're not sure about something. Can't you see it?'

The sisters were far from identical, but it was apparent they were closely related. Although Lucia's hair was the colour of copper, and

Mara was blonde, they shared the same eyes, button nose and mouth.

Lucia glanced at the photo.

'I think it *is* her,' Damian said, aware his opinion counted for nothing as far as the police were concerned. 'Try to see past how she looks now.'

'Take your time, Mrs Caslocke.' Barrett was on the edge of her seat.

'Has she said much about what happened to her?' Damian asked, buying Lucia some time to think.

'We've deliberately not pushed her until we can assess her state of mind,' Drake said, his hands in his pockets. 'All we know for sure is that she was held captive in a room under the house.'

'A cellar?'

'Not exactly.' Drake shifted his weight, looking a little uncomfortable. 'More like a cell dug out under the floor.'

Damian whistled. 'Jesus.'

'And she says she was kept chained up, at least for some of the time.'

'What about the guy who abducted her? Have you arrested him?'

Drake cleared his throat and folded his arms across his chest. 'Unfortunately, his whereabouts are currently unknown.'

'But you know who he is? You'll catch him, right?'

Drake chewed his lip. 'Our prime suspect is a man named James Finch, a self-employed handyman who'd lived in the house since his mother died. We've issued a nationwide alert for him. He won't get far.'

'You mean he's still out there?' Lucia's voice trembled.

'We'll catch him, Mrs Caslocke. Don't worry about that.'

Lucia took the photograph and held it close to her face. 'I want to meet her.'

Barrett and Drake exchanged a look.

'Have you changed your mind?' Barrett asked. 'Are you saying you believe this might be your sister, Mara?'

'Possibly.'

Damian held his breath.

'All right, but let's keep the first meeting short. We don't know how she's going to react. It's going to be a big deal for her.' Barratt crossed her legs and took a deep breath. 'And there are a few things I should explain first. As you now know, we think she's been confined in a tiny underground cell with little freedom over anything she did for the best part of twenty years. She was probably told when she could eat and drink, when to sleep and when to get up. It's possible her abductor even controlled when she had electricity and light.'

Lucia gasped.

'She's been deprived of having to make any decisions about her life for so long, this new freedom might throw up some issues. We anticipate she may experience some level of sensory overload. Everything is going to be overwhelming for her, not least seeing you again.

'Obviously, we're monitoring her closely, but don't be surprised if you find her memory is impaired, or that she can't concentrate. She might seem confused or scared. She's still in shock and maybe feeling anxious, guilty, depressed or even angry. She's open to the idea of meeting you, in fact, she's been asking for you since we picked her up. Even so, she might not want to interact with you when she actually sees you. You shouldn't take it personally.'

'I won't,' Lucia said.

'Finally, please don't bombard her with questions. I know you'll have lots you want to ask, but be patient and let her open up to you in her own time. That's really important. This is going to be a long process.'

Damian coughed. 'Will I be able to go in with Lucia?' After all the years he'd supported his wife, he wasn't going to miss out on the moment they were finally reunited.

'I think that should be all right if Lucia has no objections,' Barrett said.

Damian squeezed Lucia's hand. 'Of course she doesn't have any objections.'

'It's fine,' she said.

'In which case, let's do it,' Drake said. 'If you want to follow me, she's waiting for you downstairs.'

4

September 2004

LUCIA SIPPED from a can of Coke as she watched a herd of cattle grazing in a field on the opposite bank of the canal on one of the last warm days of September.

'It's not going to be forever,' she said, resting her head in Damian's lap.

He'd initially been sanguine at the thought they'd be studying at universities miles apart. They'd agreed to see each other every week-end, and there were the long breaks to look forward to. But as the start of term drew closer, he'd become increasingly anxious about the future, and the impact being apart would have on their relationship.

'You're missing the point,' he said. 'I'm going to miss you.'

'I'll miss you too.' She wrapped her fingers around the back of his neck and pulled his head down to kiss him. 'But we'll see each other every week.'

'It won't be the same.'

'Just don't go finding someone new,' she joked, poking him in the ribs.

He didn't see the funny side. He imagined Lucia with new, interesting friends, revelling in the infamy of having a sister who'd been abducted. They'd lap that up for sure, especially when she revealed Mara's body had never been found. He didn't like the thought of it one bit.

'Hey, if a fly lost its wings, would that make it a walk?' she said, smirking.

He wasn't in the mood.

'What was Captain Hook's name before he lost his hand?'

'Lucia, stop,' he snapped. 'We're not kids anymore.'

'What's got into you?'

'Nothing.'

'Doesn't sound like nothing.'

'Forget it,' he said, plucking the petals from a daisy. He was losing her, and there was nothing he could do about it.

'I love you,' she said. It was the first time she'd uttered the words. She laid her palm against his cheek, like the first time she'd kissed him. 'I mean it.'

He didn't know what to say. 'I've got to go.' He stood up, rolling her head off his lap. 'I told Mum I'd be back by five.'

He didn't even walk her home. He just strode off with his hands in his pockets, letting the anger boil inside him.

Lucia hadn't been particularly academic or sporty, pretty or outgoing, like some of the girls in his year. She'd been an average student at best, someone who kept her head down and steered well clear of trouble. In fact, he'd never given her a moment's notice until Mara's disappearance. Until then, he'd found her bland. Uninteresting. But a couple of weeks after she'd returned to school in the autumn term, and when the search for Mara was still in its infancy, he'd plucked up the courage to approach her, inexplicably drawn to her vulnerability and sorrow.

'I'm sorry about your sister,' he'd said, as he'd joined her at one of the wooden picnic benches outside the sixth form centre. She'd been picking at her fingernails, hiding behind her fringe.

He'd offered her a sandwich from his Tupperware box, but she'd shaken her head, squinting at him through her hair suspiciously.

'I can't imagine what it must be like.'

It was true. How could he possibly have understood what kind of hell she was going through? Nonetheless, her torment had consumed him. He'd tried to imagine her suffering, wondering what it would be like to taste the bitterness of her pain, to know what it was like to feel such raw emotion that came from losing someone close.

'It's like having an arm chopped off,' she'd said, which he thought was pretty funny at the time. But she hadn't smiled.

Mara's abduction had captivated the nation over the long, hot summer, and Damian had found it intoxicating. He'd followed every twist and turn as it played out in the newspapers and on the TV day after day, less shocked and more excited that something so dramatic had happened close to home.

The police concluded early on in their investigation that Mara had most likely been abducted. There was some speculation she'd been kidnapped by child sex traffickers. Others suggested she must have woken disorientated in the middle of the night, wandered off and fallen into the river not far from the house. The truth was, no one knew for sure.

There had been no shortage of witnesses claiming to have seen Mara over the first twenty-four hours after she went missing, but none of the sightings had proved reliable. Cranks and frauds surfaced alleging all sorts of insights into her disappearance, but none of them panned out. And with every theory shot down, the mystery only deepened.

Damian had been surprised that Lucia's parents had sent her back to school on the first day of term. She didn't seem ready to be thrust back into the school environment. And while all the other kids had flocked around her like she was a celebrity, cooing tearful sympathies or quizzing her on the details of Mara's disappearance, he'd watched her from afar.

He'd only made his move when Lucia had started to cut a lonely figure, abandoned by her so-called friends who struggled with her difficult mood swings. She'd become quiet and withdrawn, moping sulkily around the corridors between lessons with her head down and her shoulders hunched, avoiding eye contact with anyone.

Damian resisted quizzing her straight off about her sister or the trauma he suspected was eating her up. Instead, he'd won her trust by chatting about trivial things that made her smile.

'How come vampires have such neat hair if they can't see their reflections in a mirror?' he'd say.

'Did you know that if you live until you're seventy, ten years of your life would have been spent on Mondays,' she would retort.

They'd taken pride in seeing who could come up with the wackiest, quasi-philosophical observations. It had become their thing, and in time, she'd opened up. That's when he began to understand she was being tortured by guilt. She blamed herself for allowing Mara to be snatched from their tent while she slept a few feet away, and there was nothing Damian could say or do to make her feel better. As the weeks and months went on, and with the police no closer to finding her, Lucia's misplaced conviction that she was somehow responsible had only deepened.

'Why did he take her?' she would ask. 'Why not me?'

Damian had no answer. All he could do was reassure her that she wasn't to blame.

He'd never considered her as anything other than a close friend until they'd turned seventeen. The exact moment their relationship changed was fixed indelibly in Damian's memory. He would always remember how the sunlight had caught her hair and created a fiery halo around her head as they'd been working on a geography assignment together in his bedroom.

'What is it?' she'd asked, screwing up her nose as she'd noticed him staring. She'd smiled coyly, the creases deepening around her eyes, and his stomach had lurched.

'I don't know, I just... ' He hadn't been able to finish his sentence. His throat had been dry, and his chest tight. He didn't know where he found the courage, but he'd leaned across the bed, took her face in his hands and kissed her.

'Hey, what are you doing?' She'd pulled away with a grimace.

'I'm sorry,' he'd mumbled. 'Didn't you like it?'

'I didn't say that. It just came as a bit of a surprise.'

She'd adjusted her t-shirt and tried to hide a smile. 'You should give someone a warning if you're going to kiss them,' she'd said.

Then with a glint in her eye, she'd placed a tender hand on his cheek and kissed him back. Her lips had been so soft and moist, he'd thought he was going to melt.

He'd kissed a few girls before, mostly when he'd had too much to drink at parties. A quick fumble on the dance floor, too much enthusiasm and not enough experience. Lucia's kiss had been something else. It was sweet and tender and took their connection to a new level.

In their remaining year at school, Damian had spent less and less time with his friends, devoting his full attention to Lucia as she continued to fascinate and intrigue him. He hated it when they were apart, even when she'd insisted on needing space for her studies, keen to excel in her A-Levels and to make something of her life.

'I want to do well, not for me but for Mara,' she would tell him every time he tried to drag her away from her books.

She saw her education as her ticket out of town, the place that would be forever tainted with regrets and bad memories. Not only had she lost her sister, but the stress of it all had driven a wedge between her parents, who'd subsequently separated and divorced.

Richard and Linda had been crushed when Mara was abducted. The pressure on their marriage hadn't been helped by persistent rumours they were somehow involved, or at least culpably negligent in allowing their young daughters to sleep out in the garden without supervision.

In the first few days after Mara's disappearance, they'd given countless interviews to the media in the hope of encouraging someone to come forward with new information. But over time, and with the press camped out on their doorstep, they reported feeling hounded. The journalists, who'd initially been supportive and understanding, became increasingly aggressive as they looked for new angles to the story. Richard and Linda became virtual recluses, and the emotional and psychological pressure on them almost inevitably led to the breakdown of their marriage.

And yet, despite all these things, Lucia had surpassed expectations in her studies, gaining top marks in her A-Levels and securing a place at Warwick University to read economics. The only problem was that Damian was going to be a hundred miles away in Southampton. It was only a short train ride, but they might as well have been on opposites sides of the world. They were going to be apart for the first time in four years, and it tore at Damian's soul.

5

Present day

DAMIAN'S STOMACH tightened as Drake led them along a rabbit warren of corridors, down a flight of stairs and into a room filled with a dozen people working at desks. Inquisitive eyes looked up and a respectful hush fell as they filed in.

'Over to you, Helen,' Drake said, stepping away.

'Are you ready?' Barrett asked.

Lucia nodded. Damian took her hand and gave it an encouraging squeeze, feeling like a little boy on Christmas morning. In his wildest dreams, he'd never imagined this moment. He was in a turmoil of anticipation, his heart racing. Lucia, on the other hand, seemed remarkably calm. He only hoped she wouldn't disappoint him. It was a huge moment for them both.

'Just remember, please don't ask her lots of questions. She's in a fragile state,' Barratt said.

Damian took a deep breath as the psychologist opened a door into a windowless inner room. Lucia moved so hesitantly he had to fight the urge to shove her forwards.

The woman Drake had shown them in the photograph was sitting in a low chair. In the flesh, she looked ten times worse. Her skin was virtually translucent. Her face was drawn, and her shoulders sagged. Two spindly arms protruded from the short sleeves of her surgical robe, so deplete of muscle they were nothing more than bones sheathed in skin. A saline drip hung from a stand behind her chair. It looped into the back of her hand through a needle attached by a strip of plaster. She glanced up when she heard the door open and stared at them vacantly, her eyes dead.

Barrett stood in the middle of the room like a referee at a boxing match.

'Mara, do you remember your sister, Lucia?' she said.

The woman blinked twice, her expression unreadable.

'Mara?' Lucia's voice cracked.

The woman struggled to pull herself to her feet, almost losing her balance. Barrett caught her by the arm. Damian bit his lip, a lump swelling in his throat. Now he knew for sure. It was Mara. No mistake.

'I stayed alive,' she said, her voice husky, her lips dry and painfully cracked.

Lucia took a tentative step forwards and pulled Mara into a tight embrace. They stood for what seemed like hours, rocking gently with their heads buried into each other's shoulders. The hairs prickled on the back of Damian's neck and he had to bite his lip to stop his tears. He didn't want them to see him cry.

'I can't believe it,' Lucia whimpered.

Eventually the two women prised themselves apart and stood staring at each other, holding each other by the forearms.

Mara ran her bony fingers through the loose strands of Lucia's thick, red hair and touched her face lightly with her fingertips. 'You're all grown up,' she said, her face finally cracking into a smile.

'So are you,' Lucia said.

'We've missed all our birthdays.'

'We'll make up for them, every single one.'

'I'd like that,' Mara croaked.

'I'm so, so sorry. I let you down. I don't deserve you back.'

'What do you mean?'

'He should have taken me.'

'Don't be silly.' Mara slumped back down in her chair, exhausted. 'It wasn't your fault.'

'I should have stopped him, but I slept through it all and never woke up.'

'You wouldn't have been able to stop him. He was too strong.'

'I could have tried.'

'It's in the past. What's done is done.'

As Lucia pulled up a chair, Damian couldn't resist giving a little cough. He had so many questions.

'Oh,' Lucia said, glancing over her shoulder. 'This is Damian, my husband.'

He sprung forwards with his hand outstretched and a wide, friendly smile plastered across his face. 'So pleased to meet you,' he said, immediately regretting how formal he sounded.

Mara made no effort to take his hand. Her eyes narrowed as she looked him up and down. He felt uncomfortable under her scrutiny and let his arm drop to his side.

'Husband?' Mara said. 'It's funny, I didn't even consider you might be married.'

'And a mum. We have two children. A boy and girl.'

Mara looked as if she'd been slapped across the face.

'Damian,' she said at last, as if she was trying out his name for size.

'You don't remember him, do you?'

Mara looked puzzled.

'He was at St Botolph's, in my year. He looked out for me after you went missing.'

'I see.'

'We've been together ever since.'

To Damian's disappointment, Mara instantly lost interest in him. 'Did you think I was dead?' she asked Lucia, pulling her legs under her body.

'Never for one minute.'

'I don't believe you.'

'It's true. I never gave up on you. I always believed you were alive.'

'Did you look for me?'

'Of course. We never stopped looking. It was all over the papers and the TV, but no one had any idea what had happened to you. Nobody saw anything. It was a mystery.'

Mara nodded, apparently satisfied. 'Are Mum and Dad here?'

Lucia took a deep breath and took Mara's hand. 'I'm really sorry. They passed away. Dad went first and Mum a couple of years later.'

'Okay,' Mara said, showing no emotion.

'They were devastated when you went missing. They were never the same.' She didn't mention the divorce or how they'd been vilified by some sections of the press.

A morbid silence fell over the room. Damian shuffled uncomfortably, conscious of appearing like a spare part in his wife's intimate reunion with her sister. 'It's amazing you managed to escape after all this time. What happened?' he blurted out.

Mara hung her head and plucked at the material of her gown. 'I don't remember too much about it.'

'The police said you were found wandering through the woods. How did you get away?'

Barrett shot him a look, letting him know he'd overstepped the mark. 'Okay, Damian, that's enough.'

'Sorry,' he said. 'I just have so many questions.'

'And I'm sure Mara will be able to answer them all when she's good and ready.' Barrett offered Mara a reassuring smile.

'Tell me about the wedding,' Mara asked. 'What was your dress like?'

'Beautiful. Very chic. Understated.' Lucia subtly slipped her left hand under her thigh, hiding her engagement ring.

The diamond was a little on the small side, but Damian had bought it in a rush after he'd surprised them both by proposing. If he'd had the time to plan it, he'd have saved up and bought something fancy.

'Was there dancing?'

'Of course. We had a band, and the weather was perfect.'

It made Damian's heart melt to hear Lucia talk like that about their wedding day. It wasn't quite the rosy picture she'd painted, but he loved the memory she described.

'I wish I'd been there,' Mara said.

'You'd have loved it. I would have made you my chief bridesmaid.'

Mara went quiet. 'But you didn't wait for me.'

That was unfair. Mara couldn't seriously have expected Lucia to put her life on hold for all those years.

'No,' Lucia said. 'I'm so sorry, we didn't.'

6

February 2005

'I'LL SEE you next Friday then,' Lucia said, as they stood on a cold and windy platform waiting for Damian's Sunday night train back to Southampton.

'Actually, there's this thing on at the weekend with some of the lads,' he said.

'Oh?'

'Paintballing. You'd hate it. Shall we leave it a week and I'll see you the weekend after?'

Lucia went quiet. She shoved her hands in her pockets. 'Yeah, of course,' she said, turning her back to him.

And that was it. The first weekend since they'd started going out that they wouldn't be spending time together. It had been the beginning of the end. He'd broken the spell.

They'd tried kidding themselves that university wouldn't affect their relationship and had dutifully taken it in turns to make the train journey north or south every week. They'd both made an effort to get along with each other's new friends, and joined in the drinking and the parties. But Lucia changed so quickly, Damian hardly recognised the woman he'd first befriended when she was at her lowest ebb, vulnerable, lost and alone in those agonising few months after Mara had gone missing. He should have been pleased for her as he'd watched her confidence grow week by week, her circle of friends burgeoning. Instead, he resented how university life was changing her. He'd felt her slipping away from him, their time together becoming more strained until it felt like they were just going through the motions.

Their visits became less frequent, each finding excuses why they couldn't make the trip until Lucia finally sat him down and took the decision he'd sensed had been coming.

'This is really hard,' she said, sitting on the edge of the unmade bed in Damian's dingy student room one wet Sunday afternoon in April, in the hour before she was due to leave. She took his hand in her lap. 'I don't think we should see each other anymore.'

Although he'd known it had been on the cards for weeks, the shock of hearing those words still hurt. He resented that Lucia was no longer reliant on him, and that she was sharing secrets and confidences with new friends, people whose names he didn't even know.

'Why?' he said, feigning surprise. 'Have you met someone?'

'No! Nothing like that. I just think we should try a break. It doesn't have to be permanent. But a bit of space might do us good.'

'So you can go off shagging whoever you want, you mean?' Damian shouted, jumping off the bed.

'Of course not. Don't be so stupid.'

'Fine. Do what you want.'

'Damian, don't be like that.'

'Like what? You want to split up. Fine by me. But just remember I was the one who was there for you when Mara went missing and had to pick up all the pieces. And this is how you treat me? Just go,' he said, busying himself at the sink, picking at a dried speck of toothpaste, hiding the tears forming in his eyes.

'I don't want to leave it like this.'

'Get out!'

'Please.'

'Go.'

'I'll call you later,' she said.

She grabbed her case and shuffled out of his room. The finality of the door clicking shut behind her echoed off the walls.

He thought that was the end of it, that they were finished for good, that he'd never see her again. But losing her only made him want her more. She plagued his thoughts day and night, even when he was with someone else, which became a regular occurrence in the following weeks and months. His way of punishing Lucia for her betrayal.

He refused to go crawling back. He might have lost her, but he was determined to hold onto his dignity and pride. Maybe in time, she'd come back, when she realised what a good thing they'd had. Until then, he would wait and bide his time.

7

Present day

THE VOLUME ON THE TELEVISION, flickering through the window, was turned up so high Damian could hear it from the street. He let himself in the house and poked his head into the lounge where Rose was sitting primly on the sofa with her chin on her chest, snoring. He flicked off the TV, pulled the door closed, and crept up the stairs.

April's room was in darkness apart from the glow coming from her illuminated globe on the chest of drawers. His daughter's tiny body was tucked up under her favourite unicorn duvet, one arm hanging outside of the covers and her fair hair spilling across the pillow in a tangle. Every muscle in Damian's body softened as he watched her chest rise and fall, her face the picture of peace and serenity. He missed rocking her to sleep in his arms as a baby and remembered fondly taking her into their bed and letting her snuggle into his shoulder. Even the memory of her body fitting into the crook of his arm and the smell of her hair twisted his gut and filled him with such overwhelming love he never thought would be possible before they had children. It was a cliché, but he would go to the ends of the earth and back for her.

She'd been a particularly cuddly toddler. A real daddy's girl. But every day she grew a little bigger, he saw her becoming more independent until one day he knew she wouldn't need him anymore. At least for the moment, she still made a beeline for him when she was tired, climbing onto his lap, jamming a thumb into her mouth and finding that particular spot in his shoulder to rest her head. He couldn't ever imagine a day when she didn't do that anymore, but he was kidding himself.

'Goodnight, my angel,' he whispered in her ear. 'Sleep tight, and don't let the bedbugs bite.'

Dylan's room looked like there'd been an explosion in a toy factory. Action figures, miniature cars, plastic building bricks, books and dirty clothes were strewn so liberally across the floor, Damian felt like Indiana Jones running the gauntlet.

As usual, Dylan was sleeping with one leg under the duvet and another hanging out of the bed. His pillow was rucked up against the headboard, his face pressed into the mattress, and his lips contorted into an Elvis-like sneer which made Damian smile.

'Goodnight, soldier,' he whispered as he kissed his head.

Dylan drew in a deep breath and let it out with a contented sigh.

Rose was still asleep when Damian returned to the lounge with a blanket. He was about to drape it over her shoulders when she stirred, and her eyes sprang open.

'Oh, hello,' she said blinking. 'I may have dozed off for a minute.'

'They're tiring, aren't they?'

'They've been as good as gold.'

'Thanks for having them again. You're a lifesaver.'

She waved away his thanks with a liver-spotted hand. 'Always happy to help. So, how did it go?' she asked, tucking a cushion behind her back.

'Yeah, good,' he said. 'Emotional.'

'And Mara? I'm surprised there's been nothing on the news.'

It hadn't even occurred to Damian that there might be media interest in Mara being found, but he supposed it was inevitable. When she went missing, the coverage had been wall to wall for days on end. Reporters and news crews from across Europe and beyond had overrun the town. The mystery of what had happened to Mara had made the story so appealing.

It wasn't just the news crews. Apart from putting their small town on the map just as Hungerford, Hillsborough and Dunblane had been by their respective human tragedies, the story drew people from across the country. Not just mawkish sightseers but people who thought they could help with the search and couldn't stand to watch helplessly from a distance. A remarkable number turned up at the Sitwells' house, leaving flowers and lighted candles in jam jars. Women sat around holding vigils in tears, praying for news while parents in the town kept their children indoors, leaving the playgrounds empty for weeks.

'I suppose it's only a matter of time before they find out,' Damian said. 'But God help us when they do.'

Rose looked puzzled.

'Lucia's family were overwhelmed by the demands of the press at the time Mara went missing, even when they had nothing more to say. That was before they started speculating her parents must have had something to do with it.'

'I don't remember that.'

'The police moved them all into a safe house for a while,' Damian said. 'For their own protection.'

'That poor family. Did you get to see her?'

'Yeah. She's in a pretty bad way, but they think she's going to be okay, physically at least, but I don't know what kind of emotional damage she's suffered. They warned us it could take a while before she's back to normal, if at all. She said she was kept chained up for most of the day. I can't really get my head around it. What kind of sicko could do something like that?'

'Have they caught him?'

Damian shook his head. 'He vanished after Mara escaped.'

'And how's Lucia taking it all?'

'Hard to tell. It's been a massive shock for her.'

Damian ran a hand over his face, tiredness washing over his body.

He'd been running on adrenaline since Lucia had first called about Mara, and he couldn't remember when he'd last eaten.

'Lucia's boss has been great about letting her take a few days off,' he said. 'They're transferring Mara to a psychiatric hospital for the time being, so we booked a room for Lucia at a hotel nearby.'

'You should have stayed with her.'

'I couldn't leave the kids.'

'I would have been happy to have them.'

'That's very kind, but we've asked too much of you already. I'll head back down in the morning and take Dylan and April with me,' Damian said. 'They'll be so excited to find out they have an auntie.'

'Do you think that's wise?'

'Why not?'

'It's a lot for a five-year-old to absorb, and besides, you don't want to take them into a psychiatric hospital. Why not wait until Mara's better, and let them get used to the idea first?'

'I've promised Lucia that I'll be there tomorrow. She needs me.'

'Let me take the children. Honestly, they're no trouble at all.'

'No,' Damian said. 'You've been too kind already.'

He'd never been in a psychiatric hospital. His only point of reference was what he'd seen in films, but he imagined Rose was right; it was no place for children.

'You should absolutely be there for Lucia. She needs you, but leave Dylan and April with me. We'll make an adventure of it. We'll take a picnic to the park. And there's no need to rush back. I can look after them overnight if you want to stay.'

It was a tempting offer. 'If you're absolutely sure?'

'Of course I'm sure. Go be with Lucia. She needs you.'

Damian knew she was right, but he felt terrible abandoning the kids again, even if it was with Rose, who they adored like a granny. They probably wouldn't even miss him.

'All right then. Thank you. I promise we'll make it up to you,' he said.

8

December 2006

IT WAS STANDING room only at the Horseshoes as the regular Christmas Eve crowd packed into the pub for the start of the festive celebrations. Damian and his old school mates, Pete and Ralph, had arrived late afternoon with nothing else to do. They'd bagged a table in the corner which was now laden with empty pint glasses and awash with spilt beer. Damian's spirits were high, partly because of the amount of beer he'd already drunk. As much as he loved his university life, he enjoyed being back home, catching up with friends from school and acting the lark. It felt like a great time to be alive, and he was determined to savour every minute.

'Right, I'm going for a slash,' Ralph announced, standing unsteadily.

'Get another round in while you're at it.' Pete finished his pint and slammed his empty glass on the table.

'Right you are, three more pints of lager coming up,' Ralph slurred.

Damian's head was already spinning, and his stomach was bloated, but he wasn't going to be out-drunk by those two.

Fairytale of New York blasted out, and the pub crowd roared.

'I love this one,' Damian said, sliding an arm around Pete's neck and pulling him close, giddy with joy.

'One of the best, mate.'

They sang their hearts out, screaming over the din until their throats were sore. Ralph returned with three more pints as they reached a crescendo at the end of the song.

'I thought they were murdering a couple of cats,' Ralph said with a sly grin as he took his seat. 'Hey, you'll never guess who I've just seen at the bar.'

Damian sipped his pint. He couldn't feel his tongue anymore.

'Who?' Pete asked.

'Only bloody Lucia Sitwell! Never seen her in here before.'

Her name had an instant sobering effect on Damian. He sat upright with his heart racing.

'Where?' he said.

'Still keen are we?' Pete punched him playfully on the arm.

Damian strained to see through the throng of people. A gap opened up between two couples, and there she was. Her flaming hair was pulled back into a ponytail, and she was wearing dusky eye make-up, heavier than she'd ever worn before. He kind of liked it. It gave her a sophisticated edge, and he saw at that moment how well she'd grown into her looks. She was stunning.

What he didn't like so much was the guy she was with. A pretty boy. All floppy hair and chunky knitwear. Damian was disappointed. She could have done better.

'I'm going to the loo,' he said, pushing his way out from their table.

'Going to check out the opposition, is it?' said Ralph, unhelpfully. Damian ignored the barb.

His mood had changed in an instant. All he could see was Lucia. It was as if everyone else in the pub had turned invisible.

He forced his way to the front of the bar clutching a ten-pound note until he found himself standing at Lucia's elbow.

'Lucia?' he said, feigning surprise. 'What are you doing here?'

'Damian,' she squealed, throwing her arms around his neck and kissing his cheek.

'You look amazing.'

'Aww, thanks. Are you home for Christmas?'

'Yeah, I'm here with Pete and Ralph. And you?' Damian shouted over the raucous commotion at the bar.

'Just back for a few days. Thought I'd see what all the fuss was about in here.'

When she giggled, it reminded him how much he missed her laugh. Those dimples in her cheeks. The creases around her eyes. His stomach tightened, and he felt lighter than air. What a fantastic Christmas present. It must have been fate.

'It's the only place to be on Christmas Eve. Can I buy you a drink?' he asked, nodding at her half-finished glass of wine.

'Oh no, thanks,' she said, looking a little embarrassed. 'I'm actually here with someone.'

'Right,' Damian said, trying to hide his disappointment. He didn't want her thinking he was desperate.

She turned and tapped the floppy-haired chancer she'd come in with on the shoulder, interrupting his conversation with a group of lads to their right. 'Stephen, I want to introduce you to a good friend of mine, Damian.'

He spun around and shot Damian a broad grin, showing off an impeccable row of white teeth. Too late to avoid speaking with him, Damian forced a smile and shook his hand.

'Not "the" Damian?' he said, his eyes opening wide with delight.

'Stephen's staying with us for Christmas. His parents are abroad,' Lucia explained.

'So how do you two know each other?' Damian asked, not really wanting to know.

'We're on the same course at uni,' Stephen said.

'We ended up sitting next to each other in a marketing lecture, and you know, we just hit it off.' Lucia patted Stephen's arm playfully. 'We had so much in common.'

Damian wanted the ground to open up and to slip into the fiery furnaces of hell. It was too much to bear. Was she doing it deliberately to torment him?

'Oh, stop it,' Stephen teased. He looked Damian straight in the eye and winked. 'She was just after my body. It was obvious,' he laughed.

Lucia smirked. 'As if.'

'But I told her, my body's a temple. Not for the likes of an old slapper like her.'

Were they flirting deliberately to make him feel uncomfortable? Lucia squealed with delight while Damian squirmed at their private joke.

'Well, good to meet you, Stephen,' he said. 'Have a good Christmas.' He needed to get away. His good mood was being spoiled.

'You're not going, are you?' Lucia asked.

'Pete and Ralph are waiting for me.'

'We should meet up over Christmas. Do you have the same number?'

'It's probably not such a good idea.' No way Damian was going to play gooseberry on a date with those two. It was more than his stomach could bear.

'Oh, come on. It'll be fun, like old times.'

'I'm sure you two would rather spend the time together.'

'Hardly!' Stephen hooted.

'He's off again on Boxing Day when his boyfriend gets back,' Lucia said. 'We could meet after that.'

Boyfriend?

Damian hadn't seen that coming. He'd been so wrapped up in the idea that they were a couple, it hadn't even occurred to him that they could be just friends.

'You're not together then?'

'What? No!' Lucia doubled up in laughter.

'Not really my type,' Stephen said, putting on a camp voice.

'Sorry, I thought... '

'Were you jealous?' Lucia asked with a twinkle in her eye.

'Jealous? No, of course not.'

'Nothing to worry about from me,' Stephen said, throwing his hands up in surrender. 'She's all yours.'

Lucia pushed a stray strand of hair behind her ear and looked away.

'Well, in that case,' Damian said with a smile, 'we should definitely meet up before you go back.'

9

Present day

DAMIAN CALLED Lucia from the hospital car park. He waited outside on a bench in a well-tended garden with a verdant kidney-shaped lawn surrounded by colourful, herbaceous borders and sprays of grasses whispering in the wind.

'Hey,' she said, her voice surprising him as she approached from behind.

'Good morning,' he said, rising with a smile. They'd not spent the night apart since April had been born and Lucia had stayed on the maternity ward while he returned home to look after Dylan. 'I missed you.'

He hesitated as she leaned in to kiss him. She was still wearing her work clothes and looked deathly pale. Dark rings circled her eyes, and her hair was loose and untamed.

'I missed you too,' she said.

'You should tie your hair back.' He gathered a handful of it and pulled it into a rough ponytail as he kissed her. 'I like it better like that.'

'I lost my hairband.'

'And you look tired,' he said. He was in such a rush to leave the house he hadn't even thought to bring a change of clothes or her make-up bag. But then he was sure she had a compact and lipstick in her handbag. He couldn't understand why she'd not used them. It wasn't like her not to make an effort.

'I didn't sleep much. I couldn't switch off,' Lucia said.

'How's Mara?'

Lucia sat on the bench and turned her face up to the sun, closing her eyes. 'She refused to sleep in her bed. The nurses found her curled up on the floor in a nest she'd made of her blankets.'

'Really?'

'And she's being a bit difficult this morning.' Lucia sighed. 'She didn't like it when I told her I was coming out to meet you. She was kicking off when I left her. It was nothing really. She was just making a fuss. I tell you what though, she'd give April a run for her money when it comes to throwing a tantrum.' She smiled without humour.

'I'm sorry.'

'All to be expected, according to the psychologist. Just her way of adjusting. It's funny to see her bossing all the staff around though. I think she's enjoying her celebrity status.'

'They warned us it might be difficult.'

'I don't care. I'm just grateful she's back. We've missed out on so much.'

Damian took her hand and placed it in his lap. 'I never imagined this day would come in a million years.'

'You thought she was dead, didn't you?'

'Didn't *you*? In your heart?'

Lucia pulled her hand back and shook her head. 'I never gave up on her. Not once.'

A blackbird swept across the lawn low and fast, chirruping a noisy alarm.

'Has she said any more about what happened to her?'

'A little. I'm trying not to ask too many questions.'

'What did she say?'

'Bits and pieces. Nothing much.' Lucia sat forwards and buried her head in her hands. 'I know there's so much she's not telling me and, in a way, I don't want to know. I don't want to think about what he did to her, but I can't help it.'

'Don't upset yourself,' Damian said, wrapping his arm around her shoulders.

'And it was all going on while we were getting on with our lives; getting married, having kids, holidays in France, having fun.'

'We couldn't have put our lives on hold. Mara wouldn't have wanted that, I'm sure.'

'I just feel so. . . guilty.'

'You have nothing to be guilty about. We've been over this a million times.'

'Do you think they'll catch him?'

'Who knows,' Damian said. 'More likely they'll find him hanging from a tree somewhere.'

'Don't say that.'

'Why? Because hanging's too good for him?'

'Stop it, Damian.'

Lucia went quiet, wringing her hands in her lap.

'There's something else we need to talk about.'

'What?'

Damian had been mulling over how to broach the subject on the drive to the hospital, but there was no easy way of saying it. 'You do know it's only a matter of time before the press finds out Mara's alive?'

'This has nothing to do with them,' she said sharply.

'I know, but that's not going to stop them. We need to be prepared.'

'No.'

'They're going to go crazy for this story. You know what they were like when Mara went missing.'

'I'm not going through that again.' She stood up suddenly, crossing her arms.

'We're going to have to face up to it sooner or later, but it'll be different this time. I'll be with you.' In truth, Damian was secretly looking forward to the attention. He'd missed out last time, watching from the periphery.

'They don't have to know.'

'How long do you really think it's going to stay quiet? Too many people know. And then there's the police. They'll want to make a big noise about it.'

The force had been criticised at the time of Mara's disappearance when it failed to locate a white van several witnesses had reported seeing parked near the church close to the Sitwells' house on the evening Mara went missing. The police had also missed the opportunity to put up roadblocks around the town in the immediate aftermath. Finch might still have slipped the net, but with the media desperate to point a finger of blame, the police were an easy target. Now Mara had been found, it was inconceivable that they wouldn't dress it up as a huge success. Another major crime cleared up, even if Finch remained on the loose.

'We have a right to privacy,' Lucia said. 'I'll speak to that superintendent.'

'It'll be out of his hands.'

'We have to do something.'

'Let's give them what they want, and it'll blow over,' Damian said.

'You mean, speak to them?'

'Why not?'

'Because they destroyed my life and killed my parents. I don't want to speak to them.'

'That's not fair, Lucia. I know the media didn't help, but if anyone's to blame for what happened to your mum and dad, it's James Finch.'

'Yeah, whatever,' she said, inspecting the head of a bright yellow flower swaying lazily on a thin stem. 'I'd better get back. I said I wouldn't be long and I'm due to catch-up with the psychologist at one. Are you coming in?'

'Yeah, sure,' Damian said. He was still curious to find out more about the last nineteen years of Mara's life. 'Listen, I thought on the way home tonight we could stop off somewhere to eat, just the two of us. Rose said she didn't mind staying with the kids for as long as we needed.'

'Oh,' Lucia said.

'What?'

'I need to stay here, to be close to Mara. You don't mind, do you? We can go out another time.'

'Right,' Damian said, making no effort to hide his disappointment. 'The kids are missing you. They don't understand what's going on.'

'Mara really needs me right now. Dylan and April will be fine if you're there.'

'They hardly see you as it is these days, now you're working again.'

'Please, Damian, don't make this any more difficult. You think I enjoy that commute every day, getting back late and finding I've missed out on yet another bath time? But it's what we agreed, for the sake of the family.'

'How long are you planning on staying?'

'I don't know yet. I've not really thought it through. Two or three more days, I guess. I've booked the rest of the week off work. At least they've been understanding.'

'What's that supposed to mean?'

'Nothing.'

'Fine. Stay as long as you want. Just remember we're your family too.'

10

November 2008

SOME MEN SPEND months planning a marriage proposal, making sure all the details are just right; choosing the right ring, finding the perfect location, and generally stacking the odds in their favour.

Damian's proposal to Lucia tumbled from his lips before he knew what he was saying. Not that he regretted it for an instant, but if he'd planned it, maybe they wouldn't have settled on a cheap, second-hand diamond solitaire Lucia was embarrassed for her sister to see.

The thought of asking Lucia to marry him had crossed his mind before, but he'd convinced himself they were too young, too carefree. A weekend away in Bruges with its picture-postcard medieval beauty, fairytale cobbled streets, and white-washed almshouses changed all that.

They were full of coffee and waffles and giddy on each other's company, basking in the November sunshine as they walked hand in hand through the city, their breath ghosting from their mouths. As they crossed one of the countless bridges over a maze of canals, waving to the tourists on the sightseeing boats below, Damian grabbed

Lucia's wrist and twirled her into his arms. He stared into her eyes and realised he would never let her go again. The thought of her being with someone else killed him. And before he knew what he was doing, he was down on one knee.

'Lucia, you know how I feel about you. I want to spend the rest of my life with you,' he said, shrugging off his inhibitions as a crowd of excited tourists gathered around them. 'Will you marry me?'

'Are you serious?'

'Deadly,' he said. 'And if you don't say yes, you're going to disappoint an awful lot of people.' He nodded his head in the direction of the wide-eyed onlookers.

'Oh my God,' she said.

'Is that a yes?'

Those two-and-a-half years they'd been apart had tormented him. She'd told him there'd been no one else, at least no one serious. But he was sure there were others, notches on the bedpost, drunken fumbles at parties. He tried not to think about it, but the images of her with other men haunted his dreams.

'Yes!' Lucia screamed, clapping a hand over her mouth.

Damian pulled her into his arms and kissed her soft lips, feeling like the luckiest man alive. The crowd erupted into a spontaneous cheer.

'I love you,' she whispered in his ear.

'You've made me the happiest man in the world.'

'Did you plan this?' she said, suddenly pulling away from him, eyeing him with suspicion.

'I wish,' he said, lowering his gaze. 'If I had, I'd have bought a ring. I'm sorry.'

'Don't be silly. I don't need a ring.'

'Of course you do. Every bride-to-be needs a ring.'

And so they went off in search of one that Damian could afford on his meagre earnings. It was still early days in both of their careers, and the creative agency where Damian had ended up wasn't exactly paying a fortune.

They settled on a simple diamond solitaire they found in a little antiques place on the outskirts of the city. The man in the shop said it dated back to 1914 and they imagined a tragic story of it belonging to a young Belgian woman who'd lost her fiance to the war. The gold band was thin and worn, and you almost needed a jeweller's glass to see the diamond. But Lucia loved it, and all Damian craved was Lucia's happiness.

11

The inside of the hospital didn't look anything like he'd imagined. The outside resembled a prison with its high chain-link fences and rolls of razor wire, but inside it reminded him of his university halls of residence. He'd pictured foreboding, dark corridors, padded cells, beds fitted with restraints and the strains of tortured moaning. But after passing through a series of airlock doors and handing over his mobile phone and keys, they stepped into a bright and airy atrium decorated with a collage of colourful drawings and paintings, where patients were wandering around freely in casual clothing. There wasn't a strait-jacket in sight.

Lucia led Damian into an annexe off the main building, pointing out a lounge behind a set of closed double doors on their left.

'They've got a pool table, and the patients can play table tennis,' she said as if she was pointing out the attractions at a holiday camp. 'They do arts and crafts in there too.'

Damian nodded, trying to look interested, but he was still stewing from Lucia's revelation that she wasn't intending to return home that evening. He tried to see it from her point of view, what it must be like to be reunited with a sister she'd not seen in nineteen years. It had been a shock to them all, but he meant it when he said the children needed her. They all did. It was fantastic that Mara had been found alive, but what price were they going to pay?

'Mara has a lovely room with a window and her own bathroom,' Lucia said. 'It's more like a hotel than a hospital.'

'Sounds great.' He didn't mean it to sound as petulant as it came out.

'Try to show some enthusiasm, will you?' Lucia snapped. 'After everything she's been through, just try to be nice, okay?'

'We've all been through a lot, Lucia.'

She scowled at him. 'Grow up, Damian. She needs my support right now. Our support. This isn't going to be easy on any of us.'

'Okay, okay,' he said, throwing his hands up in submission. His bad mood wasn't going to change her mind about not coming home, and it was true, Mara needed them. She had no one else.

'Her room's just here. She'll be waiting for me.'

A scream pierced the quiet, echoing off the walls. A nurse stumbled out of a room into the corridor, clutching a hand to her ear, a scarlet stream of blood running through her fingers.

Damian and Lucia froze.

Lucia reacted first, running towards the nurse. 'What's going on? Mara?' she said, putting her head around the door where the nurse was standing looking dazed.

'She bit me,' the nurse said, inspecting the hand she'd clamped to her head. 'The bitch bit me.'

Her ear and neck were covered in blood, and it was already soaking into the collar of her tunic. She reached for an alarm on the wall, setting off a deafening siren.

Inside the room, Mara was sitting on the floor in the corner, her back against the wall, her eyes screwed tightly shut, and her knees tucked up against her chest.

'I was only trying to help her with her buttons,' the nurse said.

Heavy footsteps pounded along the tiled corridor, and suddenly they were surrounded by burly men in scrubs. Lucia was shoved out of the way, and Damian grabbed her arm to pull her to safety.

'Stop it! Don't hurt her,' Lucia yelled at the mass of brawn and muscle.

Someone clattered past with a metal trolley stacked with medicine bottles, instruments and dishes. Over Lucia's shoulder, Damian saw Mara's arms and legs thrashing. A needle. A syringe. Hands trying to hold her down. A confusion of shouts and orders. Mara's pitiful screams drowned out.

'You're hurting her!' Lucia fought against Damian, but he held her back, worried she'd get hurt.

'Let them do their job,' he said.

And then almost as quickly as it had kicked off, order was restored. The shouting stopped, and the thrashing ceased. Two male nurses lifted Mara's body onto the bed, and everyone quietly left the room, leaving Damian and Lucia standing outside, looking stunned.

'Why don't you come with me?' said a voice from behind them. 'Let's talk while your sister sleeps off that sedative.'

'What've they done to her?'

'She attacked one of the nurses.' Helen Barratt, the psychologist from the police station, was standing with her hands in the pockets of a long, brown knitted cardigan which reached the top of her knee-length leather boots. 'They had to sedate her for her own safety.'

Lucia glanced into the room where Mara was on her back in a ruck of bedsheets, her eyes closed.

'Will she be all right?'

'She'll be out for a few hours, but hopefully, when she wakes up, she'll be calmer.'

'I don't like what you did to her,' Lucia said, shrugging off Damian's grip on her arm. He'd forgotten he was still holding her back.

'I promise she's in excellent hands. Let me get you both a coffee. We need to talk.'

HELEN BARRATT'S office was on the second floor behind a series of locked doors she accessed with a swipe card around her neck. They sat in comfy chairs around a low table. Damian felt as though they were about to embark on therapy. It was that kind of set-up.

Barratt crossed her legs and smiled with practised ease. 'I'm sorry you had to see that, but it's nothing to worry about.'

'You overreacted,' Lucia said. She was tense and upset. 'It was heavy-handed. Unnecessary.'

'I know it's upsetting, but we have a duty to protect our staff. We can't let patients go around attacking nurses.'

'I'm sure she didn't mean it.'

Barratt raised an eyebrow and pulled a pair of black-framed Harry Potter-style glasses from the top of her head. She slid them on and opened a folder she'd grabbed from her desk. 'We always knew it would take time, but it's such an extraordinary case none of us can really predict what's going to happen with Mara and how she's going to cope. That said, it's not unexpected that someone who's been locked up for the best part of twenty years by a violent, controlling and abusive kidnapper is going to have difficulty coping with their newfound freedom. Our job is to rehabilitate her to the best of our abilities.'

'How long's that going to take?' Damian asked, wondering about the coffee Barratt had promised.

'It's impossible to tell. We're in uncharted territory, but in my experience people can be remarkably resilient and I would expect Mara to make a full recovery. How long it will take, I can't say, but, handled in the right way, this could even be a positive growth experience for her.'

Lucia nodded, twisting her wedding ring around her finger, her jaw tight and her back straight.

It was hard on her. All she wanted was for her sister to be well and to pick up the pieces of their lives where they'd left off. Damian wasn't sure where that left him or the kids, but they'd cross that bridge. The important thing was to get Mara better so she could stand on her own two feet. Eventually, they'd need to think about where she was going to live and the support she'd need, but that seemed a long way down the road based on what they'd just witnessed.

'I was keen that Mara was reunited with her family as soon as possible,' Barratt continued, resting the folder on her knee. Damian tried to decipher the scribbles on the top sheet of paper but could only make out the odd word which in isolation made no sense. 'She's responded positively to you, Lucia, but now you've had a chance to get reacquainted, I need to explain some of the difficulties we're likely to encounter along the way. This morning's episode is unlikely to be the last.

'We know Mara was taken when she was just eleven,' Barratt said, 'so she's spent the majority of her life in captivity. The chances are that has severely stunted her emotional and intellectual development. To what extent, we don't know. What we plan to do is make sure she feels safe and has a degree of autonomy over her life, letting her reintegrate into the world at her own pace.

'At the moment, the hospital remains the best place for her. We'll help her come to terms with what happened and show her how she can rebuild her life. Don't expect the trauma she suffered to ever be totally erased. It's key that we start with letting her regain her independence, which means we'll be giving her choices over everything; what she has to eat and drink, when she goes to bed, what time she wakes up, even how she wants her room to look. There will be times, like today, when she becomes angry or confused, but that's part of the process. It's her way of dealing with the trauma.'

Damian pictured the nurse staggering out of Mara's room with blood streaming down her neck. 'Is she dangerous?'

Lucia shot him a look.

Barratt cocked her head to one side and narrowed her eyes as if that idea had never occurred to her.

'I saw what she did to that nurse,' Damian added, imagining Mara throwing herself at the poor woman and burying her teeth into her ear like a crazed animal.

'Challenging, maybe,' Barratt said. 'I wouldn't exactly say dangerous. She's having to learn the boundaries all over again, and there are bound to be hiccups. She's been regularly beaten and abused, starved of love and affection, which means she's struggling with her emotions. Sometimes that's going to come out in a violent, physical reaction. It's to be expected, but nothing to worry about.'

Damian wasn't so convinced. If all she'd known for the last nineteen years was violence, it stood to reason that was the currency she was going to trade in. It worried him how easily Lucia could end up as her next victim.

'Your role will be vital in her rehabilitation, Lucia,' Barratt continued. 'She needs you to make her feel safe and empowered.'

'Whatever it takes. I'll stay with her until she's better. It's the least I can do.'

'Lucia feels responsible,' Damian said, placing a hand on his wife's knee. 'They were in the tent together when James Finch abducted Mara. Lucia has always felt guilty that she slept through it and did nothing to stop him.'

Barratt shook her head and leaned forwards. 'Lucia, you mustn't blame yourself or worry about what happened in the past. We need to focus on the future, and the best you can do for your sister now is to be there for her.'

'Does she know Finch is still on the loose?' Damian asked, wondering what impact that threat might have on her mental stability.

'We've taken the decision not to disclose that information to her at present. We don't feel it would be helpful, so please avoid the subject when you're talking to her.'

'Absolutely,' Lucia said, nodding her agreement.

'Just be yourself around her, and you'll be fine. She's still a young woman, and she may surprise us all with how quickly she adapts. The best we can all do now is to be there for her when she needs us.'

12

Damian took Lucia for lunch in town while Mara slept off the sedative. They found a cheery café with tables on the pavement outside and a gleaming stainless steel coffee machine hissing and steaming on the back counter. They ordered lattes and club sandwiches and sat in a window overlooking the street.

'What's wrong?' Damian asked, noticing Lucia hadn't eaten much of her food.

She set down her latte and took his hand. 'You know Mara needs me, right?'

'And we'll do whatever we can to help her.'

Lucia chewed her bottom lip. He recognised that look. She was mulling over something he wasn't going to like.

'I have to be here with her until she gets better. I can't leave her on her own, it's not fair. It might be a few weeks. Or a few months. I don't know.'

'A few months?'

'You understand why, don't you?'

'What about Dylan and April?'

'It won't be forever.'

'And work?'

'I have a few weeks' holiday left, and I'll ask for compassionate leave for the rest. They'll understand. But you heard what the psychologist said; I need to be with Mara to help her get better.'

'*I* need you. The kids need you.'

Damian pulled his hand away. How could she even consider abandoning them for so long?

'You'll cope fine without me, I'm sure. Please, don't make this any more difficult than it is already.'

'What am I supposed to tell the children?'

'I'm not leaving them,' she said. 'You can bring them to visit at weekends and in time, we can even introduce them to Mara.'

'I'm not sure that's such a good idea.'

'Why not?' Lucia frowned.

Damian raised an eyebrow. 'You saw what she did to that nurse.'

'She was frightened and scared. She didn't mean any harm.'

'Even so, we need to think about what's best for the kids. We want you home with us.'

'I know. But the kids will be fine. It's only temporary, and I promise to make it up to you when Mara's better.'

He could tell she'd made her mind up and there seemed little point arguing. 'Fine,' he said reluctantly. 'Do what you have to do.'

'Thank you. I love you.'

'Yeah, I know.'

Maybe he should have put his foot down and made Lucia see sense. If he had, everything might have turned out differently. Perhaps if he'd stood his ground and insisted, instead of giving in so easily, he wouldn't have lost his wife.

'Are you going to eat the rest of that?' he asked, pointing at Lucia's untouched sandwich.

'No, you can have it.'

Lucia's phone rang, vibrating on the table with an insistent buzz. She picked it up, frowned when she looked at the screen and put it to her ear.

'Hello?'

'Who is it?' Damian mouthed.

She scowled and waved a dismissive hand at him. 'But why?' she said. 'I don't understand.'

Another short silence. Damian put the remains of Lucia's sandwich down and wiped his hands on a napkin.

'I'm begging you, please don't.'

'Is it Mara?' Damian whispered.

'No, absolutely not. You have no idea what it was like last time. I can't face it again.'

Lucia hung up and slammed the phone on the table.

'Who was that?' Damian asked, fearing he already knew the answer.

'The police,' Lucia said. 'They're going to make an announcement to the press about Mara being found.'

13

Lucia sat shaking. The colour had drained from her face, leaving her skin deathly pallid.

'Lucia?' Damian touched her lightly on the arm. 'What did they say?'

But she wouldn't answer. She just sat staring blankly out of the window. Damian picked up her phone and called the last number. It rang twice before it was answered.

'This is Damian Caslocke. You called my wife a moment ago. What the hell did you say to her?'

'Mr Caslocke,' said Superintendent Drake, his familiar south London drawl instantly recognisable. 'We thought it best she knew that our media team took a call within the last hour from a journalist.' He hesitated. 'I'm sorry, they know about Mara. We've not confirmed anything yet, but it's forced our hand. We can't hold off making a statement for much longer.'

'Can't you deny it?'

'You mean, can we lie to the press?' Drake sounded exasperated. 'No, we can't, especially as several reporters are sniffing around the house where Mara was held. They know something's going on, so I wanted to give your wife the heads-up at the earliest opportunity. Are you at home?'

'No, we've been at the hospital all morning.'

'I'd probably try to lie low for a bit.'

Damian's head was spinning. 'How did they find out?'

'It can be difficult to keep a lid on things like this. The information could have come from any number of sources; maybe someone at the hospital.'

'Or one of your team,' Damian said.

'It's not really the time for recriminations, Mr Caslocke. The fact is we need to come up with a strategy to handle the story. There's going to be significant interest, so we think the best option is to hold a press conference in the morning, but that's not going to stop the speculation this evening. We'll have to put out a statement of some kind tonight. We have no choice.'

'What statement? What are you going to say?'

'We'll have to confirm that Mara has been found alive.'

As if on cue, Damian's mobile buzzed, lighting up with a news notification.

Sources report 'significant new lead' in hunt for missing Mara Sitwell who disappeared from her home 19 years ago.

Damian deleted it with a swipe of his finger. 'How long can you delay?'

'We'll have to put something out within the next couple of hours, I'm afraid. That's all the time we've got.'

Damian's stomach cramped. Out of fear? Anxiety?

No, excitement. Only a handful of people currently knew the truth about Mara, but within a few hours, the whole world was going to know. They were about to become celebrities.

Damian pushed the thought from his mind. It was the last thing Lucia would want.

'What about Mara's rights? This is an abuse of her privacy,' he said.

Damian could imagine the superintendent shaking his head on the other end of the line. 'The public has a right to know,' he said. 'And I should warn you, the press are going to be clamouring to speak to your wife, and Mara too.'

'Out of the question,' Damian said. There was no way Lucia would agree to speak to the media after the way her family had been treated, and he doubted Mara was in any fit state to give interviews. 'The press have done enough damage.'

'Look, we need to talk through the options as a matter of urgency, but we don't have much time. Can you come to the station? My team can advise you on the best options.'

'Now?'

'We don't have time to waste.'

Damian glanced at Lucia, who was lost in her own thoughts, tugging at her bottom lip.

'We'll be there as soon as we can.'

AT THE STATION, they were shown straight into a large conference room on the second floor that was buzzing with low-level chatter. Not the light, inconsequential gossip of parties, but the studious discourse of professional people facing a challenge. Superintendent Drake pushed through a crowd of uniformed officers and civilians to greet them. He showed them to seats around an oval table.

'Okay, thanks everyone for attending at short notice,' he said, calling the meeting to order. 'It's unfortunate that the news about Mara Sitwell has leaked, but let's remember this is a positive story and we should look to capitalise on the interest. After all, Mara is alive and well, and that's the main thing.'

Lucia looked up, startled. 'She's three stone underweight, sleeps curled up on the floor and has difficulty remembering the simplest things,' she said. 'She's hardly well.'

Drake held up an apologetic hand. 'I'm sorry. Bad choice of words. What I meant is the story is going to take on a life of its own, no matter what we do.' He glanced around the table and spoke slowly. 'As you'll know, we intend to confirm later this afternoon that Mara has been found alive, and we fully expect that will trigger massive press interest nationally, and possibly internationally. With that in mind, we've taken the decision to hold a press conference first thing tomorrow morning.'

The door squeaked open, and Helen Barratt slipped in mumbling apologies. She sat at an empty space at the table, nodded a friendly greeting in Lucia's direction, and pulled out a notepad and pen from a leather briefcase.

'Kate, perhaps you can explain the next steps,' Drake said, addressing a woman in a cheap, beige suit, who had heavily-rouged cheeks and short, spiky hair.

'Kate Blandford, Head of Media Relations,' she said, looking directly at Damian and Lucia. 'I think it's important you prepare yourselves. There's going to be a huge appetite for information. Obviously, we can provide some context around how Mara was found and the ongoing investigation into her abductor, but what they'll really want is to hear from Mara herself.'

'No way,' Lucia said, her shoulders tensing.

'I can understand your reluctance, Mrs Caslocke, but you should at least discuss it with your sister.'

'Mara's in no position to make that kind of decision at the moment,' Barratt said, laying down her pen. She gave Blandford the same "I'm only saying this because I'm your friend" smile Damian had seen in her office. 'In my professional opinion, her mental health remains in a fragile state and exposure to the media may do more harm than good at this stage.'

'I understand,' Blandford said. 'In which case, they'll want to hear from the family. Now, I believe Mrs Caslocke that you're the only close family member?'

'That's right,' Damian said, answering for Lucia, feeling sidelined.

'In which case, you're going to be in high demand. How do you feel about giving interviews?'

'I'm not interested,' Lucia said.

'Lucia's family were harassed by the press when Mara first went missing,' Damian explained. 'It put an unbearable toll on them all, and honestly, it's taken a long time for Lucia to get over it.'

'That may be so, but it's not going to deter the media pursuing you. On a positive note, you might be offered money for your story. I'd think carefully about how that might help Mara as she begins to rebuild her life.'

'Absolutely not,' Lucia said.

'Please, take some time to think about it seriously.'

'I have, and it's not happening.'

Blandford sighed. 'I'm not sure you realise the enormity of what's about to happen here. They may not leave you alone. My advice would be to tackle it head-on, no matter how much you hate the idea. Get it over with and move on with your lives.'

'She's my sister. It has nothing to do with anyone else. How would you like it if I started nosing around in your private business?'

'I'd hate it,' Blandford said. 'But it's not happening to me. It's happening to you, and I'm trying to prepare you for it the best I can. At least if you give interviews, you'll have a degree of control over the story. If you say nothing, they'll speculate and say what they like.'

Lucia's head dropped, like a punch drunk boxer.

'Okay, here's another option,' Blandford continued.

Lucia looked up, hopefully.

'What about offering an interview on a pooled basis?'

'What's that mean?' Damian asked.

'One interview to one broadcaster and one newspaper, on the understanding it would be shared with all the other interested media outlets. In exchange, the press would agree to respect your privacy and not bother you further. It's a win-win situation.'

'Sounds like a reasonable option,' Damian said.

'Do I have a choice?' Lucia asked.

'I can't force you to do anything,' Blandford said, 'but I would urge you to seriously consider it.'

'When do we need to decide?' Damian asked.

'Unfortunately, time isn't on our side. You need to decide soon.'

'And you'd arrange it all?' Damian was already picturing how the interview would look. A darkened room. Carefully trained spotlights. Tears and tight close-ups on Lucia's face as she pondered a lost childhood with a sister cruelly snatched from her too young.

'I'd personally take care of everything,' Blandford said. 'You don't have to make your mind up straight away. Sleep on it. See how things play out this evening and tomorrow morning after the press conference.'

Lucia nodded. Damian took that as a sign that at least she was considering it.

'Where are you staying?' Drake asked.

'Lucia's booked into the Travelodge so she can be close to the hospital.'

Drake glanced at Blandford and raised an eyebrow.

'I would suggest finding a quiet B&B. The last thing you need is to bump into a journalist staying at the same hotel,' Blandford said.

It was a good point Damian hadn't thought of. His phone buzzed again. He checked it under the table. Another news notification.

Reports that Mara Sitwell, who disappeared from her home in Sussex 19 years ago, has been found alive. Follow live updates on Sky News.

Damian swallowed hard. It had begun. The news machine was turning. It was out of their control. The only choice they had now was how much they chose to engage with it.

14

When they'd finished at the station, they took the police advice and moved Lucia out of her hotel into a quiet guesthouse on the outskirts of the town. It wasn't a palace, but it was quiet and out of the way. With ivy smothering the porch and chickens roaming the garden, it was twee almost to the point of absurdity. At least the owner, a middle-aged woman who dressed ten years too young for her age, was more interested in talking about herself than quizzing them.

Damian thought it was best to stay the night with Lucia. The press conference had been scheduled for the next morning, and there was so much for them to think about.

'What do you think I should do?' Lucia asked, emerging from an en-suite bathroom, brushing her hair. Her face was flushed, and she looked drawn.

'It's not my decision. You have to do what you think's right.'

'What about Dylan and April? I need to think about the impact it would have on them.'

Damian smiled. 'They'll be fine.'

'So, you think I should do it?'

'The press aren't going to go away if you refuse. You heard the woman at the station.'

'We'll see,' Lucia said.

Damian desperately wanted her to face the cameras but knew if he pushed too hard, she was likely to kick back against him and refuse. It had to be her own decision, or it wasn't going to happen at all.

They ate early at a quiet pizzeria, keeping their heads down, half expecting reporters to jump out at them at any moment. It felt like they were riding the calm before the storm.

After they'd eaten, Lucia wanted to return to the hospital. Mara had come around from the sedative and had been asking for her.

'Will you come with me?'

'You could probably do with some more time alone without me,' Damian said. 'I might go for a drive to clear my head. I'll pick you up later.'

He wasn't sure when his desire to visit the house where Mara had been held had first surfaced in his mind, only that it had now become an itch he was desperate to scratch. He couldn't think about anything else. Soon, pictures of the house would be all over the news, shared with the world. He wanted to see it for himself before it became public property.

The house wasn't difficult to find based on a few scraps of information Drake had revealed. He knew it was in woods north-west of the town, in a remote spot several miles away from the nearest property. Damian scanned a map on his phone and identified three possible properties.

He knew he'd found it when he saw blazing lights from a distance. A ramshackle building with rotting window frames, a moss-ridden tiled roof and a crooked chimney was lit up by an array of powerful spotlights. A task force of men and women in white forensics suits were swarming all over the place.

Damian parked a short distance from the house in a narrow lane crowded with vehicles, among them a fleet of police cars and a TV news satellite van. A small group of people had gathered on the road, held back behind police tape. It annoyed him that they'd beaten him to it. He'd expected the police but thought he'd be able to watch alone, not have to share the moment with reporters and news crews.

God knows how they'd found the house. A TV cameraman was tracking a white-suited figure carrying a bulging plastic bag out of the property.

He should have walked away, or at least kept his distance, but he was drawn by an impulse he couldn't control. It thrilled him to be there in an unexpected way, to be so close to where Mara had been held captive. Where she'd suffered so much pain. Adrenaline spiked his nerves, and as he ran his tongue over his dry lips, his fingers tingled.

'Gives you the creeps just looking at the place, doesn't it?'

Damian glanced at a young woman standing to his left, smartly dressed in a neatly tailored jacket over a blue sheath dress. Long hair flowed down to her waist, and she had a big leather bag slung over her shoulder.

'Do you live locally?' she asked.

'No,' he said, catching an intoxicating breath of her musky perfume.

'So what brings you here?' Her grey eyes were the shade of innocence.

'Curiosity, I suppose. I heard this is where they found Mara Sitwell.'

'News travels fast. Do you remember the case?'

'Of course.'

He'd talked about his memories of Mara only once before when she'd first gone missing. The newspaper clipping was secreted away in a shoebox hidden in the loft. At the time, he'd been pretty proud of himself, painting a picture of a girl he hardly knew with such vivid description he might well have been her best friend. In the end, it only made a few paragraphs in a longer background piece, but the sight of his name in print had excited him.

'The rumour is, she'd been kept prisoner in a hole under the floor all these years.'

'That's horrific.'

'I know,' the reporter said.

'I used to know her.' The words slipped from Damian's mouth

before he could help himself. 'I was in the same year at school as her sister.'

His pulse was racing. What the hell was he doing?

The woman turned to face him, her eyes lighting up. 'Tell me, what was she like?' she asked.

15

'It couldn't have happened to a nicer kid,' Damian said. 'She was always so happy. Always smiling. It was such a shock when she went missing.' The words he'd trotted out all those years ago came flooding back.

The woman stole a glance over his shoulder. He could see in her eyes she thought she'd struck gold.

'Tanya Hayes, Daily Mail.' She extended a delicate hand. Her nails were painted the same blue as her dress.

'I didn't realise you were a journalist.'

'Is that a problem?'

Damian hesitated. 'No, I suppose not.'

'Perhaps there's somewhere quiet we could talk?' she said, with a suggestive smile.

His stomach lurched. He was already smitten with her pretty features, the spray of freckles across her nose and the way the skin crinkled around her eyes. 'My car's just down the road,' he said.

'What's your name?'

'Richard,' he said, fishing the name out of nowhere. 'Richard Hawkins.'

'Well, Richard Hawkins, shall we go?'

As they walked in silence to his Audi, Damian tried to suppress the vague feeling of guilt niggling at the back of his mind. What harm could it really do? He'd given a false name, and she'd probably not even use the interview anyway.

Damian held the passenger door open for the reporter, catching a satisfying glimpse of thigh as she climbed in, crossed her legs and adjusted her skirt.

'Do you mind if I use a recorder?' she asked, pulling a mobile phone out of her bag as he climbed in behind the steering wheel.

'That's fine.'

'And it would be really great if you didn't talk to any other reporters. My editor's quite particular about getting exclusive insights into stories.' She gave him the full doe-eyed look he was sure she reserved for every mug persuaded to talk.

'No problem.'

'For the record, tell me again how you know Mara Sitwell.'

'We were at the same school, at least for a short time, before, you know, she was taken.'

'In her first year at St Boltoph's?'

'That's right.'

'How well did you know her?'

'She was the sister of a girl in my year.'

'Lucia?'

'That's right,' Damian said.

'Tell me what you remember about her.'

'She was an intelligent kid. And popular. You never saw her on her own. Kind too. No one had a bad word to say about her.'

Tanya nodded her encouragement, her eyes fixed on Damian's face. 'So it must have had a devastating impact on the school when she went missing?'

'Of course. We had no idea what had happened. People said she'd been kidnapped, but I don't think any of us really understood the gravity of it.' Damian recalled the stunned shock they'd felt when rumours began to ripple around that a girl had been abducted, the sense of disbelief. It was the closest he'd ever come to real horror, and it left him giddy.

He didn't really know Mara at all, but as impressionable teenagers, they'd all convinced themselves they remembered her better than they did. The oddest thing was the collective mourning that broke out at school when they returned after the summer break, especially among the girls who teetered on the edge of hysteria in those first few weeks back. Huddles of them comforted each other in the corridors, crying fake tears that streaked their mascara. The boys were more gung-ho, threatening to form vigilante gangs to hunt down Mara's kidnapper, and boasting about the cruel justice they planned to mete out once they'd found him. It was all talk, of course, but it seemed to make them feel better.

'Richard? Are you okay?' Tanya asked.

'Talking about it brings back all the memories, that's all.'

'I'm sorry,' she said. 'It must have been so hard on you.'

Damian blew out a lungful of air through pursed lips. 'We didn't know how to process it, so probably imagined the worst, but then knowing there was a guy out there, in our town, snatching kids out of their gardens. It was terrifying. Have the police told you anything?'

'Not much.'

'What about the guy who abducted her? Did they say anything about him?'

'We've got a name, that's all. James Finch. He lived in the house alone.'

Damian smiled. Not quite alone, but he knew what she meant.

'You ever heard of him?' she asked, her eyebrows raised.

He shook his head and slipped his hands under his thighs. The first time he'd heard Finch's name was when Superintendent Drake had mentioned him.

'Wouldn't surprise me if he'd topped himself,' Tanya said, shifting in her seat. Damian stole another glance at her legs. 'So you said you knew Mara's sister?'

'That's right.'

'Are you still in touch with her?'

'Sorry, no.'

'Do you know where her family live?'

He thought she was interested in what he had to say, but he began to wonder if she thought he was just a route to get to the family. 'I heard her parents died.'

'That's a shame. I'd love to talk to Lucia. We'd pay good money for that interview.' As her eyes locked on Damian's, a silence hung between them.

His mind wandered into treacherous territory. How much would they pay? An interview with Lucia had to be worth thousands, if not tens of thousands. It could set them up for life. Or at least pay for the kids' education and maybe a nice holiday or two. He guessed it depended on how badly they wanted the story.

'It was a long time ago,' he said coldly. 'I never kept in touch with her, I'm afraid.'

'I'm sure we'll find her, probably through social media. Most people tend to leave tracks in the digital snow these days.'

Good luck, Damian thought. Lucia detested social media. She never understood why anyone would willingly want to document their private lives in public.

He shrugged.

'Well, if anything else occurs to you, or you hear anything, give me a call.' Tanya dug into her bag, retrieved a black, leather purse and pulled out a business card. 'We pay good money for tips,' she said.

'Sure.' Damian placed the card on the dashboard. Her details might come in useful if he could persuade Lucia to talk.

'Thanks for your time, Richard. Can I take your number?'

'Why?'

'Just in case I need to double-check my facts.'

He couldn't see the harm. He watched her scribble it down in a notebook.

'Will you be using my name?'

Tanya cocked her head and screwed up her nose like she was about to explain the facts of life to a child. 'We don't tend to use anonymous quotes. Names lends the piece authenticity,' she said.

'That's fine.'

Tanya pushed open the door.

'Will it be in the paper tomorrow?' Damian asked, jumping out of the car, but she was already striding off, her hips shimmying, head held high, and her long hair cascading down her back.

He watched her walk away with an unsettling rattle of regret. He shouldn't have talked to her, but he'd not been able to stop himself. He'd betrayed Lucia, but at least he'd had the sense not to reveal his real name. If he kept his mouth shut, there was no reason he wouldn't get away with it.

The buzz of his phone in his trouser pocket made him jump.

Lucia's name screamed at him, lit up on the screen.

Shit.

He took a deep breath. 'Hi,' he said, trying to sound untroubled. 'What's up?'

16

Lucia was already waiting, arms folded across her chest when Damian pulled into the hospital car park.

'Where have you been?'

'Just driving.' It came out a little high-pitched. He sounded guilty. 'How's Mara?'

'A bit groggy.' Lucia yanked on her seatbelt as Damian turned the car around.

'No more incidents?'

'No.'

'And did you warn her about the press conference?'

'I mentioned it in passing, but I'm not sure how much she took in.'

He doubted Mara had any idea what a press conference would involve anyway. How could she have any understanding of how things like that worked after being isolated from the world since she was a child?

'Have you given any more thought to whether you'll do the interview?' Damian glanced at Lucia, but she turned away from him, looking out of the window.

'I'm not doing it.'

'Okay,' he said. There was still time to change her mind.

His phone buzzed in its snug cubbyhole next to the gear lever. He ignored it, but a few seconds later, it buzzed again.

'Who's texting you at this time of night?'

As Lucia snatched up the phone, a spike of panic made Damian's heart beat faster. What if it was Tanya Hayes sending some follow-up questions? How would he explain that?

Lucia went quiet. Too quiet.

'What is it?'

'The police have confirmed they've found Mara,' she said, putting the phone back in its place.

He'd completely forgotten they were planning to put out a statement. Now the world would know, and their lives would never be the same again. His stomach fizzed in anticipation.

'They were going to find out sooner or later,' he said, but he knew his words were meaningless to Lucia. She'd never understood why the press took so much interest in a story she felt was a private affair.

He parked in the gravel driveway at their guesthouse, and they crept up to their room. Damian was dying to switch on the TV to see how the story was playing out, but he resisted, for Lucia's sake. Instead, he undressed and slipped into the unfamiliar bed, relishing the chill of the sheets on his skin.

'Everything's going to be okay,' he said, reading Lucia's tension as she sat at the dressing table removing her make-up.

'No, it's not,' she said. 'When they find us, it's going to be hell all over again. I don't think I can stand it.'

'Then do the interview. Give them what they want.' Damian puffed up a pillow and stuffed it behind his head.

'Why should I?'

'Because if you don't, they'll never leave us alone. How long do you think it'll take for the press to find out where we live? They could make us prisoners in our own home.'

'I don't want to talk about it anymore.'

'You can't bury your head in the sand forever.'

'Damian, stop.'

'All right, fine. But just think about it for a bit.'

Neither of them slept much that night. The room was hot and

stuffy, even with the window pushed fully open. Lucia was up several times, and when she did go back to bed, she tossed and huffed so loudly that sleep eluded Damian too.

They both finally admitted defeat at around six and rose bleary-eyed and short-tempered. Damian slipped out to a nearby supermarket for orange juice and croissants to eat in their room, while Lucia called the kids, reassuring them they'd be home soon. She promised them presents to placate their howls of protest. By eight-thirty they were back at the hospital.

Lucia didn't even bother to argue when Damian told her he wasn't going in. He wanted to find somewhere to watch the press conference on TV. He thought about sneaking back to their room, but he was desperate for a decent coffee, so drove into town and looked for a pub where they might have one of the news channels on in the background.

Eventually, he found a sports bar with wall to wall TV screens. A young barman who was opening up agreed to let him switch on the news. Damian settled in to watch the build-up to the press conference and was surprised to discover the story that Mara had been found alive was already dominating the run order. A ticker-tape rolled along the bottom of the screen still announcing the previous evening's developments as breaking news.

'Mara Sitwell found alive after being held in captivity for 19 years, police confirm.'

It was followed by an additional line about the hunt for her kidnapper.

'45-year-old James Finch sought by Sussex Police on suspicion of child abduction.'

Two experts, a psychologist and a criminologist, had been wheeled into the studio to discuss the story. Their views were intercut with commentary from a reporter standing live outside the police station a few miles away from where Damian was sitting. He turned up the volume as the reporter outlined the scant details the police had revealed so far. She recapped the mystery of Mara's disappearance with old footage from the original police investigation and the familiar, grainy school picture of Mara that had been widely used at the time she'd gone missing.

'That poor kid,' said a male voice over Damian's shoulder. A scruffy guy with scraggy, greying stubble, who was nursing a pint of lager, was transfixed by the TV.

'Yeah,' Damian said, unwilling to encourage him into conversation. He didn't want to miss a second of the coverage. He was enthralled, sitting on the edge of his barstool, waiting to hear what the police would say.

The reporter put a finger to her ear as if she was receiving an update, and the screen cut to a shot inside the building where Superintendent Drake was taking a seat at a table, a serious expression painted on his face.

He had nothing new to say. Mara had been discovered in woodland not far from her family home. She was currently receiving psychological assistance. It was believed she'd been held at a nearby property where she'd been incarcerated for long periods in a cell under the floor. She'd been manipulated and controlled by her captor. Her family had been informed, and she'd been reunited with her sister.

That was it.

Drake ended by explaining that the man suspected of Mara's abduction was on the loose and a nationwide manhunt was underway. James Finch should be considered dangerous and wasn't to be approached, he added.

'What kind of fucking animal could do something like that?' the man over Damian's shoulder grunted into his beer.

As Drake wrapped up his pre-prepared statement, the questions from reporters came as thick and as fast as the camera flashes that lit up his face. They all wanted to know about Mara's mental state. How had she coped? What details of her captivity had she been able to provide? How big was her cell? How had she managed to escape? They were as hungry for the details as Damian had been.

'What was her relationship with Finch?' one reporter asked.

'She didn't have a relationship with him,' Drake replied, which Damian figured must have been blatantly untrue after nineteen years sharing the same house.

'I reckon she was in on it from the beginning.'

Damian turned on his stool to face the guy behind him, irritated by his constant commentary. 'What?'

'You're telling me that in nineteen years she never had a chance to escape? It was only one bloke.' He scrunched up his weathered face in disbelief. 'It don't add up to me. I reckon she was in cahoots with him.'

'He kept her chained up in a cell under the floor,' Damian said. 'How do you think she was going to escape?'

The guy shrugged and took another long draught of his beer. But he had a point. It was something that had been troubling Damian from the moment they'd found out Mara had survived her ordeal. It seemed inconceivable that during all that time in captivity, Mara had never once had the opportunity to run away or raise the alarm.

Damian had seen enough. He headed for his car and drove straight to the hospital. He dialled Lucia's number as he drove.

'I'm heading back to the hospital,' he said. 'Can I come in?'

'Of course.' Lucia hesitated for a moment. He heard a rustling as if she was getting up and moving. 'I'll meet you at reception if you get yourself signed in.'

'Great. See you shortly,' Damian said, hanging up.

It was about time to start asking some serious questions.

17

A small crowd of reporters had already gathered at the entrance to the hospital. As Damian slowed, a photographer stepped off the grass verge and pointed his camera through the windscreen, firing off a handful of frames. At first, Damian thought he'd been recognised until he saw the photographer do the same with the car behind. He was just playing the percentages game and hoping to get lucky.

Damian put it out of his mind as he parked and made his way inside the hospital through the usual airlock doors and signing in process, handing over his mobile phone and leaving it with his keys in a safe box. Lucia seemed pleased to see him, her mood having lifted since he'd dropped her off earlier. She strode along the corridor towards the reception desk with a broad grin on her face.

'I'm glad you came,' she said.

'I thought it was about time I put in the effort to get to know my sister-in-law. It sounds weird, doesn't it?'

'Not as weird as discovering your missing sister is alive after nineteen years.'

'How is she?'

'Better. I don't know, she seems perkier, less daunted by the world today. Do you want to grab a cuppa? Mara's taking a quick shower. She wanted to freshen up before you arrived.'

They headed into the lounge and sat in two upright armchairs cradling tea in plastic cups from a dispensing machine.

'Did you catch the press conference?' Damian asked.

'No,' Lucia said. 'Did you?'

He nodded. 'There was a lot of interest in how Mara had survived for all that time. Has she started talking to you about it yet?'

Lucia blew on her tea before taking a delicate sip. 'Not really,' she said. 'I'm trying to let her take the lead like the psychologist advised.'

'Aren't you curious, though?'

'Of course I am, but she'll tell us when she's ready.'

'Has she not even said anything about how she managed to get away?'

'They were in the garden.' A skinny teenager in a fleece tracksuit loped past the window.

'Outside?' Damian asked, surprised. 'I didn't think Finch ever let her out of the house?'

'She said they had a vegetable patch which he let her look after. A couple of days ago, he took his eye off her for a moment, and she ran.'

Damian puzzled it through in his head for a moment. Something didn't add up. After nineteen years, why would Finch suddenly get sloppy and let her get away so easily?

'Seems odd that he suddenly became so careless.'

'I don't know, Damian, I wasn't there. I'm telling you what she told me. Who knows what went on inside that house.'

'I just find it all a bit strange.'

'Everything about this is strange. You're letting your imagination get carried away.' Lucia finished her tea and tossed her cup in a bin. 'Let's see if she's ready. I think it would do her good to get to know you.'

Damian followed Lucia along the corridor, preparing what he would say. He wanted Mara to know he was on her side, for her to like him and to open up to him. Perhaps she'd reveal things to him she couldn't or wouldn't to Lucia. But first, he needed to win her trust.

His mouth was dry, and his stomach in knots as they approached Mara's room. Her door was open, and there was movement inside. Suddenly the memory of the nurse stumbling out with blood streaming down her neck flashed through his mind. He remembered her eyes wide with shock and terror, her skin pale. He'd not given it much thought since, but now he remembered vividly the rush of people into the room; Mara's unearthly screams, brute force and the fury of controlled violence. He shuddered, and his feet slowed.

Lucia reached for his hand. 'Here we are,' she said, smiling at him sweetly.

Mara was hanging up a towel on a radiator. She turned at the sound of Lucia knocking and grinned when she saw her sister.

'Hi,' she said.

'Look who I found.' Lucia pulled Damian into the room.

Mara's smile slid from her face. Even in a couple of days, her cheeks had taken on a ruddy glow, and her skin had lost a little of the green tinge, although her red t-shirt and faded jeans only accentuated how thin she looked.

'You're looking better,' Damian said, not sure whether it was appropriate to shake her hand or hug her, or whether physical contact was even a good idea. Indecision won over, and he stood awkwardly with his hands in his pockets, unable to hold her intense gaze. It was like she was looking through his skin and peering into his soul. 'How are you settling in?'

'Fine.' As Mara ran a hand over her shaven head, Damian noticed a faded bruise on the back of her arm. 'Although it's all a bit unsettling being around people all the time. I'm not used to that.'

'I can imagine.'

'Can you? Really?'

Damian's cheeks flushed. 'No, of course not.' He laughed, his nerves getting the better of him. 'I don't suppose you ever thought you'd see Lucia again?' The words tumbled out of his mouth before his brain had a chance to process what he was saying. He winced at his own crassness.

'Actually, I always knew we'd be together again. I never gave up hope.'

Damian tried changing the subject. 'Did Lucia tell you you're an auntie? Dylan and April are going to be super excited to meet you.'

Mara seemed unmoved. 'What do you do?' she asked, sitting on the end of an unmade single bed that had been crammed into one corner next to a cheap, matching faux pine wardrobe and chest of drawers which made the room look more like a bedsit than a hospital ward.

'I'm a freelance web designer.'

Mara frowned.

'I don't think Mara's familiar with the internet,' said Lucia, looking amused at Damian's discomfort.

'We didn't have a computer,' Mara said.

It stood to reason. That would have made it far too easy for Mara to reach the outside world.

'You've missed out on so much. It's going to be fun showing you so many things,' Damian said.

Lucia brushed past his shoulder and picked up an empty jug from the chest of drawers. 'You're out of water,' she said. 'I'll go and fill it up while you two get to know each other.'

A pang of anxiety gripped Damian at the thought of being left alone with Mara. He leaned casually against the wall as if it was no big deal.

'How did you two meet?' Mara asked when they were alone.

'We were at school together. Lucia was a mess when you were . . . '

' . . . taken,' Mara said, finishing his sentence.

'I was a shoulder to cry on.'

'Do you love her?'

'Of course, I do,' he said. What sort of question was that?

'Okay.'

If she had no idea about the internet, how could she have any concept of what it was like to love somebody? For the last nineteen years, she'd only known one other person. Maybe she'd fallen in love with him. Damian had heard of cases in America where that had happened. It wasn't unheard of, just one of those inexplicable psychological phenomena.

'There you go, fresh water,' Lucia said, breezing back into the room with the jug brimming. She placed it on the chest, which looked strikingly bare. None of the usual assortment of cosmetics and accessories you might expect to find in a woman's bedroom. No make-up or hair straighteners, perfume or hairbrushes.

'Right, just popping to the ladies,' Lucia said, trotting out of the room. 'You two carry on.'

Damian watched her leave and listened to her footsteps echoing down the corridor. When the sound had faded away, Mara turned her gaze on Damian with a look that sent a chill down his spine.

'I expect you'll be glad to get out of here,' he said, to break the uneasy tension.

'Pass me some water. I'm thirsty.'

He scowled at her rudeness but bit his tongue. If Dylan or April had spoken to him like that he'd have hit the roof. But he knew it was important to make allowances. There was plenty of time to teach her some manners.

'You want me to pour you a glass?' Damian tugged his hands from his pockets and pushed himself off the wall.

'No. Pass me the jug.' Mara remained cross-legged on the bed, making no effort to move.

Damian huffed, picked up the jug and a plastic beaker, and handed them to Mara. She snatched them from him without a word of thanks.

'You're welcome,' he said, under his breath.

Mara's lips curled in a snide grin, and without taking her eyes off him, she lifted the jug and hurled it onto the floor.

The crack of plastic echoed off the walls like a shotgun. Water sprayed everywhere, splattering Damian's legs. Mara took a lungful of air and let out a preternatural scream like an animal possessed.

Damian stood on the spot staring at her, unable to move. Feet hammered along the corridor, and Lucia burst breathlessly into the room.

'Mara! What the hell's happened?'

She padded through the puddles of water, and wrapped her arms around Mara's puny body, pulling her into her chest and shushing her quiet. Mara's screams quietened as quickly as they'd started, only to be replaced by an inconsolable sobbing.

Lucia glanced at Damian. 'What did you do?' she asked, with an accusatory growl.

'Me?'

'He threw the jug across the room. I don't know why,' Mara howled.

'No, I didn't! She did it!'

Mara screamed again.

'Damian! You're upsetting her.'

Two nurses appeared in the doorway and assessed the mess with looks that said they'd seen it all before and worse. 'Everything okay here?' one of them asked.

'It's fine,' Damian said.

'Damian, please just go. Can't you see, she's upset. You being here isn't helping.'

He threw his hands up in defeat. 'Fine,' he said. 'I'll go.'

'Wait in the lounge. I'll find you in a bit when Mara's calmed down.'

'Whatever,' he said, throwing up his hands in despair and casting a final petulant glance at Mara, who was clutching her sister tightly.

As he turned to go, he was sure she smiled at him, a wicked grin of delight that filled his belly with venom.

18

Damian trudged back to the lounge, deflated. He'd hoped to make a positive impression on Mara, but it was clear he had some way to go. He had no idea what he'd done to upset her, and her tantrum with the jug of water had left him speechless. He put it down to her state of mind, reminding himself what she'd been through. God knows anyone would have been screwed up after what she'd endured.

He fished in his pocket for some loose change and grabbed a tea from the dispensing machine. As he watched two thin streams of watery-looking liquid trickle into a plastic cup, he heard the lounge door brush open, and footsteps approach from behind. When he checked over his shoulder, he was surprised to see the nurse who Mara had bitten, a thick bandage taped to the side of her head. He nodded and smiled, hoping she wouldn't recognise him. He stepped to one side as he added a pod of foul-tasting long-life milk to his tea.

'You're here with Mara Sitwell, aren't you?' the nurse asked, slotting a handful of coins into the machine and prodding a keypad.

'She's my wife's sister,' Damian said, nervous she was about to tear a strip off him for Mara's behaviour. 'I'm sorry she bit you,' he added, feeling pressured to apologise.

'It's not your fault,' the nurse said with a shrug. 'Just be careful.'

'I'm sorry?'

The machine clunked and whirred as it dispensed a dirty trickle of black coffee into the nurse's cup.

'She'll try to convince you there's nothing wrong with her, but she's in pain,' the nurse said. 'Keep a close eye on that one.'

'What are you trying to say?'

The nurse poured two sachets of sugar into her coffee, stirring them in slowly and deliberately, but she didn't elaborate.

'She's going to get better, isn't she?' Damian persisted.

'Maybe' she said. 'In time and with the right support.'

Damian opened his mouth to reply, but she was already walking off, heading for the door.

'Wait,' he said, but she didn't stop. The door clattered shut behind her.

Damian was left stunned and confused. The psychologist said she was confident Mara would get better in time. She said there was no reason she wouldn't make a full recovery. Had she been lying?

'There you are.' Lucia's voice snapped Damian out of his thoughts. 'What the hell was all that about?'

'I could ask you the same thing,' he said.

'Mara says you threw the jug across the room for no reason.'

'Why would I do that?'

'I don't know, Damian, why would you?'

'Come on, Lucia. Seriously? I'm not the one being held in a psychiatric unit.'

Lucia ran a pale hand over her forehead, sweeping her fringe out of her eyes. 'I need some fresh air. Let's walk.'

The grounds surrounding the hospital buildings would have been an oasis of calm with their wide borders filled with brightly-coloured dahlias and rudbeckias if not for the eight-foot metal fence encircling them.

'What did you say to her?' Lucia asked as they strolled along a meandering path through a freshly-cut lawn.

'Nothing.'

'You must have said something.'

'I asked whether she was looking forward to getting out of hospital. It was small talk. That's all. Then she asked me to pass the jug, and she went all psycho.'

Lucia shot Damian a disapproving look. 'You've got to remember everything's new to her. She's a bit disorientated.'

'We're all trying to adjust.'

Lucia sighed. 'There's not much left of the Mara I remember.' They stopped to face each other. Lucia's eyes were rimmed red. 'It's so much harder than I thought it would be.'

'Nobody said it was going to be easy.'

'And what if she never gets better?'

'Of course she will, with your love and the support of the shrinks here.'

'Don't call them that.' Lucia smiled.

'Hey, how many psychologists does it take to change a light bulb?'

'Damian don't.' Lucia's hair shimmered in the sunlight as she shook her head.

'None, but the lightbulb really has to want to change.'

She punched him playfully on the arm. 'That's really inappropriate. Someone might hear.' Lucia glanced over her shoulder. At least it had put a smile back on her face.

They carried on walking.

'I think she's testing us,' Damian said. 'She wanted to see how we'd react, whose side you'd take.'

'That's ridiculous.'

'She asked me earlier if I loved you.'

'What did you say?'

'What do you think? And when I tried to tell her all about Dylan and April, and how excited they'd be to meet her, she didn't show a jot of interest.'

'She's spent most of her life being told she'd been forgotten by her family, and now she's coming to terms with the fact that not only am I married but she's the aunt to two young children. She's confused. She doesn't know what to think.'

'She'll get used to the idea.'

'Perhaps we should bring the kids to meet her?' Lucia suggested.

'I don't think she's ready yet.'

'You're probably right.'

'We have plenty of time ahead of us.'

Lucia stopped walking abruptly. Damian could see immediately something was troubling her.

'What is it?'

'There's something I need to ask you.'

Now she had him worried. 'What is it?'

'We're the only family Mara's got.'

'And we'll make sure she's given the best help, even if it means going private. We'll find the money.'

'That's not what I mean.' Lucia fiddled with her wedding ring.

'What then?'

'When she's better, I want her to come and live with us.'

'Live with us?' Damian spluttered. 'It's a bit early to be thinking about making those sorts of plans.'

'Why?'

'I'm not sure, especially with the kids in the house. She might be dangerous.'

Damian pictured Mara stalking through their house in the dead of night, a kitchen knife in her hand, her eyes glassy and unseeing. He shook the image away.

'She's not dangerous!'

'You don't know what she is. She's certainly damaged,' Damian said, the nurse's words echoing around his head.

'It's going to take time, but she'll get better. What did you think was going to happen to her?'

Damian hadn't really thought about it. Everything had happened so fast. 'I guess I thought we'd help her to find a place of her own, in time. Get her set up and standing on her own two feet. She's not going to want to come and live with us.'

'She can't live on her own. Not yet, at least. She has no idea how to cope. If she's with us, at least we can help her and maybe when the time's right, we can find her a flat. She can have the attic room for now.'

'And what about all our stuff?'

'We'll chuck it or give it to the charity shop.'

Damian wasn't sure he was ready to give up his guitars to make space for Mara, but that was the least of his worries. After what he'd witnessed with the nurse, he didn't want her anywhere near the house or the children. 'It's not practical,' he said.

'The house is plenty big enough if we have a clear out.'

'The kids are at an important stage at school. A disruption like that could really impact their education.'

'Oh, come on, Damian.' Lucia threw up her hands. 'Now you're just making excuses. She's my sister. I want her to move in with us.'

'Sounds like you've made up your mind already.'

'I have, but I was hoping I'd have your support. I'm not talking immediately. It would be in a few weeks or months after Mara's been through therapy and only when the medical staff give us the go-ahead. We're the only family she's got. I can't turn my back on her.'

'Can I sleep on it?'

'If you must.'

The sweeping path brought them back to the entrance of Mara's ward. Sliding doors hissed open, and a rush of artificially chilled air beckoned them out of the humidity. Damian tried picturing what life would be like with Mara living with them. Maybe it could work if she was supervised, he just couldn't shake a dark unease.

'Did you give any more thought to doing an interview for the press?' he asked as the sliding doors kissed shut behind them. 'There were already some reporters at the entrance when I arrived.'

Lucia's jaw fell open. 'What, here?'

Damian nodded. 'You can't ignore it, and they're not going away.'

'You really want me to do it, don't you?'

'I think it's for the best. Get it over and done with and we can move on with getting Mara better.'

Lucia tugged at the lobe of her left ear as she turned the idea over in her mind. 'And you really think they'll leave us alone after that?'

'They won't if we try to hide from them.'

'Okay,' Lucia said, fixing him with a stern stare. 'But on one condition.'

'Name it.'

'I'll do the bloody interview but only if you agree to let Mara come and live with us.'

19

Two chairs had been arranged side-by-side, ringed by an array of spotlights, while black sheets over the windows blocked out all the natural light in the room. A couple of men in saggy jeans and loose-fitting t-shirts were running cables and setting up cameras and audio equipment with the quiet diligence of professionals who'd been doing their job for years.

When Damian and Lucia slipped in at the back with Kate Blandford, the police media relations chief, nobody seemed to notice. Lucia's hand was hot and sweaty, and she'd gone quiet. A sure sign she was battling with her nerves. It had been a major concession on her part to consent to the interview, and until they'd walked into the police station that afternoon, Damian wasn't sure she was going to go through with it.

They'd spent the last hour with Kate talking through some of the questions that might come up and how Lucia should answer them. She spoke about being honest but seemed keen Lucia didn't comment on the police investigation, particularly as James Finch was still on the loose. Damian suspected it was because she didn't want Lucia highlighting their failure to find Mara when she first went missing.

A middle-aged woman with a golden blonde bob set rigid with

hairspray and immaculate, if not severe, make-up came striding over with a huge beam on her face.

'Mrs Caslocke, I'm June,' she said, with a practised, disarming smile. 'I'm going to be doing the interview today. It's so good of you to agree to speak to us.'

Lucia shook her outstretched hand and returned her smile with neither warmth nor humour.

'Have you done a TV interview before?'

'No.'

'Well, there's nothing to worry about. Try to ignore the cameras and treat it like we're having a chat in the pub. We'll make it as painless as possible. Okay? Any questions? No? Well, you try to relax, and I'll be with you shortly, as soon as we've set everything up.'

She trotted off in her kitten heels to consult with one of the cameramen adjusting the height of a tripod.

'She seems nice,' Damian said.

'I feel sick.' Lucia looked pale.

'You'll be fine as soon as you get started. And then it'll all be over.'

Damian checked his watch. They were due to start at two. Another ten minutes to kill. Ten minutes for Lucia to get cold feet.

'Do you want some water? Or something to eat?' he asked, noticing a table laden with bottles of water, plates of pastries and a bowl of fruit.

'No.' Lucia licked her dry lips.

'Shall we sit down while we wait?'

'I'm fine, Damian. Stop fussing.'

'Calm down. You're getting yourself worked up into a state.' He tucked a stray strand of hair behind her ear and checked how she looked again. It was important she made a good impression.

'You must be Mara! How wonderful you made it. Thank you so much.' June rushed across the room, her smile wide and welcoming.

Mara had appeared at the door with Helen Barratt, her psychologist, at her side. Her eyes opened wide as she took in all the lights, cameras and bustling activity. If Lucia had been overwhelmed, God knows what Mara must have thought about it all.

'I'm so pleased to meet you at last. My name's June, and I'll be doing the interview, but I just wanted to say before we start, on a personal note, how terribly brave we all think you are. I mean, to survive something so horrific, it beggars belief. I don't think I would have had your courage.'

The cameramen and a couple of make-up girls stopped what they were doing and seemed enthralled by Mara's presence like she was A-list movie star.

Mara stared at June as if she didn't know what to make of her fawning platitudes. Her lips turned up into a slight, wry smile as she stared at the presenter, as though she was judging her and finding her lacking.

'We're so excited to hear from you finally,' June carried on, her sycophantic prattle seeming to know no end.

'No problem.' Mara's face finally softened.

'And can I say how incredible you look, given everything you've been through.'

Damian had thought the press would be happy Lucia had agreed to be interviewed. But as the negotiations progressed, it became clear they really wanted Mara, to get a first-hand insight into her experience, how she'd been kidnapped, how she'd survived and how she'd managed to finally escape from James Finch.

'Let's at least ask her what she thinks,' Kate Blandford had suggested to Lucia. 'Then, we could make sure the interview is done on our terms.'

For the first twenty-four hours, Lucia had held firm. She wouldn't even consider broaching it with her sister, adamant she wasn't in a fit state.

'She's supposed to be making her own decisions. It's not going to help you mothering her. That makes you no better than Finch,' Damian had said.

He'd probably overstepped the mark, but it had worked. Lucia finally relented and asked Mara if she had any desire to speak to the press about her ordeal. Mara had surprised everyone by not only agreeing to it but enthusiastically embracing the idea. If anything, she seemed energised by the opportunity.

Helen Barratt took a little more persuading, but when she saw how childishly over-excited Mara appeared at the prospect of being on TV, she waived her concerns and gave the green light. She even thought talking about her ordeal to a stranger might help Mara's recovery.

Lucia caught her sister's eye and when June finally pulled herself away, wrapped Mara in a suffocating hug as if they'd not seen each other in months.

Not for the first time, Damian felt like a spare part. He left them to it and wandered over to the refreshments table. He helped himself to a bottle of water and a banana from the fruit bowl, careful not to bring the scaffold of apples, oranges and kumquats crashing to the floor.

'Are you staying to watch?'

Mara's voice startled him. When he glanced over his shoulder, he saw Lucia had been taken to one side and was being fussed over by one of the make-up girls who was attacking her face with a thick brush.

'I wouldn't miss it for the world.'

'Why?' Mara reached for an apple, letting her fingers brush across its waxy red skin before pulling her hand away, empty.

'I'm as interested as anyone to know more about what happened to you,' he said.

She'd still not spoken about it much to either him or Lucia and the longer she'd refused to talk, the more his curiosity had gnawed at him. Like the rest of the world, he wanted to know what kind of life she'd led in captivity with Finch.

'So are you ready for your big moment?' he asked.

'I guess so.' Unlike Lucia, she appeared calm and relaxed, totally unfazed by all the people in the room, or the cameras and the lights.

'Good, because you shouldn't worry about it. They're not here to catch you out.'

Mara frowned. 'Why would they try to catch me out?'

'Well, they won't. That's what I'm saying.' Damian flushed hot and cold. Mara still had this unsettling effect on him.

She grabbed a bottle of water and took a sip. 'What first attracted you to Lucia?' she asked.

'What do you mean?' It wasn't the first time she'd quizzed him about his relationship with Lucia, but every time she brought it up, he had an unnerving feeling she was testing him.

'You were both so young.'

'I don't know,' he said. 'We were friends for a long time first.'

'You didn't answer my question.' Was that a hint of irritation in her voice? 'What attracted you to her?'

'It's obvious, isn't it? Come on, she's beautiful.' Damian laughed nervously, feeling too awkward to spell out that he adored the colour of her hair, the spray of freckles across the bridge of her nose, and the way she always looked like she was floating on air when she walked.

Mara pressed her lips together and shook her head. 'No,' she said. 'I don't think that's it.'

What the hell did she know? The only attention she'd received in the last nineteen years was from the psychopath who'd abducted her. It didn't exactly equip her to preach to him.

'Love's a mysterious beast.' He laughed.

'I'm glad she's back in my life, but I hated Lucia every moment I was in that house. Isn't that terrible? I know now it wasn't her fault, it was just the way my mind was wired about it.'

'That's crazy.'

'I know it must sound weird, but sometimes you can't help the way you feel about things. I couldn't understand why he chose me over her, and I resented her for it.'

'Have you told her?'

'I've forgiven her now, so it doesn't really matter. Do you think she loves you?'

'Of course,' Damian said. 'Why do you ask?'

'She said you were her rock.'

'She told you that?'

'Yes.'

Damian sighed. 'She was in so much pain when you went missing. She blamed herself. She still does. And it nearly destroyed her. It was lucky I was there for her.'

'Were you attracted to her because she needed you?'

'Of course not.'

'Hey, you two. What are you talking about?' And suddenly Lucia was there, standing with them, her face caked in far too much foundation.

'Nothing,' Damian said, sounding instantly guilty.

Mara gave him a knowing smile as she watched his obvious discomfort.

'Come on, spill the secret.'

'Mara was just telling me how much she's looking forward to finally being able to tell her story,' he said. 'Isn't that right?'

'That's right,' Mara said.

'Right, everyone ready?' June bounded over with a clipboard in her hand. 'We're good to go if you lovely ladies could take your seats.'

'Good luck,' Damian said.

Mara grabbed her sister's hand and led her across the room, virtually dragging her to the two seats now brightly illuminated under the powerful spotlights. Mara crossed her legs and sat back casually inspecting her fingernails, while Lucia perched on the edge of her chair with her back straight and looking like she'd rather be anywhere else in the world but in that room.

20

The day they finally brought Mara home, grey clouds blanketed the sky, and the first threat of autumn was heralded on a bone-chilling north-easterly wind. It had been six weeks since she'd given her one and only interview, and it had been hailed a storming success. The press and public had taken Mara to their hearts. They couldn't get enough of her; the little girl who'd been robbed of her childhood and her innocence, and stoically survived against the odds.

There'd been an hour-long special on the BBC, and all the major TV and radio news programmes had used the footage extensively in their bulletins. Sketch writers filled thousands of column inches describing her as indomitable and heroic, fearless and plucky. Experts and pundits had crawled over every word she'd spoken and studied her body language for hidden meaning. She was praised for her honesty and fortitude in the face of overwhelming cruelty and, overnight she'd become the nation's darling.

And yet while most medical experts had agreed her deep psychological scars would take years to heal, she'd been discharged from psychiatric care less than two months later. Too soon, in Damian's opinion. He'd remained nervous about Mara moving in with them, but Lucia was adamant, reminding him of the deal they'd struck in return for her reluctant appearance in front of the TV cameras. Damian understood Lucia's deep desire to reconnect with Mara and why she wanted her to live with them, but it was Dylan and April's safety he was concerned about.

When they collected Mara from her room, she was unusually pensive, chewing her lip as she sat on the bed next to a solitary holdall they'd bought for her to fill with her few meagre possessions. Lucia did her best to lighten her mood, talking excitedly about the room they'd prepared in the attic, how the children couldn't wait for their new auntie to move in and how life was going to be just perfect. But Mara's feet dragged as they walked to the reception desk to sign out like she was a condemned prisoner walking to her execution.

In the car, Mara insisted on sitting in the passenger seat up front with Damian, relegating Lucia to the back. She spent the journey home with her knees pulled up to her chest and gnawing her fingernails, grunting at any questions they asked.

'Here we are at last,' Damian said, as they pulled up outside the house, relieved to finally be home and to see no sign of any reporters lurking outside.

As Lucia jumped out of the car, hardly able to contain her joy, Mara took her time studying the grey Victorian villa they'd transformed into a home. Even Damian felt a rush of excitement. He'd spent the week clearing the attic room of junk, while Lucia dusted, vacuumed and polished until the whole house shone.

They'd agreed not to repaint the room until Mara had seen it, keen to let her make her own choice on colour, heeding Helen Barratt's advice about how they could best help her re-establish her place in the world.

'What do you think?' Lucia asked.

'Yeah, it's nice.' Mara sounded distinctly underwhelmed.

Damian did his best to see it from her perspective. It was a strange house in a strange town, and she was facing a new life full of uncertainty. Her nineteen years in captivity had done little to prepare her for any of it. It was bound to be daunting.

Damian grabbed Mara's bag from the boot and followed the two women into the house. Rose was standing in the doorway to the lounge, the TV on in the background. She watched Mara with thinly veiled suspicion. 'The children are in their rooms playing. They've been no bother,' she said.

'Thank you so much,' Lucia said. 'We do appreciate it. This is my sister, Mara.'

'Yes, yes,' Rose said, pulling on her coat. She couldn't get away fast enough. 'I'll leave you all to it. I'll see you later.'

'Let me walk you to your door,' Damian said.

'Don't be silly.' She patted his arm. 'I'm only across the road.'

'Come on, I'll show you around.' Lucia grabbed Mara as Damian shut the front door.

He followed discreetly behind them, trying to gauge Mara's reaction as they worked their way through the ground floor, into the lounge, the dining room and the kitchen they'd had extended into the garden. Mara pressed her nose to the glass of the bi-fold doors looking out over the leaf-strewn lawn.

'It's a real sun trap in the summer.' Lucia watched her sister with her hands on her hips. 'You can go out there whenever you like, but come on, let's go and find Dylan and April, and I'll show you your room.'

Mara trailed behind her sister, taking it all in, only hesitating briefly on the stairs to check out the framed family photos on the wall. Pictures of Damian and Lucia's wedding. Shots of the kids when they were babies. A montage of the life they'd lived without her.

Damian had discovered a great deal about Mara from the TV interview. She'd come across as wounded but not defeated, damaged but resilient as she talked about her hopes of catching up on lost time with the sister who'd never given up hope she was still alive. She'd cried in all the right places, appeared upbeat about her future and addressed all the questions with an endearing mixture of politeness and vulnerability.

Mara seemed to warm to her interviewer, answering candidly about how she'd been snatched from her garden, her terror when she was thrown into a pitch black cell and chained to the wall, and how her food, water and even light had been rationed. She explained tearfully about the beatings she'd endured almost daily, her determination to never give up trying to escape, and how she was slowly adjusting to her new freedom.

The only time she faltered was when she was asked about James Finch. She'd refused to condemn him, insisting that he'd often shown her great kindness. He'd brought her as many books as she could read, she'd said, let her watch carefully selected television programmes and allowed her to sit with him when she'd been good. He'd made sure her education didn't suffer, insisting she studied all the core subjects and even taught her how to cook. At times, she spoke about James Finch with the sort of affection a daughter might talk about her father. Damian had found it profoundly disturbing.

'It's all perfectly normal,' Helen Barratt had told them later. 'You have to remember Finch was the only person she had any contact with for all that time, as far as we know. It's only natural she developed a deep connection with him, as a way of surviving.'

Still, it seemed pretty odd to Damian.

Mara remained tight-lipped about the precise details of her escape, brushing off June's questions with the vague excuse that it had all happened so quickly. She'd been allowed out into the garden, she'd said, and Finch had left her alone briefly. Spotting her chance she ran and never looked back until she became lost and disorientated in the woods. It was the same story she'd given Damian and Lucia, but it left him with as many questions as it had answered.

They were naive to think that after giving the interview it would be the end of it, although the agreement with the press had been clear. One interview on the condition they would be left alone for Mara to begin the long process of healing. It didn't prevent a small group of journalists remaining stationed outside the hospital, nor camping outside their house for several days after her interview was broadcast.

At first, Damian found their presence an irritation as they persisted in thrusting microphones under his nose and shouting questions at him every time he walked out of the front door. But eventually, he felt sorry for them. What a job to have to stand around outside someone's house all day hoping to be tossed a meagre scrap of information or a snatched soundbite. There were days when the temptation to speak to them gnawed at his guts. It would have been so easy. He imagined his name and picture splashed across the front pages as he gave them a rare insight into Mara's new life.

But he never did. He remained resolute. Lucia would never have forgiven him if he'd crumbled.

'Come on, slowcoach,' Lucia shouted from the landing.

As Mara caught up, Lucia pointed out the family bathroom at the top of the stairs.

'Dylan! April! Auntie Mara's here!'

Dylan appeared from his room, clutching a plastic spaceship and sporting a sheepish smile. 'Hi,' he said, looking down at his feet.

'Hello,' Mara said, looking equally awkward.

They'd introduced Mara to the kids a few times over the previous few months so they could get to know each other, but Mara had always been cold with them. Uninterested even. Damian knew it broke Lucia's heart, but they couldn't force her to love the children.

April was lying on her bed, engrossed in a book.

'April, Aunt Mara's here,' Lucia said. 'Aren't you going to say hello?'

April glanced up with a put-on smile. 'Hello,' she said, without making any effort to put her book down.

Mara looked around the room briefly and backed out onto the landing.

'What's this room? she asked, reaching Damian and Lucia's bedroom at the front of the house.

'I'll show you.' Lucia threw open the door. 'We've only recently had it re-done. It's all Farrow and Ball.' She ran a hand over the nearest wall.

Mara frowned.

'It's posh paint.' Lucia laughed. 'It costs a fortune, but everyone uses it.'

'I like this room.' Mara drifted to the window overlooking the street. 'It's lovely.'

'If you stand on tiptoes, you can see the sea,' Damian said.

The estate agent had described the house as having sea views, which he always thought was stretching it a bit, but technically it was true. If you stood tall, and craned your neck, on a good day, you could catch a glimpse of the English Channel at the end of the street.

They watched, enchanted, as Mara glided around the room, running her fingers over the oak wardrobes and through the fronds of their areca palm in its earthenware pot.

'We even have an en-suite.' Lucia pointed to the door in the corner behind the bed.

Mara squealed with delight as she peered inside. 'It's amazing,' she cooed.

She wandered back to the bed, ran her hand over the Laura Ashley duvet cover and collapsed on the mattress, sinking deep into the soft memory foam.

Damian wrapped a hand around Lucia's slim waist and pulled her close, his fears temporarily dispelled. Maybe they could make it work with Mara living with them after all. It was certainly good to see Lucia so happy.

'Shall we take you to see your room? It's upstairs in the attic,' Lucia said. 'Damian's cleared it out, but we've not painted it yet. We thought you'd like to choose the colour. You can have Farrow and Ball if you'd like.'

Mara sat up, her face darkening. 'But I like this room.'

'This is our room. You have your own room upstairs.'

Mara stood and walked slowly towards them, her eyes narrowing, her jaw clenched tight. 'I want this room,' she repeated.

21

'This is exactly what I was afraid of,' Damian said, as he lay in bed with the rain hammering on the roof so loudly he wondered how he was going to sleep. 'She's only been here a matter of hours, and already she's caused chaos.'

'Nobody said it was going to be easy.' Lucia dumped a dirty cotton wool pad into a bin under the dresser as she removed her make-up. 'But you know what the psychologist said about letting her make her own choices.'

'Even if that means turfing us out of our own bedroom?'

'It'll only be for a night or two. I'll talk to her again in the morning.'

'I get the point, but we need to set some boundaries, or she'll run rings around us.'

Lucia sighed. 'I'll talk to her.'

She slipped off her clothes and pulled on a pair of cotton pyjamas before sliding into bed.

'I just think we need to get this right from the start or it's not going to work,' Damian said.

'I'll take her shopping tomorrow for a new duvet set, and maybe even go looking for paint. I'll talk her around.'

'Don't take too long about it.' Damian rolled over and reached to switch off his bedside lamp.

'You begrudge her being here, don't you?'

'Of course not,' he lied.

'But you don't like it.'

'You never said I had to like it.'

'She's my sister. What was I supposed to do, throw her out on the street?'

'We're not qualified to look after her needs,' Damian said. 'And at some point, she needs to learn how to cope on her own. We could have set her up on her own with some care support.'

'What she needs is her family. She's had no one for the last nineteen years. She needs to be with people who love her.'

'What about the kids? They need us too.'

'They'll get used to each other.'

'And at what cost to this family?'

'Mara *is* family.'

Lucia rolled over and switched off her light as the rain intensified, clattering on the roof tiles like a million stamping, angry feet. Damian lay on his back and stared at the ceiling.

'Do you think the police will catch James Finch?' he asked, not feeling in the slightest bit sleepy.

There had been plenty of sightings of Finch after the police appeal, from Cornwall to Scotland, and as far away as the Czech Republic, Portugal and Norway, but so far he'd remained tantalisingly elusive. Maybe he'd had help. Someone somewhere must be harbouring him.

'What if he comes looking for her? Maybe it would be better for her own safety if Mara lived somewhere else. We don't want to put her in danger again.'

'For the last time, Mara isn't going anywhere. She's staying with us.'

'Don't say I didn't warn you,' Damian said with a sigh.

Lucia sat up suddenly. 'It's what we agreed when I did the interview you insisted on. And as far as James Finch is concerned, I wouldn't be surprised if he was dead in a ditch somewhere. I don't care. And even if he was alive, he'd be an idiot to come anywhere near this house. Now go to sleep. We'll talk to Mara in the morning.'

'Fine. But there's something I have to tell you, something Mara said to me before the interview you did for the TV.'

'Damian, I'm tired. It's been a long day.'

'Yeah, sure,' he said, rolling over. 'It can wait.'

'Goodnight.'

The light went out, and darkness enveloped them, but Damian's eyes stayed open, staring into the gloom. His mind was racing as fast as his heart, and he knew sleep was going to elude him for a while.

22

After convincing Mara she would have more privacy at the top of the house away from the children, she finally agreed to move into the attic room. She'd made Damian paint it twice, once in a hideous candy pink and again in a more sober pale lavender, and chose a duvet cover decorated with princesses and unicorns, which seemed more appropriate for a child than a grown woman.

'How long is Auntie Mara staying with us?' April asked, in that way kids have of asking the most telling questions framed in the most innocent tone.

It was a late afternoon in October when the hazy light of the day was dipping over the horizon. April was picking at a plate of spaghetti at the kitchen table an hour or so before Lucia was due home.

'Why? Don't you like her being here?' She'd never asked about Mara before, so Damian wasn't sure where her question was leading.

April pursed her lips and rolled her eyes to the ceiling as if she'd never considered the thought before. 'I'm not sure,' she said. 'She never wants to play dolls with me.'

Damian put the glass he was drying away in a cupboard and slung the tea cloth over the handle of the range.

'We've talked about this, remember?' he said, drawing up a chair at the table. 'Auntie Mara has never known any children before.'

'What, none?' April screwed her face up in disbelief.

Dylan looked up from his iPad and gave his father a silent, knowing look. Damian was sure he knew more about what had happened to Mara than he was letting on. The other kids at school must have been talking about it. Perhaps it was time for another chat with him.

'No. And because she's never known any other children, she finds it hard to know how to play. Now, eat up. Mum'll be home soon, and you're not even in your jim-jams yet.'

Lucia was late back that evening, caught up in an ongoing train drivers' strike that had been dragging on for months. They shared a bottle of Californian Pinot Noir over dinner, and Damian rubbed Lucia's feet as they suffered through a predictable and plodding crime drama on TV. Mara rarely joined them in the evenings, preferring to eat on her own in her room.

'I think we need to talk to Dylan again,' Damian said, as the news headlines came on at ten.

Lucia sat up and stretched. 'About what?'

'I think he knows more about what happened to Mara than we realise. Don't you think it would be better for us to talk to him about it than for him to pick up rumour and innuendo at school?'

'I still think he's too young to understand.'

'He's a bright kid. I think he knows we're keeping the truth from him.'

'Fine,' Lucia said, standing up and sweeping away their coffee mugs. ''Talk to him if you think it'll help.'

Damian hesitated. 'And I think April's uncomfortable around your sister. She was asking how long Mara's staying with us.'

'April will get used to her being here soon enough.'

'Maybe we should talk to her psychologist?'

'And say what?'

'She could give us some advice on helping April to cope.'

'Don't be ridiculous. April doesn't need help.'

Damian switched off the TV and the standard lamp in the corner.

'I know you're trying to do your best for Mara,' he said, following Lucia into the kitchen, 'but don't forget Dylan and April need your love and support too.'

'Are you saying I'm neglecting them?'

'No! Of course not. I'm just saying that you're not here all the time, so you don't see the effect it's having on them both, the way I can.'

Lucia turned on him, her eyes blazing. 'Don't you dare try to make me feel guilty about going back to work.'

'I'm not criticising. I'm just pointing out I see things you can't because you're not always here.'

'That's really not fair, Damian.'

'You have to admit you've been completely wrapped up with Mara these last few months. And I understand that, but just bear in mind the impact on the rest of us.'

'I'm too tired for this. I'm going to bed. We'll talk about it in the morning.'

As Damian climbed into bed with their cross words playing over in his mind, he regretted not clearing the air. There was nothing worse to breed resentment than going to bed on an argument.

Lucia turned off her bedside lamp and rolled over without a word. Damian read for a short while, but when he tried to sleep, he found he couldn't switch off, so lay sweating into his pillow for what seemed like hours.

He must have drifted off at some point because he woke with a start, the room still swathed in darkness. He squinted into the gloom, letting his eyes adjust to the night, his head foggy. He checked his phone. It was gone two in the morning. Outside the window, a cat yowled. His mouth was dry, and his tongue furry. He needed a glass of water.

He swung his legs out of bed, grabbed his dressing gown from the back of the bedroom door and slipped out onto the landing. The door swung closed behind him, and he took a hesitant step, his brain struggling to rationalise the disquiet niggling him. Something was out of kilter. Not quite right. He was in almost complete darkness, the only light coming from April's room. He was sure the night light on the landing had been on when they'd gone to bed, softly illuminating the carpet along the skirting board.

He glanced into April's room with a chill tingling his skin. He was certain he'd pulled her door shut when he'd checked on her before bed. He recalled tiptoeing around the detritus of dolls and toys scattered across the floor, pulling the duvet up to her chin and planting a delicate kiss on her soft forehead. The stripped pine door had definitely clicked shut as he'd backed out of her room. And yet there it was, wide open, the glow from April's globe spilling out onto the landing.

His first thought was that April had been up in the night. But it was unlike her. Usually, if she woke before morning feeling ill or needing the bathroom, she'd holler for her parents.

And yet he'd heard nothing.

'April?' he whispered, his sleep-deadened senses now fully alive.

He poked his head into her room and checked her bed, half expecting to find it empty. To his relief, her arms were hanging over the edge of the mattress and her hair was a messy tangle over the pillow. Her breathing was slow and regular. He watched her for a moment, his heart swelling. Although she'd started school and often exhibited the precocious sauciness of a teenager, while she slept, she looked like an angel.

Satisfied nothing was amiss, he reached to pull the door closed, but something in the corner of the room caught his eye. He gasped as he saw Mara sitting frozen in her pyjamas on the chair in the corner. Her body was rigid, her hands resting on her knees. She hadn't noticed Damian in the doorway, or if she had, she'd ignored him.

'Mara?' Damian whispered. 'What are you doing?'

Nothing.

She didn't move a muscle, only continued to stare at April sleeping oblivious in her bed.

He edged towards her wondering if perhaps she'd been sleepwalking. He'd heard about people going into catatonic trances, awake but unaware of their surroundings. Was it a psychological symptom of the kidnapping? Whatever it was, it gave him the creeps.

'Mara, are you awake?'

Still she didn't respond. He didn't want to frighten her, but she couldn't stay in April's room. Damian waved his hand in front of her face, but she didn't even blink.

'Mara!' he hissed as loudly as he dared.

April moaned in her sleep and rolled over. She scrunched up her face as she rubbed her nose with the back of her hand and took a deep breath.

Damian was at a loss. He was nervous about touching Mara in case he startled her, and she screamed, and besides, he wasn't sure if that's what you were supposed to do with people in catatonic trances.

He needed Lucia. She'd know what to do. He tiptoed back to their room, switched on his bedside lamp and found her wrapped up in the duvet like a butterfly in a cocoon. He rocked her shoulder gently, not wanting to startle her.

'Lucia, wake up.'

She groaned and muttered something incomprehensible.

'I don't know what to do. Mara's in April's room.'

Lucia's eyes peeled open, blinking as she struggled to focus on his face. 'What time is it?'

'The middle of the night,' Damian said. 'You have to come and talk to her.'

Lucia pulled herself up on her elbow, her eyes narrow slits. She glanced at her bedside clock and frowned. 'It's two in the morning.'

'Mara's just sitting in April's room staring at her like she's in some kind of trance. I didn't know what to do. Quickly, come and see for yourself.'

'For God's sake,' Lucia mumbled, sliding her legs out of bed.

Bleary-eyed, she stumbled across the room and out onto the landing as Damian held the door open.

'I'm worried if April wakes up and sees her in her room, she'll freak out.'

'All right, calm down. I heard you.'

Lucia stepped cautiously into April's room, looking first at the bed and then at the chair in the corner.

'There's no one here,' she said, raising an eyebrow.

'What do you mean?' Damian squeezed past and looked for

himself, expecting to see Mara sitting frozen in the same spot where he'd left her.

But the chair was empty.

'I swear she was here a minute ago,' he blustered. 'I'm not making it up.'

Lucia tiptoed across the room and smoothed down April's hair before planting a kiss on her head.

'Well, she's not here now,' she whispered, shooing Damian out of the room and quietly pulling the door shut.

The night light on the landing had been switched back on, casting its reassuring glow along the floor like an emergency light in a stricken aircraft.

'But I saw her!'

'If this is some kind of joke, it's not very funny.' Lucia stomped back to their room.

Damian began to doubt himself. But no, he was sure he hadn't imagined it. He'd seen Mara clearly.

'I didn't dream it if that's what you think,' he said as Lucia climbed back into bed.

'Go back to sleep, we'll talk about it in the morning.' She rolled over, plumped up her pillow and pulled the duvet over her shoulders.

'It was as if she was awake but couldn't see me. It was really weird,' Damian persisted. He had to make her believe him.

'Turn the light out and go to sleep.'

Reluctantly, Damian crawled back into bed. The sheet was rucked up from his earlier restlessness. He punched his pillow into shape and turned off the light with a sigh, concentrating on slowing his racing heart rate. But he couldn't shake the thought of Mara sitting motionless in April's room, then started to worry about waking to find her in their room, her eyes blank and unseeing. It made him shudder, and as he lay there wide awake, he resolved to fit a lock to their door first thing in the morning.

23

Damian woke to the sound of Lucia's alarm. He peeled his eyes open and was immediately struck by a sense of dread, a tight knot of anxiety coiled in his gut. And then he remembered how he'd found Mara in April's room, a silent, spectral presence watching his daughter sleep in some kind of otherworldly trance. And like a ghost in the night, she'd vanished the moment he'd dragged Lucia out of bed to investigate. Maybe he'd dreamt it. A symptom of the turmoil in his mind. But no. Mara's presence had been as real as the insistent bleat of the alarm.

Lucia rolled over and silenced the clock. She stretched and yawned.

'How did you sleep?' she asked, turning her head to face him, strands of red hair plastered to her forehead.

'Not great,' he said. 'How about you?'

'Yeah, fine.' Either she'd forgotten he'd woken her in the middle of the night or she'd pushed it out of her mind.

'Got to get up. I'm going to be late,' she said, sliding out of bed and shuffling bare-footed towards the en-suite across the stripped pine floorboards.

While she showered, Damian woke the children, battling with

them to wash and get dressed. Then he herded them downstairs and began his well-rehearsed breakfast routine, orchestrating everything like a symphony conductor; kettle on, bread in the toaster, orange juice on the table next to the butter and jam, glasses, plates and cutlery out, cereal packets lined up on the side. As he waited for a cafetière of coffee to brew, he hooked Dylan and April's lunch boxes out of the fridge and zipped them into their school bags.

The toaster popped up at the exact moment Lucia walked into the kitchen, her hair tied back in a ponytail, her skin glowing.

'Perfect timing,' Damian said, burning the tips of his fingers as he grabbed the toast and dropped it on a plate.

Lucia poured herself a mug of coffee and sat with the children at the table. Dylan could barely drag his eyes away from his iPad, head-phone buds plugged in while he shovelled cereal into his mouth. Lucia was no better, scrolling through her emails on her phone as she ate. At least April wasn't distracted by a device, even if she was spreading too much butter on her toast and getting jam all over her hands.

For a moment, they looked like any ordinary family sitting down to eat breakfast together. But since Mara had moved in, they had become anything but ordinary. Little things they used to take for granted had changed, like the way they used to listen to the news on the radio in the morning, but ate now in silence for fear of the children hearing something unsavoury about Mara's ordeal.

'Daddy, are unicorns real?' April asked, wiping her fingers on the tablecloth.

'Some people think so, yes.'

'Well, are they?'

'What do *you* think?'

'I think they're real.'

'Then they must be,' he said.

Lucia finished her coffee and dropped her mug in the sink. 'I'd better get going,' she said, grabbing her bag and kissing Damian's cheek. 'Be good for Dad, kids. See you tonight.'

Dylan shrugged off her attempt to hug him. April reached out sticky fingers, but Lucia skilfully sidestepped her grasp and planted a kiss on the top of her head.

'Right, go and brush your teeth and get your shoes on. We need to leave in ten minutes,' Damian warned the children as Lucia swept out of the door.

The school was a short distance from the house, a brisk walk that usually cleared Damian's head. But not that morning. The vision of Mara sitting in the darkness in April's room haunted him, and as much as he tried to rationalise her behaviour, he couldn't shake the feeling it was just plain weird. She'd only been sitting there, watching. But who knew what was going on inside her head after years of abuse and trauma. It was foolish to think she could simply settle into normal family life. What had Lucia been thinking? They needed help. Some support. But they'd hardly heard from Mara's psychologist since she'd been discharged from the psychiatric hospital.

They arrived at the school gates a few minutes before the bell. April and Dylan ran off without a backwards glance and instantly disappeared among a seething mass of screaming children in the playground. Once, Damian would have stayed to chat to some of the mums, putting off the start of his working day. But now he went out of his way to avoid them. He sensed their furtive glances and whispered gossipping whenever they saw him, all bursting to ask him about Mara.

Instead, he turned straight for home. He had a big project to finish, and if he got his head down, there was every chance he could break the back of it before pick-up.

The clatter of dishes came from the kitchen as he let himself into the house and hung his jacket on a hook in the hall.

Mara was at the sink, washing up the breakfast bowls and plates Damian had abandoned in his haste to get the kids to school on time. Even though she'd put on weight, her jeans and hoodie hung limply off her tiny frame. She glanced over her shoulder and caught him watching. He shuddered at the memory of her blank eyes as she'd sat rigid in April's room the previous night.

'You're back,' she said as if nothing had happened.

'I didn't expect to see you up yet.'

'I was hoping to catch Lucia before she left.'

Damian shrugged. 'She went off in a rush this morning. She'll be home by seven tonight.'

'No problem. It can wait.'

A troubling silence filled the room as Damian struggled to think of something to say. Should he tackle her about what had happened, explain to her it was unacceptable to go into the kids' rooms while they slept?

'Do you fancy a coffee?' he asked. Maybe if they sat down and talked, he could find a way of bringing up the subject.

Mara peeled off a pair of rubber gloves and hung them over the tap. 'Sure,' she said. 'Why not.'

They skirted around each other in an embarrassed dance as Damian filled the kettle and she pulled out a chair at the table, watching him heap ground coffee into the cafetière.

'It's good to see you up and about so early,' Damian said, waiting for the coffee to brew. He leaned casually against the worktop, trying to look relaxed, but feeling anxious.

'I've not had a chance to tell you how grateful I am to you for letting me stay. I know it couldn't have been an easy decision.'

'Don't be silly. You're family,' Damian said.

'It won't be forever.'

'Stay as long as you need,' he found himself saying. 'There's no rush.'

'I'm sure you don't want me hanging around.'

'Well, I expect you'll be wanting a place of your own soon.'

'Of course,' Mara said, sounding less than enthused.

'I can help you find a job, maybe in one of the local shops. I'll keep my eye out for anything that crops up.'

'What is it you do again?'

'Computers,' he said. 'I develop websites.'

'And look after the children.'

'In between keeping my clients happy.'

'It's a shame Lucia has to go out to work. She must miss out on so much with Dylan and April.'

'It makes financial sense for me to stay at home,' Damian said.

He ignored Mara's raised eyebrow. He took two mugs from the shelf over the microwave and poured from the cafetière.

'Why? Does Lucia earn more than you?' The idea seemed completely alien to her.

'I'm a freelancer so I can work from home and fit it around childcare.'

'Doesn't it bother you?'

Damian stared at Mara across the kitchen. Was she deliberately trying to get a rise out of him? 'It's not the nineteen seventies,' he laughed, hoping to disguise his irritation.

'That's great you feel that way. You guys have obviously talked this through, and it's amazing you're able to make it work.'

'There are loads of guys I know who stay at home with the kids while their wives work. I think it's liberating.'

'Absolutely. You shouldn't care what anybody else thinks.'

'What about you, do you think you'd like to have children one day?' Damian asked, steering the conversation away from his domestic arrangements.

'God, no!'

'Why not?'

'I'd always be worrying about them.'

Every parent was anxious about keeping their children safe, but Damian had long ago accepted you couldn't think like that or you'd go mad. Like his mother used to say, you can't wrap them up in cotton wool. But of course, for Mara, it was different.

'I'd never be able to let them out of my sight,' she continued. 'I'd forever be thinking the worst was about to happen.'

'Yes,' Damian said. 'I can understand that.'

He took a seat at the table opposite Mara as a pregnant silence fell between them. Damian cradled his mug and sipped at the coffee, savouring its bitterness, noticing the loudness of the clock ticking on the wall, and how Mara had bitten her fingernails down to the raw skin at the tops of her fingers.

'Can I ask you something?' he asked. 'About what happened last night.'

Mara looked startled. 'I wondered if you might bring it up,' she said. At least she had the decency to look embarrassed.

'You saw me?'

Mara nodded, sucking in her bottom lip, like a child with a guilty conscience.

'Why didn't you say anything?'

'I was frightened. I didn't expect to see you.'

'Is it something that's happened before?'

Mara frowned. 'Before?'

'I guess it's the symptom of some kind of post-traumatic stress,' he said. 'It's probably nothing to worry about. Do you remember what happened?'

'Of course.'

'And you remember going into April's room? Can you remember what you were thinking?'

Mara's eyes narrowed. 'What do you mean?'

'I'm not angry. I'm trying to help you.'

'But I didn't go to April's room.'

'I saw you, Mara, remember? You were sitting on the chair in the corner in the dark, just staring at April as she slept. You gave me quite a shock.'

'I never left my room last night.'

Damian sighed. So she had been sleepwalking, or at least that's what she wanted him to believe. 'You don't remember anything?'

Mara frowned. 'I remember seeing you, but not in April's room.'

'Then, where?' She was talking in riddles. She must have been confused.

'You came into *my* room. You frightened me.'

'What? No, I didn't. You're confused. I woke up to get a glass of water and noticed April's door was open. When I went in, I found you sitting there, watching April.'

Mara shook her head. 'No, that's not right,' she said. '*You* were in *my* room, at the end of my bed, staring at me. I was so scared I couldn't move or speak.'

'No, that's not what happened. You're getting muddled up.'

'I know what I saw, Damian. You came to my room last night, and you stood over my bed, watching me while I slept.'

It was worse than Damian thought. She was delusional.

'I don't want to mention it to Lucia. She'll only get upset, but you have to promise me never to do that again,' said Mara. 'You really frightened me.'

24

Damian collapsed into the chair at his desk in his study, his mind a whirl of self-doubt and confusion. Mara had been so convincing, so utterly sure of what she'd seen, she had him questioning his own mind. The look in her eye had been pure fear. Was it possible he'd unknowingly crept up the stairs and let himself into her room? He cast his mind back, trying to grasp at the flimsy memory of waking, of stumbling onto the landing, the niggle of uncertainty, pushing open April's door and finding Mara sitting motionless in the tub chair in the corner. He was sure he hadn't dreamt it. If he'd climbed the stairs to Mara's room, surely he would have remembered.

But what concerned him most was Mara confiding in Lucia, telling her he'd sneaked into her room. He knew Lucia was desperate to reconnect with her sister, and there was a distinct possibility she would believe Mara despite his protestations.

Damian flipped open his laptop, hoping work would distract his mind, but he screwed up his password twice, his fingers fumbling on the keyboard.

He almost missed the gentle tap at the door. He froze, hands poised in mid-air, listening for movement outside.

'What is it?' he called out.

The door clicked open, and Mara peered in.

'Am I disturbing you?'

Damian swivelled his chair to face her, trying to look casual. He didn't want to give her the satisfaction of seeing she'd wormed her way under his skin. 'No, it's fine,' he said, the words catching in his throat. 'What's wrong?'

'Can I come in?' She slunk across the room and sat on the sofa along the back wall where Damian took his early afternoon naps before school pick-up.

'I was thinking I'd like to do something to thank you both for letting me stay,' she said, sitting demurely, the picture of innocence. It was like the conversation in the kitchen had never happened.

'There's no need,' Damian said, desperate for her to leave him alone.

'No, I really want to. I thought it might be nice if I cooked you a meal. It's the least I can do.'

The way her demeanour had changed so quickly unsettled him. One minute she was accusing him of prowling in her room, the next she was offering to cook for them. It was the last thing he expected.

'A meal?'

'I could have something ready for when Lucia gets home.'

'Tonight?'

'Why not?'

'It's a bit short notice.'

'Did you have something planned?'

Damian considered the packaged quiche lorraine in the fridge they were going to have. 'Not really,' he said, wondering how he could put her off.

'Tonight it is then. I know this recipe for chicken casserole that Lucia would love,' Mara said, beaming broadly. 'You have to simmer the thighs in white wine with lardons and olives.'

'Where did you learn that?'

She glanced at her hands, hesitating before answering. 'I used to cook for him sometimes. He said I had a talent for it.'

'James Finch taught you?'

'You look surprised. He taught me about taste and seasoning and how flavours work together.'

Damian raised an eyebrow.

'He wasn't a monster,' she snapped.

'He kept you chained up in a cell under the floor, Mara.'

'You wouldn't understand.'

'Explain it to me then.'

'I don't want to talk about it.'

And that was the problem; she never wanted to talk about James Finch. Her relationship with him was the one area she shied away from in the TV interview, and Helen, her psychologist, had warned them against prying. But the longer she kept quiet about it, the more suspicious Damian had become about what she was hiding. He knew there was something. He'd read up about Stockholm Syndrome and how hostage victims often formed strong bonds with their captors as a survival mechanism, but he struggled to understand how Mara could talk about Finch with anything other than utter disdain. When she did mention him, she told them she hated him for stealing her childhood, but her tone suggested something else, something warmer. Damian wondered if she'd been in love with him.

'You never talk much about him,' he said. 'Why is that?'

'Why do you think?'

'You must have been close?'

She hesitated, studying Damian's expression. 'Admit it, Damian, you want to know if I was fucking him, don't you?' She spat out the words with such venom, he was taken aback.

'No,' he protested, although that was precisely what he was thinking.

'Then ask me.'

Their eyes met, and she held Damian's gaze with a steely look of defiance. He tried to read her, but her expression was cold and hard.

He licked his lips. 'Did you ever sleep with him?' he asked.

Mara continued to stare at him, her jaw tight and the veins in her scrawny neck pulsing. 'Fuck you.'

'But you loved him, didn't you?' he pressed. 'After all that time cooped up in that house together, you must have developed strong feelings for him.'

She refused to answer, but neither would she look away.

'And something else that's always troubled me,' he continued. Now he had her full attention he wasn't going to miss the opportunity. 'When you escaped, you were half-starved, weak with hunger and barefooted. How did you outrun him?'

She blinked twice but otherwise looked utterly unfazed. 'Do you want me to cook or not?'

'Why won't you answer?'

'I don't have to explain anything to you. You weren't there. You don't know anything about it.'

'So help me understand.'

'I'll need ingredients. You'll have to take me shopping.'

Damian glanced at the clock. It had already gone ten, and he hadn't even logged onto his computer yet. 'I'm busy today, Mara. Maybe you could cook another day.'

Her face darkened. 'I think Lucia would be disappointed, but if you really don't want me to... '

'Tell me what really happened the day you ran away from James Finch.'

'I've already told you. Now are you taking me shopping or not?'

'All right, all right,' Damian said. She wasn't going to be broken quite so easily. The answers to his questions would have to wait for another day.

'Great,' she said, jumping up and clapping her hands with glee. 'I'll go and get my coat.'

25

They drove the first few miles in silence with Damian watching Mara from the corner of his eye. Even though she'd been in the car before, she was like a child visiting a new country, observing everything they passed with an enthusiastic curiosity which he might have found endearing if he didn't know her better.

He'd thought carefully about where to take her. She'd rarely left the house since moving in with them, and she remained wary of strangers and large crowds. On the few trips she'd taken into town with Lucia, she'd become anxious and panicked when confronted with bustling streets of shoppers. So with that in mind, Damian avoided taking her to the large supermarket where they usually shopped and opted to head for a small farm shop on the outskirts of town where it was quieter and less intimidating. Somewhere Mara was less likely to be recognised.

'Did Finch really keep you chained up in your cell?' he asked as they turned onto a short section of dual carriageway.

Mara craned her neck to watch a buzzard soar high into the grey sky on broad, outstretched wings. 'Do you doubt it?'

'It's just that it's so horrific I can't imagine what kind of person could treat another human being like that, let alone an eleven-year-old girl.'

'Only for the first few months, until he could trust me,' Mara said. 'Then I was allowed to join him in the house sometimes, although I always had to sleep in my room.'

Room? Did she mean her underground cell? It was an odd way to describe it. In her interview, Mara had explained how Finch had forced her to carry out chores to keep the house spotlessly clean, and how he'd beaten her for any minor transgression. But there was something else she'd said that had remained at the forefront of Damian's mind. She'd said she preferred the beatings to the days she was left alone in her cell without any human contact. It was one of the saddest things he'd ever heard, a testament to the depth of her suffering and the total physical and emotional control Finch had held over her.

'Did you ever think you'd escape?'

'Of course, even when he told me everyone I loved had forgotten about me,' Mara said.

'I think I'd have given up.'

'If I'd given up, I would have died,' she said. 'And I wasn't ready for that. I wasn't going to let him win.'

They pulled up into a rough gravel car park outside the farm shop, a low wooden building with a flat roof and an air of decay. It wasn't much to look at from outside, but after being recommended by a well-known chef in a Sunday newspaper it had become a mecca for food lovers. At weekends, it was almost impossible to find a parking space.

'You don't have to come with me,' Mara said, unclipping her seatbelt. 'I can cope perfectly well on my own.'

Damian hesitated. She'd never been shopping on her own, and he wasn't sure how Lucia would feel about it. But what the hell, she had to learn some independence sooner or later or she was never going to cope when left to her own devices.

'Are you sure?'

'Yes. I won't be long.'

'Fine. I'll be right here if you need me,' Damian said, happy to have some time on his own.

'Do you have any money?'

He pulled a twenty-pound note from his wallet. 'Is that enough?'

Mara shrugged. 'I guess so,' she said. He'd forgotten she had absolutely no idea about the value of anything.

As she marched across the car park and disappeared into the shop, he felt a release of tension in his body. He rolled his seat back, flicked on the radio and fell into a light sleep to the slow beat of an old acoustic ballad.

He was woken by the sound of Mara battling with three bulging plastic bags as she struggled into the car. Damian fixed his seat back into an upright position and rubbed his eyes. He hadn't realised how tired he'd been.

'Did you get everything?'

'Yes,' she said. 'We can go now.'

A light rain started to fall as they drove home, coating the windscreen with a fine layer of mizzle. 'It wasn't supposed to rain,' Damian said.

'But it's good for the garden.' Mara stared vacantly out of the window.

'Do you mind me asking questions about what happened when you were taken by Finch? The psychologist said we're not supposed to pry.'

'It's fine. Lucia's always pussyfooting around me like I'm made of glass. She never asks me anything.'

'She's afraid of upsetting you.'

'Why?'

'Because she worries about you. She always did. She still feels guilty about the night you were taken. She thinks she let you down.' Damian wanted Mara to know the agony her sister had endured and how it still gnawed at her conscience.

'I used to wish it had been her instead of me,' Mara said.

'And now?'

But she didn't reply.

26

On the way to pick up Dylan and April from school, Damian called Lucia. She answered straight away.

'I thought I'd better warn you,' he said. 'Mara's cooking for us tonight. I've left her in the kitchen prepping.'

'Cooking?'

'She was insistent. She wants to thank us for having her. You'd better not be late. I don't think that would go down too well.'

As Damian reached the school gates, still on the phone, he nodded and smiled at a mum of one the kids in April's class.

'That's sweet. I'll do my best to get away on time.'

'You need to do better than that. She'll be furious if you're late.'

'Okay, okay. I'll be there.'

'This is really important, Lucia. I had to take her shopping.'

'Where?'

'The farm shop out of town. I thought it would be quieter than the supermarket.'

'And?'

'It was fine.'

A stream of children appeared from the main school building, coats and bags and jumpers dragging behind them.

'Listen, Damian, about last night... '

Oh shit. He thought she'd forgotten. 'Yeah?'

April loped across the playground with her face set like thunder, her satchel scuffing along the ground.

'It doesn't matter. We'll talk tonight.'

Damian let out the breath he was holding. 'Okay, gotta go. See you tonight. Remember, don't be late.'

'Hate school.' He caught April's bag in one hand as she slammed it into his stomach.

'Why, what's happened?'

But she was already stomping off. 'April, wait!' Damian shouted.

He scanned the playground for Dylan, who appeared with two of his friends sauntering along deep in idle chat. Behind him, April's teacher was waving at Damian, trying to catch his attention.

'Mr Caslocke!'

'Come on, Dylan, your sister's stormed off in a huff,' he said, turning his back on the teacher trotting towards them. Whatever storm was brewing in whatever teacup, it could wait. He was worried about April reaching the road on her own. Five-year-olds in a huff tended to have little concern for their own safety.

He pushed through a meandering throng of mums and grabbed April's hand as she slipped between two parked cars.

'Hey, sweetie, you shouldn't run off like that. What's happened? Why are you so upset?'

'I don't want to talk about it.' She yanked her hand free and crossed her arms over her chest.

'Okay, fine. We'll talk about it when we get home.'

'What's wrong with her?' Dylan asked, prodding his sister in the back of the head.

'Hey!' she screamed, swiping violently at his hand and missing.

'Dylan, enough!' Damian shouted. 'Leave your sister alone.'

THE SMELL of frying onions welcomed them home. Mara was at the hob with an array of diced ingredients laid out in dishes on the side.

'Smells good,' Damian said, pinching a cube of red pepper and popping it in his mouth.

Mara picked up one of their long-handled Sabatier knives and began chopping up chunks of fatty bacon with the dexterity of a Michelin-starred chef.

'Did Finch let you use knives?' Damian asked, perching on the edge of the kitchen table watching the blur of rapid cuts in awe.

'Only under supervision. He kept them locked up in the drawer where I couldn't get them most of the time,' Mara said, without looking up.

'It certainly looks like you know what you're doing. Can't wait to taste the results.'

Without the worry of having to cook their evening meal, Damian concentrated on feeding the kids and making sure they were bathed and ready for bed when Lucia returned home. True to her word, she was on time for a change. He greeted her at the door with a chilled glass of wine.

She gave him a 'what's going on?' look as she caught the aroma coming from the kitchen. Damian shrugged.

'I guess we shouldn't knock it,' she whispered, kicking off her heels.

'The kids are both in bed, but we've been banned from the kitchen. Why don't you read them a story and have a quick bath.'

'A bath before dinner? How decadent.'

'You might want to have a word with April too,' Damian said, lowering his voice. 'She's had a bad day at school but won't tell me what's wrong.'

Lucia rolled her eyes and padded softly up the stairs.

27

Damian found it an odd experience to dress for dinner in his own house. He showered and shaved and even pulled on a clean shirt with the smart jeans he reserved for special occasions. Then he reminded himself this *was* a special occasion. It felt like they'd finally turned a corner with Mara.

As he checked his hair in the mirror, Lucia emerged from the bathroom dressed to kill. She'd taken his recommendation and was wearing her emerald Karen Millen pencil dress, her skin still flushed from the heat of the bath. She'd piled her hair on her head in a messy updo, and she smelled divine.

'You look stunning,' Damian said, kissing her cheek.

'You've scrubbed up pretty well yourself.'

'Did you get a chance to speak to April?'

'She says it was nothing, a silly squabble with her friends. It'll have all blown over by the morning.'

'Anything to do with Mara?'

'What? No, of course not.'

'Is she being bullied?'

'She's fine, Damian. Forget about it.'

Mara met them in the hall as they descended the stairs and

ushered them into the dining room. Flickering candles and the twinkle of fairy lights over the fireplace had transformed the room into something magical. Soft music completed the romantic effect. Lucia immediately burst into tears.

Mara looked crestfallen. 'Have I done something wrong?'

'No, it's amazing,' Lucia sobbed. 'You didn't have to go to so much trouble.'

'It was nothing.'

Lucia threw her arms around her sister and pulled her into a crushing hug, her tears threatening to streak her make-up. After all the effort she'd gone to to make herself look nice, she was going to ruin it.

'Why don't we sit down,' Damian suggested.

Lucia dabbed her eyes with a tissue and checked her mascara in the mirror over the mantelpiece. 'Good idea. Whatever you're cooking, it smells incredible.'

'I almost forgot. I bought a fancy bottle of white wine. It's chilling in the fridge,' Mara said, hurrying away.

She was halfway out of the door when Lucia noticed what Damian had already spotted. 'You've only laid two places. Aren't you going to join us?'

Mara shook her head. 'This is your treat. You should spend some time together.'

At last, she was talking sense. For the last few months, Lucia had been so preoccupied with her sister, she'd barely had any time for Damian or the kids. A romantic meal for two at home was better than nothing.

'Damian, tell her,' Lucia said, pleading with him with her eyes.

'Lucia's right,' he said. 'You should definitely eat with us after all the trouble you've gone to.' He tried to sound genuine even though it was the last thing he wanted. Mara's presence around the table would have soured everything.

'I'm more than happy eating in my room, and I'm not going to argue about it. Tonight is for you two.' Mara slipped out of the room before Lucia could protest.

'I feel bad,' Damian said. 'I had no idea she was planning this just for us.'

'Should I force her to come and eat with us?'

'She needs to make her own choices, remember?' Damian said, grasping gratefully at Helen Barratt's advice.

'I just thought it would be nice for all three of us to sit down together for once.'

Damian reached for Lucia's hand. 'Maybe next time,' he said with a sympathetic smile.

Mara returned with a bottle of wine in one hand and balancing a bread basket and a bowl of olives in the other.

'Wine?' she asked, placing the bread and olives on the table.

'Lovely, thank you.' Lucia held up her glass.

'Could I just grab a beer?' Damian asked.

'But I've got wine,' Mara huffed, staring at him with ill-concealed disdain.

'Fine, I'll have wine.' He didn't want a fight to spoil the evening. It had been so long since he and Lucia had sat down for a meal, he was determined not to let Mara ruin it.

'It's a nice Sauvignon. The man in the shop recommended it.'

'Sorry,' Damian muttered. 'It looks like a good choice.'

As Mara filled his glass, Lucia reached for a chunk of bread from the basket, but her hand stopped mid-air. Her eyes opened wide. 'Oh God, we can't have this in the house,' she said, her voice pitched with alarm.

'What's wrong with it? It's artisan.'

'It's covered in seeds!'

'So?'

Damian grabbed the basket. Sure enough, the crust of the bread was coated in a smattering of black and brown seeds. Among them were at least a dozen almost translucent sesame seeds, like under-ripe apple pips. Innocuous but deadly.

'Jeez, Mara, what were you thinking?' Damian said, banging the basket on the table.

They'd striven to keep the house sesame-free ever since Dylan had suffered a severe reaction as a toddler. They'd identified the cause of a random but violent vomiting episode to a hummus dip. A series of blood tests at the hospital had confirmed his reaction had been to sesame.

The paediatrician's words of warning still echoed through Damian's memory; if Dylan was exposed again, it could cost his life. Anaphylactic shock could cause his throat to constrict, and he might be unable to breathe. If he didn't receive immediate medical treatment, he could die. The doctor's words were delivered with a harsh solemnity that condemned them to a life of fear and worry.

They went home in shock, cleared out the kitchen cupboards and disinfected the work surfaces. They checked all the labels on the packets and jars of food they already had in and read up on the subject voraciously, realising that eating out with Dylan would be a minefield that would be best avoided in future.

Over time, they learnt to live with their fears. It became second nature to check the lists of ingredients on the back of supermarket packets, scanning the tiny print for allergen advice and avoiding bread that had been produced in a bakery where the risk of contamination was high or that hadn't been pre-packed in a sesame-free environment. Thankfully, in the four years since his diagnosis, Dylan had never had another reaction, but it didn't mean they weren't always on their guard.

It was easy to see how Mara might have forgotten about Dylan's allergy. Lucia had mentioned it a couple of times, but Damian wasn't sure if Mara had taken it in. Why would she? It was the least of her worries. He doubted she even understood the danger.

'Dylan has a severe allergy to sesame,' Damian said, enjoying the view from the moral high ground. 'If Dylan had eaten this, it could have killed him.'

'But he's not eaten it.' Mara's brow furrowed.

'That's not the point. We don't ever have sesame in the house.' Lucia pushed her chair back and grabbed the breadbasket.

'I'm sorry,' Mara said, hanging her head. 'I didn't know.' She snatched the basket from her sister. 'I'll get rid of it.'

'Look,' Damian said, reaching for a drawer in the sideboard. One of Dylan's out-of-date auto-injectors was buried under a pile of napkins. 'Dylan always carries one of these in case of an emergency. It could save his life, and if you're living with us, you need to know how to use it.'

He took an orange from the fruit bowl on the side and showed her how to flip open the pen's cap and stab the needle hard into the flesh of the fruit.

'It delivers a shot of adrenaline,' he explained. 'If you think Dylan might be having a reaction, don't ever be afraid to use it.'

'I'm sorry. I'll throw the bread away,' Mara said.

'It's okay, you didn't know. No harm done,' Lucia said, returning from the brink of her meltdown.

Mara shuffled out of the room with the bread, muttering her apologies. Lucia sunk her head in her hands. 'What the hell were you thinking, Damian? How could you let her bring that into the house?'

'Hang on, this isn't my fault.'

'You were with her when she went shopping, weren't you?'

Damian opened his mouth to reply and then clamped it shut again.

'After everything we've done to keep Dylan safe.'

'I didn't see her pick up the bread,' he said.

Lucia looked like she was about to say more but stopped when she heard Mara's footsteps in the hall. Her sister appeared with one of their big blue Le Creuset pots leaking wispy tendrils of steam. She put it down in the middle of the table and removed the lid to reveal a delicious smelling casserole.

'Bon appetite,' she said.

'Please come and join us,' Lucia said. 'You've made plenty.'

'Absolutely not. I've served up a plate in the kitchen. I'm going to eat in my room.'

'I feel bad.'

'There's a programme on TV I wanted to watch anyway.' She hesitated.

'Everything okay?' Lucia asked.

'Actually, there was something I wanted to ask. I'd like a lock on my bedroom door.'

'A lock?' Lucia glanced at Damian, looking perplexed.

'I'd feel safer, especially at night.'

'Are you having trouble sleeping?'

'A little.' Mara's gaze shifted towards Damian, her eyes narrowing. 'I know it's silly, but I'm worried someone might come into my room while I'm asleep.'

'You poor thing. You should have said something before.' Lucia stood and threw her arms around her sister.

Mara buried her chin into Lucia's shoulder, her arms around her waist, but she kept her eyes on Damian. He swallowed hard, fearing she was about to tell Lucia she'd woken to find him in her room. He readied himself with a protestation of innocence.

'It's only been recently. I didn't want to make a fuss.'

'After everything you've been through, you're entitled to make a fuss. We want you to feel safe in our house, so if you want a lock, we'll fit one for you. Isn't that right, Damian?'

He almost choked on his wine. 'Sure.'

'Damian will do it first thing tomorrow, won't you, darling?'

Mara shot him a thin, knowing smile.

'Of course,' he said. 'Whatever it takes to make Mara feel safe.'

28

If Mara thought she could get away with holding a false threat over him, she'd have to think again. Damian had done nothing wrong, and he wasn't going to be blackmailed. If she really wanted a lock on her door, he'd do it, but that would be the end of it.

'What's wrong?' Lucia asked, catching him lost in his thoughts.

'Nothing. This really is delicious, isn't it?' He forked another mouthful of chicken into his mouth. As much as he hated to admit it, it was a superb dish. The chicken melted in the mouth and the flavours were perfectly balanced, the sharpness of the white wine offset by the saltiness of the bacon.

'I guess it's in the genes. Mum was a great cook,' Lucia said.

'Are you sure everything's okay with April?'

'There was a bit of silly name-calling. Nothing to worry about. I expect it'll all be forgotten by tomorrow.'

'Was it about Mara?'

'I don't know.'

'Lucia?'

'Maybe, but look, you know what kids are like. They can be cruel. I'm sure it's nothing serious.'

'Do I need to speak with Miss Heggarty?' At least he knew now why she'd been trying to catch his attention in the playground.

'Let's see how things are in a few days.'

Lucia pushed her plate to one side and topped up their glasses with the last of the wine, shifting her chair back from the table. 'I forgot to say, the police called earlier.'

Damian raised an eyebrow and lowered his fork.

'They're going to scale back the investigation. They don't have the resources to keep looking for Finch.'

'Seriously? But what if he attacks another child?'

'Drake said their leads have virtually dried up. He gave me the impression that . . . I don't know, maybe I was reading too much into it, but I get the impression they think Finch might be dead.'

'Nothing more than a scumbag like him deserves.' Whatever he thought about Mara, Finch was the real villain.

'I suppose it would spare Mara having to face him in court.'

'But don't you think a trial would have given her some closure, at least,' Damian said.

'Maybe.' Lucia sighed. 'All things considered, she's doing well, don't you think? And this meal is a real step forwards.'

The problem was that Lucia only saw what she wanted to see. The truth was that Mara spent most of her time shut away in her room. She rarely went outside the house and seldom spoke about her time in captivity. Damian couldn't see how she was adjusting at all. It didn't help that she'd hardly seen her psychologist since she'd moved in. Mara was supposed to be getting regular therapy, but Damian couldn't help but feel they'd been abandoned.

'I don't know,' he said. 'What about this business with the lock for her door? Is she worried Finch is going to come back for her?'

'It gives me the creeps to think he might still be out there.'

'He'd be an idiot to turn up here,' Damian said.

'But until they find him, or his body, we won't know for sure.'

'You'll give yourself nightmares. Put him out of your mind. You'd be better off concentrating on getting Mara better.'

'Do you think I'm doing enough for her, especially now I'm back at work?'

'You've given her a home, a family. You've done plenty.'

Lucia shook her head. 'I can't fail her again. I owe it to her to protect her from him.'

'We've been through this. You didn't fail her. You were fourteen when she was taken. There was nothing you could have done. There's only one person responsible for what happened, and that's James Finch. Stop blaming yourself.'

'I can't just switch off how I feel,' she snapped.

'Maybe we should get you some counselling.'

'Don't be silly! I'm not a crank.'

'It's not being silly. You need some help.'

'I don't want to talk about it anymore. It's getting late. Let's clear up and go to bed.'

It's what always happened when Damian tried to tackle Lucia's pent up feelings of guilt. No matter how often he told her she wasn't to blame, he couldn't seem to get through. Whenever he tried to broach the subject, she shut him down, like it was too painful to discuss. Tonight wasn't the night to push it. She needed professional help.

Damian checked his watch. It was much later than he'd realised. He stood to clear the plates.

'Bugger, I've forgotten to do the sandwiches,' he said, scraping chicken bones from Lucia's plate onto his own. He usually juggled making the kids' lunches around preparing dinner, but Mara offering to cook had thrown out his routine.

'I'll do them while you clear up.'

'No, you have work in the morning. It'll only take me two minutes. Why don't you go to bed. I'll be up in a jiffy.'

'Are you sure?'

'Of course.'

'You're an angel.' Lucia moved close and planted a soft kiss laced with promise on Damian's lips as she stroked the nape of his neck.

He placed his hands on the thin material of her dress, taut over her hips, and pulled her to him.

'I didn't tell you how amazing you look tonight,' he whispered in her ear, with a frisson of excitement. It had been a while since they'd made love, Lucia's worries that Mara might hear them having not only dampened her libido but suffocated it and buried it deep underground.

'Is that right?' she said with a suggestive smile as she pulled away from him. 'Don't be too long. I'll be waiting for you upstairs.'

As she sashayed out of the room, rolling her hips, she shot Damian a coy glance over her shoulder.

He practically ran into the kitchen, his arms laden with plates and cutlery and the heavy Le Creuset pot with the remains of the casserole. Most of the dirty dishes went into the dishwasher, but he left the wine glasses on the side to wash up in the morning. He quickly wiped down the work surfaces with a damp cloth, clearing up the mess Mara hadn't bothered to clean, ignoring the nagging irritation that she'd left it for someone else to do.

Humming to himself, he laid out four slices of bread on the chopping board. He'd been going through the same routine for so long that making Dylan and April's sandwiches came as naturally to him as tying his own shoelaces, so he let his mind wander, imagining how the rest of the night would play out. He thought about Lucia's well-toned body, the curve of her hip, the swell of her stomach and of her long, smooth legs wrapped around his body.

He twirled flamboyantly on his heel to reach the fridge, yanked open the door and grabbed a tub of supermarket own-brand spread and a packet of ham. Thirty seconds later he had two sets of sandwiches cut into neat squares and wrapped in cling film. He retrieved the two lunch boxes from the draining board, thankful he'd remembered at least to wash them up after the kids had returned from school, and stacked the sandwiches neatly inside.

Next, he peeled and quartered two apples, chopped two carrots into batons, wrapped them in more cling film and popped them in with the sandwiches and a tube of yoghurt each. Job done. And in record quick time.

He checked the back door was locked, killed all the downstairs lights and hurried to bed. On his way, he locked and bolted the front door and checked on Dylan and April.

Dylan was on his back with his mouth open, breathing heavily.

April was curled up in a ball with the duvet wrapped tightly around her body. He couldn't help but glance at the chair in the corner, remembering how disconcerting it had been to find Mara sitting motionless in her cotton pyjamas, staring at his daughter. He shuddered and eased the door closed.

Their bedroom was in semi-darkness, the only light coming from the lamp on Damian's side of the bed. He imagined how Lucia had stripped out of her dress and had climbed naked between the sheets to wait for him, her hair fanning out over her pale, freckled shoulders.

He unbuttoned his shirt with trembling fingers, anticipating the warmth of Lucia's skin against his own naked body.

'Lucia?' he whispered. She was on her side with her back to him, the duvet pulled up to her neck.

He kicked off his jeans, slipped into bed and switched off the light. He rolled into Lucia's body, tucking his knees behind her legs.

'Lucia,' he breathed in her ear, kissing the tender skin on her neck.

But her breath came slow and deep, a sure sign she'd already succumbed to sleep.

He rolled back onto his pillow, stared at the ceiling and rued his own stupidity for forgetting to prepare the kids' lunches earlier.

29

Damian was startled by the phone ringing in the hall. It was rare for anyone to call that number, especially during the day. Most people rang his mobile, so he didn't pick up, assuming it was someone trying to sell him something he didn't want.

It stopped but immediately started ringing again.

With a weary sigh, Damian flipped his laptop closed and trudged into the hall.

'Hello?'

'Mr Caslocke?'

The prim voice was familiar, but he couldn't immediately place it. 'Yes?'

'It's Maggie McGuire, from St Joseph's.' There was a strain to her voice that made him nervous. 'I'm afraid there's been an incident.'

He immediately thought of April. Whatever she'd done must have been serious for the headteacher to call. He held his breath, praying she'd not hit or bitten another child. If she was being bullied, Damian wouldn't have put it past her to have stood up for herself. What if she was being suspended? Or worse, expelled?

'Is it April?' Damian asked, expecting the worst.

'April? No,' said Mrs McGuire, sounding perplexed. 'It's Dylan. I'm afraid we've had to call an ambulance.'

Her words hit him like a battering ram in his chest, and he felt like he was falling down a deep, dark chasm.

'Dylan collapsed in the dining hall about twenty minutes ago. He's had a suspected allergic reaction. The paramedics are taking him to hospital. You should get there as soon as you can.'

'Jesus,' Damian said, catching his breath. 'How?'

'Mr Caslocke, we can talk about this later, but right now Dylan needs you.'

'Did you use his injector pen?' he asked, scratching the stubble on his chin, puzzling how to make sense of what he was hearing.

A pause on the line. Was that a sigh?

'Yes, of course, we did, but you know yourself it's prudent to call an ambulance after someone, especially a child, has had a reaction.' Mrs McGuire hesitated again. 'He was struggling to breathe, even after we'd injected him.'

'Right, yes, I see,' he heard himself stammer.

'Mr Caslocke?'

'Yes?'

'Dylan's teacher, Mrs Anand, has gone with him in the ambulance. She'll meet you at the hospital.'

'Right, thank you,' Damian said, hanging up and staring into space.

He always knew this moment was a possibility, but he never honestly expected it to happen. They'd been so careful and the school so diligent in putting in protective measures. He couldn't work out what had gone wrong. He'd always imagined he'd be one of those people in a crisis who sprang into action, doing what needed to be done. But he was rooted to the spot, paralysed with shock.

A lump solidified in his throat, and he had to fight back the tears, pushing away his darkest thoughts. Losing a child was the worst pain he could imagine.

He snatched up his keys and rushed out of the door, fumbling with his phone as he climbed into the car.

'Dylan's been taken to hospital,' he blurted out when Lucia

answered her mobile. 'I'm on my way now. Can you meet me there?' He fired the words at her like bullets.

'Slow down, Damian. What's going on?'

'He's had an allergic reaction. The school's just phoned. They had to call an ambulance.'

'Is he all right?'

'I don't know.'

'Okay, I'm on my way.' He heard her packing up her things and rushing for the door. It was at times like these he wished she didn't work so far away. He needed her to help him through this.

He dumped the car on double yellow lines outside the hospital and raced into the accident and emergency department, pushing ahead of a small queue at a reception counter.

'My son's been brought in by ambulance,' he said breathlessly. 'Dylan Caslocke,' he added, glancing at the woman's computer screen.

'Mr Caslocke?'

He spun around at the sound of his name.

'He's through here.' Mrs Anand looked as shell-shocked as he felt.

She led him through the waiting room and into a treatment area beyond. She pointed to a room at the far end of a short corridor where Dylan was sprawled out on a bed surrounded by a team of doctors and nurses in a busy hubbub of activity, working with a calm urgency.

He looked so helpless, lying unconscious, his bright red school jumper contrasting with the pallid complexion of his skin. Plastic tubes poked down his throat and ran off his arms, while a monitor displaying incomprehensible graphs and numbers beeped in the corner.

Damian stood in the door, unable to move as he watched the team of strangers working on his son, feeling helpless and terrified in equal measure.

He wasn't aware of the nurse who appeared at his side until she touched him lightly on his arm. 'Are you his father?'

She wore heavy glasses and her dark hair, streaked with the first strands of grey, was pulled away from her face in a loose ponytail. Behind the thick lenses, Damian saw kind eyes.

He nodded. 'Is he going to be all right?' He'd held back the tears as he'd raced to the hospital, but now faced with the stark reality of Dylan's precarious situation, raw emotion crushed him. His face crumpled and tears pricked his eyes.

'They're doing everything they can for him,' the nurse said. 'I know it looks scary, but his blood pressure is stabilising, and his SATs are coming back up. Why don't you hold his hand. Let him know you're here.'

She coaxed Damian closer to the bed as another nurse made room for him with a reassuring smile. He took Dylan's hand and was shocked how cold and limp his fingers felt. His face was almost unrecognisable, his lips and eyes puffed up grotesquely like he'd been ten rounds with a heavyweight boxer.

'Does he know I'm here?'

'Speak to him and tell him,' the nurse said.

'Dylan, it's okay, Dad's here,' Damian said, a little self-consciously.

He stood like that, gripping his son's hand and praying for a miracle for the next fifteen minutes as the team worked around him. Eventually, the beeping from the machine monitoring Dylan's heart slowed to a more regular rhythm, and the team's frantic urgency became less intense. The room thinned out, and a doctor who'd been issuing orders finally acknowledged Damian with an understanding smile.

'He's lucky the school called an ambulance when they did,' he said, shoving his hands in the pockets of his white coat. 'His airway was closing up, and we had to help him breathe. He's out of danger now, but we'll need to move him onto the ICU to monitor his recovery.'

'Thank you, doctor,' Damian said, wiping his sleeve across his nose. 'Thank you so much.'

'You're welcome.'

'Can I get you a coffee?' the nurse with the thick glasses asked.

'No, I'm fine, thank you. We're normally so careful with his food. I don't understand how this could have happened.'

'Don't blame yourself. The school did the right thing calling 999 straightaway. Their quick actions probably saved his life.'

Damian wasn't surprised. St Joseph's had been incredibly proactive when they'd first told them about Dylan's allergy, almost revelling in having a special case. They kept several adrenaline injector pens in the school office, and half a dozen teachers had received first aid training in how to use them. And pupils were banned from bringing food containing sesame onto the premises. They'd gone over and beyond what Damian would have expected. So how had Dylan still managed to come into contact with sesame?

'He could have died,' Damian said, stroking the back of Dylan's hand. He was still unconscious, but his breathing was more regular and less inhibited than when Damian had first walked into the room.

'But he didn't,' The nurse said. 'Why don't you go and wait outside while we prep him. You can come with us when we take him up to the ICU.'

Damian nodded. With his own adrenaline levels dropping, a wave of exhaustion washed over him.

Mrs Anand was in the waiting room looking worried.

'Is everything okay?' she asked, jumping up from her seat.

'They're taking him up to intensive care, but he's over the worst.'

'Thank God.'

'I just don't understand what happened. The school's normally so careful.'

Mrs Anand bit her lip and lowered her gaze. She had the look of someone who was holding something back.

'What is it?' Damian asked, a sick feeling twisting in his gut.

She reached into a leather bag slung over her shoulder and pulled out a clear plastic freezer bag. She held it up between her fingers so Damian could see what was inside. He stared at it with disbelief.

'It was in Dylan's lunchbox.'

'No, you've got it wrong.' A hot flush brought a bead of sweat to Damian's brow.

He looked more closely at the sandwich and the ragged slither of ham poking out from between two slices of thick, roughly cut bread. A small bite, about the size of Dylan's mouth, had been taken out of one corner.

'Do you have any idea how it ended up in his lunch?' Mrs Anand asked, raising her eyebrows like she was accusing him.

Blood rushed in Damian's ears, and his head pounded. He couldn't take his eyes off the bread, its crust thick with seeds. Black ones. Brown ones. Even little translucent tear-shaped ones like misformed apple pips. Deadly sesame seeds.

'I didn't do it,' Damian gasped. 'It wasn't me.'

30

Lucia could hardly bear to look at Damian across the table where they were sitting nursing cups of tea amongst the clatter of plates and cutlery as the staff in the hospital café prepared to close for the day.

'I don't understand how this could have happened,' she said. 'How did that bread end up in Dylan's packed lunch?'

'I don't know,' he said. 'I've been asking myself the same thing.'

He couldn't believe he would have made such a dangerous error. There had to be another explanation.

'Why can't you just admit you were tired and made a mistake? You left it to the last minute to make the lunches, and you weren't concentrating on what you were doing,' Lucia said, pointing aggressively at Damian's chest.

'Because that's not what happened,' he said. 'I wouldn't have been so careless.'

It's true, he had been in a rush, but he remembered clearly stacking the dirty dishes in the dishwasher and putting the wine glasses to one side. He recalled his niggle of irritation at having to wipe down the work surfaces after Mara had left them in a state, and he was sure he took the bread from the sliced loaf in the bread bin.

The safe pre-packaged bread he always used to make the sandwiches. But there was no way of proving it.

'Do you realise how serious this could have been? Dylan could have died.'

'Yes, of course I do. You don't need to keep reminding me. I feel bad enough as it is.'

'How could you have been so stupid?'

'Hang on, this wouldn't have happened if Mara hadn't brought that bread into the house in the first place.'

'So you're going to blame Mara?'

'You'd warned her about Dylan's allergy, and she ignored you.'

'You were with her when she went shopping and must have seen her buy it!'

Damian took a deep breath and cradled his tea. 'Let's not argue,' he said. 'It's not what Dylan would want.'

'So what happened? Did the sandwich fairy switch the bread in the middle of the night?'

Maybe not the sandwich fairy. There was only one other person in the house who could have tampered with the kids' lunches, but why would Mara do something like that? Was she trying to get back at him? She knew Lucia would assume Damian was to blame. She'd already accused him of sneaking into her room while she slept, so he wouldn't have put it past her. But this was taking things to a whole new level. If she'd put Dylan's life in danger to score petty points against him, he'd kill her.

'Well?'

'I think Mara might have done it.'

Lucia looked at Damian open-mouthed for a second or two, her eyes narrowing as if she was wondering if he was making a sick joke. 'You've got to be kidding.'

'She was the only other person who could have done it.'

Lucia folded her arms and stared at him. 'Honestly, Damian, you're pathetic.'

'How can you be so sure it wasn't her?'

'Because she's my sister! Would you just listen to yourself for a minute.'

'She's mentally ill. She can't be trusted.' The words spilt out before he could stop himself.

'Give her a break, will you. You've been like this ever since she moved in. I don't know whether it's jealousy, or you feel threatened by her, but get used to her being around. She's not going anywhere.'

'We'll see,' Damian muttered under his breath.

'What?'

'Nothing.'

'I think you'd better go.'

'Fine,' he said, pulling himself out of his seat. 'So you're going to stay here, are you?'

'Yes, of course I am. Dylan's my son.'

'Right, well I'll see you later,' Damian said, marching off without a backwards glance. At least if Lucia was staying at the hospital, it would give him a chance to confront Mara.

31

As he drove home, Damian tried to think rationally. He was sure he hadn't used the seeded bread to make Dylan's sandwich, which left only one explanation. Mara must have waited until they'd gone to bed, then sneaked down to the kitchen in the night. It was so cold, so pre-meditated, it made him shudder. What was worse, Lucia had immediately jumped to her sister's defence, unable to believe Mara had had anything to do with it.

Maybe all those years of suffering had twisted Mara's mind, and she no longer knew the difference between good and bad. Or was there something more calculated about her behaviour? Had she intended to make Lucia believe Damian had put his own son's life in peril?

If only he could prove Mara had tampered with Dylan's lunch.

And then a thought struck him with such dazzling clarity, he wondered why he hadn't thought of it before.

He put his foot down and let his speed creep up, his thoughts entirely focused on getting home and searching the kitchen. He found a space near the house and mounted the kerb in his hurry to park. He jumped out, blipped the locks and already had his door key in his hand when he remembered April. Cursing under his breath, he turned on his heel and headed across the road.

'Daddy!' April squealed, pushing past Rose as she threw open the front door. April wrapped her arms around Damian's waist and buried her head in his stomach.

'Hey, sweetie. Have you been a good girl?'

'Good as gold,' Rose replied on April's behalf. 'How's Dylan?'

'Over the worst of it, although he gave us a bit of a shock. April, go and grab your coat and bag. We need to get you home.'

'Do you know what happened?'

'He had a reaction to something he ate. That's all we know,' Damian lied.

'His allergy?'

'We're not really sure.' He didn't have the time or the inclination to begin a discourse on how sesame seeds might have ended up in his son's lunch. There was only one person he wanted to have that discussion with. 'We won't stop. Thanks again for helping out.'

April reappeared with her coat hanging off her shoulders, and her bag clutched to her chest. Damian ushered her out and across the road. Their house was swathed in an unusual silence.

'Hello?' Damian called out as April ran inside, peeled off her shoes and darted upstairs. 'Anyone home?'

Nothing.

He figured if Mara was in her room with her door closed and her TV on, she wouldn't have heard him. Perfect.

April's footsteps padded across the landing and Damian heard the creak of a loose floorboard in her bedroom. Slipping off his jacket, he headed towards the kitchen with his pulse threading keenly through his veins.

'Hey,' Mara said, startling him as she appeared in the doorway of his study, the room in darkness behind her.

'What are you doing in there?'

'Nothing. Looking for a pen,' she said, her face a vision of innocence. 'How's Dylan?'

Damian could barely bring himself to look at her, his fury seething inside. 'He's in intensive care. He could have died.'

'Shit. I'm sorry. But he's going to be okay, right?'

'With luck, yes. Lucia's staying with him overnight.'

Mara blinked twice. 'Okay,' she said.

'Did you find one?'

'What?'

'A pen.'

'Oh, yes, thanks.'

Damian could see she was empty-handed and had been blatantly snooping around while everyone was out, but she didn't even have the decency to look embarrassed. 'Anything else you need?' he asked, hoping she'd pick up on the sarcasm.

'No, I was just heading up to my room.'

She floated across the hall and vanished up the stairs. Damian waited until he heard her door shut, then marched into the kitchen with his sights set on the bin under the sink.

To his surprise, it was empty. He was sure it had been half-full the night before. In fact, he remembered thinking it needed emptying as he scraped the leftover chicken bones from the meal Mara had cooked off their plates. He poked around the freshly fitted bin liner and concluded that Mara must have emptied it in her attempt to cover her tracks. The bins were his job, so it was unlikely Lucia had done it.

He raced outside to the two wheelie bins in the side return; a blue one for recycling and a green one for household waste. He threw open the lid of the green bin and pulled out a bulging rubbish sack, ripping open the plastic with his fingers, letting its contents spill out all over the flagstones. The smell of rotting food hit the back of his throat and made him gag, but undeterred, he picked through the slimy mess of blackened vegetable peelings, balls of used kitchen towel, plastic wrappers and some kind of unidentifiable gunge that might have been the remnants of the pasta bake he'd made at the weekend.

Among the waste were a few slices of the seeded bread, but it wasn't what he was looking for. To prove Mara's guilt, he needed to find the sandwiches he'd made, or at least the bread he'd used and that he suspected Mara had thrown out. But there was nothing in the sack.

'Bitch,' he hissed under his breath. She was more devious than he'd given her credit for.

He grabbed another stinking bag from the bin and ripped it apart, diving in with his bare hands. Nothing. No sandwiches. Not even a single slice of bread. In frustration, he threw an empty carton of soup against the wall, splattering it with a trail of tomato red.

'What did you do with them?' he growled, wondering how she'd managed to smuggle the sandwiches out of the house. She'd probably thrown them into one of the neighbour's bins.

With his anger simmering, he thundered back inside, stopping only to wash and dry his hands at the kitchen sink, scrubbing off the muck and the smell, before bounding up the two flights of stairs to Mara's room.

He banged on the door and tried to shoulder it open, forgetting about the bolt he'd fitted that morning.

'Mara, open up, it's me,' he shouted.

The TV in the background fell silent.

'What is it?'

'I need to talk to you. Open the door!'

The bed squeaked, and footsteps creaked across the floor. The newly-fitted bolt shot back with a click and Mara opened the door just wide enough that Damian could see one eye staring at him.

'What did you do with them?' he demanded, shoving the door so hard she was bowled backwards, stumbling to catch her balance.

She squealed, her eyes wide. 'What are you doing?'

'You took Dylan's sandwiches.'

'What are you talking about?'

'Don't play games with me, Mara. I'm not in the mood. I know what you did. Admit it.'

Mara shook her head as she backed away, fear and mistrust in her eyes. 'I didn't do anything.'

'Stop lying!' Damian shouted as he thumped the wall.

'You're scaring me.'

'What did you do to Dylan's sandwiches?'

'I never touched them.'

'Liar!'

'I swear.'

'You put seeded bread in Dylan's lunchbox. You knew he was allergic and you went ahead and did it anyway. Why? Were you trying to kill him?'

'No! Of course not.'

'So why did you do it?'

'Why would I touch Dylan's sandwiches?'

'I've done nothing but make you welcome in my house, and this is how you repay me?'

'I didn't touch Dylan's lunch. I promise.'

'You must really hate us. You obviously despise the idea of Lucia having a family of her own now. So who's next? Me? April?'

'You don't know what you're saying.'

'I'm onto you, Mara.'

'You're insane.'

As Mara backed up against the far wall, Damian felt an unexpected thrill. He was enjoying intimidating her. She looked so frail, her limbs so thin and her skin almost translucent, and yet he saw the defiance in her eyes, and he knew instantly he was right. Mara was to blame for nearly killing his son, and he'd never forgive her for that.

'I'm sorry for everything you went through, but if you hurt my kids again, I'll kill you. Is that clear?'

'For the last time, I didn't do anything! Maybe you should take a closer look in the mirror, Damian. You made Dylan's sandwiches. Who's to say you didn't use the seeded bread?'

Damian shook his head and tutted. It was pathetic that even now she was trying to pin the blame on him.

'You were tired. You'd been drinking. Maybe you made a mistake,' she continued.

'How dare you. I'd never hurt my son.'

'But it's convenient to blame me, isn't it? You never wanted me here.'

'That's not true.'

'Isn't it?'

'No.'

'You planned this so you could turn Lucia against me. Except she doesn't blame me, does she? She blames you.'

'Shut up!' Damian yelled, his hand balling into a tight fist as the fires of rage burned in his chest. 'Don't try to twist this.'

'Face the truth, Damian. You're the one who nearly killed your own son.'

Every fibre of Damian's being screamed at him to hit her, to pummel her body into a pulp. She was wrong. He didn't just hate her. He despised her with a passion. She'd come into their lives, and she wanted to destroy them. He could see it clearly now. And rather than loving Dylan and April as an adoring aunt, she considered them nothing more than a nuisance. A problem to sweep away.

'Enough!' he yelled.

'What are you going to do, hit me?' The way she said it, taunting him like she thought he couldn't or wouldn't do it only increased his fury. He raised his arm, his fist shaking.

'Daddy! Daddy! What are you doing? Why are you shouting at Auntie Mara?'

April was standing in the door, clutching her favourite doll by its arm, her face creased with worry. Her eyes were fixed on Damian's fist.

Damian lowered his arm, a sick feeling swelling in his stomach. The anger dissipated as quickly as it had risen, and a flush of shame grazed his cheeks. To think April had almost caught him hitting Mara.

'I'm so sorry, honey. I didn't mean to shout,' he said, stooping to his daughter's level.

But instead of jumping into his outstretched arms, she stood motionless, staring at him with such confusion and disgust, it nearly broke his heart.

Damian was angry with himself for letting Mara get under his skin and for allowing April to witness his naked aggression. He'd never hit anyone, let alone a woman. What kind of message would that have sent to his daughter? He was supposed to protect her from the world, to show her the path of righteousness and yet she'd caught him at his worst, about to commit an unforgivable crime.

'Come and give Daddy a hug,' he pleaded.

But she shook her head solemnly, turned away and ran down the stairs.

32

Damian slept fitfully, painfully aware of the aching emptiness in the bed as he lay worrying about Dylan and how he'd lost his temper in front of April. And yet when his alarm sounded, he had to force himself to wake up having finally fallen into a dreamless sleep. He rose feeling groggy, his eyes heavy. He checked his phone. No missed messages from Lucia which he took as good news.

April was already dressed by the time he'd showered and shaved. She ran downstairs full of boundless joy, and as they ate breakfast together at the kitchen table, she chatted incessantly about inconsequential nonsense, never once mentioning how she'd caught him with his fist raised to Mara. But then she didn't even ask after Dylan or question why her mother was absent, although since Lucia had returned to work, April had become increasingly accepting that Lucia wasn't always around.

Damian was thankful they made it out of the house without seeing Mara. The thought of bumping into her on the stairs or skirting past each other on the landing left him feeling queasy. He was embarrassed she'd been able to get under his skin so easily, forcing him to overreact, but he shouldn't have threatened her. Would he really have hit her if

April hadn't appeared? The thought scared him. He wasn't used to losing control.

When they reached the school, April ran off across the playground towards a group of her friends without saying goodbye.

Damian walked briskly home, jumped straight in the car, drove to the hospital and phoned Lucia from the car park.

'How's the poorly soldier this morning?'

'Much better.' Lucia sounded distant and weary. 'They moved him out of the ICU and onto the children's ward late last night.'

'That's good news.'

'He might even be able to come home later, once the doctor's given him the once over. Where are you?'

'Outside. I'll come and find you.'

Dylan was sitting up in bed, playing a game on Lucia's phone. His face was still puffy, especially around the eyes, but he had some colour in his cheeks.

'Hey, sunshine,' Damian said, ruffling his son's hair. 'How're you feeling?'

'I'm okay,' he said, glancing up at Damian briefly before returning his attention to his game.

'You had us worried there for a minute. Didn't you see there was sesame in your sandwiches?'

Dylan shook his head.

'Don't worry. It's not your fault.' He felt Lucia's eyes boring into the side of his head. 'I should have checked before I packed your bag. But you're okay now, and that's the main thing.'

'Did you speak to Mara?' Lucia asked.

'Let's not talk about this now,' Damian said, pulling up a vinyl-covered chair alongside Dylan's bed. 'We'll discuss it later.'

'I hope you haven't upset her?'

He bit his tongue and smiled at Dylan. 'What are you playing there?'

'It's just a game, Dad.'

A youthful-looking doctor with gelled hair arrived just after ten, accompanied by an older nurse. He had the easy manner of a man used to working with kids, making Dylan laugh with puerile jokes delivered in a thick Northern Irish brogue. After a quick glance through his notes and checking Dylan's vital signs, he declared he was happy to discharge him.

'Dylan shouldn't suffer any lasting damage,' he said, with a more sombre tone as he turned to Damian and Lucia. 'But he was lucky. The school did exactly the right thing, but you really need to make sure Dylan isn't exposed to sesame again.'

'No, of course. I'm sorry,' Damian said, hanging his head and feeling suitably chastened.

They drove Dylan home and for the rest of the day let him watch TV and play on his iPad, following the doctor's advice to keep him off school until the swelling around his face had gone down, and his body had had time to recover.

'What did you say to Mara?' Lucia asked as she and Damian sat at the kitchen table later. The stress of the last twenty-four hours had taken a toll on both of them. Lucia had dark rings around her eyes, and Damian doubted she'd slept much in the hospital.

'Nothing.'

She raised an eyebrow. 'You didn't speak to her at all last night?'

'Only briefly. I told her we were lucky Dylan hadn't died.'

'And pointed the finger of blame at her, I suppose?'

'No,' he lied. 'Although I might have asked if she'd touched Dylan's lunch.'

'For Christ's sake, Damian.' Tea sloshed out of Lucia's mug as she slammed it on the table. 'Why would Mara have anything to do with Dylan's lunch?'

'I don't know. I've been asking myself the same thing.'

'I told you, I didn't go anywhere near it.' Mara's gravelly voice made them both jump. Damian had no idea how long she'd been standing at the door.

Lucia gasped. Mara's left eye was almost completely closed up, its socket bruised a darkening shade of purple.

She scraped her chair backwards. 'What the hell's happened to you?'

Mara lowered her gaze and lifted a couple of fingers to touch the top of her cheek. 'It's nothing,' she said. 'I walked into a cupboard.'

'Let me take a look.'

Mara tried to push her sister away, turning her face to the wall. 'It's nothing. I'm fine,' she said, but eventually relented and looked up to the ceiling as Lucia held her head in two hands to examine the damage more closely.

'You've got a real shiner coming up,' Lucia said. 'You need to put some ice on it.'

As Lucia crossed the room towards the freezer, Mara fixed Damian with a knowing stare. A spike of fear chilled his bones.

'Honestly, it's nothing to worry about. It'll go down in a few days. They usually do,' Mara said, a reminder that violence and bruises were nothing new to her.

'Here, put this on it.' Lucia handed her sister a bag of frozen peas. 'It'll help with the swelling.'

'You should take more care,' Damian said.

Mara touched the bag to her face and winced.

'Do you want some tea?' Lucia asked.

'No, I only came down to see how Dylan was and to say I'm sorry about the bread. I totally forgot about his allergy, and now I feel terrible. He could have died because of me.'

'Stop,' Lucia instructed her with a dismissive wave of her hand. 'It's not your fault. You didn't put the bread in his sandwiches.' She shot Damian an accusatory look.

He resisted the urge to protest. There was no point. Lucia had already made up her mind that he was guilty.

'Even so, it wouldn't have happened if I hadn't been so careless. So I've been thinking, it's probably for the best if I move out. You've both been so kind letting me stay, but you need your own space, without me.'

Damian sat up straighter. He hadn't been expecting that. Perhaps his words had sunk in after all.

Lucia looked horrified. 'What? Don't be ridiculous. You don't have to move out.'

'Maybe it's for the best,' Damian said. 'We should support Mara to do what she wants. If she's decided she wants to get her own place, we shouldn't stand in her way.'

'No, I won't hear of it,' Lucia said. 'The best place for you is here, surrounded by your family.'

Mara smiled coyly. Damian knew she was playing games again, safe in the knowledge Lucia would never stand for her moving out. 'Do you really mean it?'

'Yes, of course.' Lucia grabbed her sister by the arms and held her tightly. 'You're not ready to live on your own, and why would you want to when you have everything you need here?'

'But she needs to learn to cope on her own at some point,' Damian said, seeing the window of opportunity to rid themselves of Mara closing.

'It's only been a few months, Damian. She needs more time. I'm not going to argue about this. There's no way I'm letting you move out.'

Mara glanced in Damian's direction with the trace of a self-satisfied smile.

'At least we should talk about a timescale for her going,' he said. 'Don't you think it would give us all something to work towards? It would be good to give Mara a goal.'

'Why are you so keen for her to leave?'

'I'm not,' Damian said, even though it was precisely what he wanted for the sake of their marriage and the children's safety. If only he could make Lucia see the threat her sister presented.

'The problem is I've been neglecting you, haven't I?' Lucia said, gripping Mara's hands. 'Let's be honest. I should have taken more time off to be with you. I'm so sorry.'

'Don't be silly. You've been amazing.'

'I've made up my mind. I'm going to give you the time you need. Whatever it takes, I'm going to be there for you.'

'You've already used up your annual leave for the year,' Damian said, his irritation growing.

'I'm going to speak to work about taking a six-month sabbatical, or at least until Mara has properly recovered.'

'Six months?' The idea of Lucia being out of work and unpaid for that long sent Damian's head spinning. 'We can't afford for you not to work.'

'We'll manage,' she said. 'We can dip into our savings and tighten our belts for a bit. And that way I can spend more time with Mara. It's the least she deserves.'

Mara's face cracked into a broad grin. 'Do you really mean it?'

'Of course I mean it. I'll speak to them tomorrow.'

'Can we discuss this first?' Damian asked, feeling like he was being railroaded into a decision Lucia had made without considering any of the consequences.

'No,' she said. 'I've made up my mind, and that's all there is to it.'

33

A grey squirrel with a bushy tail appeared confidently close to Damian's feet. It stopped with its paws raised and its nose twitching before bounding off towards a sycamore tree shedding its autumnal leaves. He watched it scamper up the gnarled trunk in short, staccato movements and disappear along a twisted branch, before the sound of April's voice shouting for him to watch her descend the slide snatched his attention back again. He gave her a thumbs-up as she launched herself with a squeal of delight, shot down the ramp and landed on her backside in a fit of giggles. On the far side of the playground, Dylan had made friends with two other boys of his age. They were in a tight, conspiratorial huddle, chatting.

Damian was glad to have time alone with the children again, even though he'd initially been surprised when Lucia had announced she was taking Mara away for the weekend. The retreat, as she insisted on calling their trip to a spa hotel in Berkshire, was supposed to be an opportunity for the sisters to bond while they were pampered with pedicures, hot stones and facials. It couldn't have come at a better time. Mara's presence around the house had become increasingly suffocating since she'd appeared in the kitchen sporting a black eye, and without her there, even for a couple of days, Damian felt able to relax again.

As April clambered up the ladder to the top of the slide, he turned his attention to his phone. He thumbed through his Facebook feed, full of the usual crap from friends he'd long since lost touch with in real life, and who now seemed to spend their entire time posting sweaty-faced post-Park Run pictures or snaps of their ugly children.

The bench sagged as a lone figure sat down.

'Hello, Damian.'

He glanced up and almost dropped his phone. 'Tanya,' he gasped.

'Or should I call you Richard?'

Damian's cheeks flushed as he remembered the fabricated name he'd given the journalist when they'd chatted outside the house in the woods.

'I'm sorry. I lied to you.'

'And I thought I could trust you.' She smiled weakly. 'How are things going with Mara?'

Damian slipped his phone in his pocket and looked nervously around, afraid of being spotted talking with a journalist. April was racing towards the swings, and Dylan and his new friends were kicking through piles of scorched leaves.

It would be so easy to tell Tanya everything, how Mara was scarred beyond help by what she'd been through and how she was ripping his family apart. How he didn't feel safe in his own home anymore and that he feared for the safety of his young children. He took a deep breath, the air damp with the moisture from earlier rain. 'It's fine,' he said.

'And your wife? How's Lucia coping? It must have been strange for her.'

'No comment,' Damian said, coolly.

'Come on, Damian, lighten up. I'm only making conversation.'

'We both know that's not true.'

Tanya sighed, pulled the collar of her coat up around her neck and crossed her legs, giving him another tantalising glimpse of her thighs. He was sure she did it deliberately, just like when she'd climbed into his car, and he'd tripped out the imagined memories about Mara from school. But he knew trouble lay there and averted his gaze.

'I'm not interested in talking to you, Tanya. We've made it clear from the beginning we needed privacy to help Mara rebuild her life. She's given her interview, told her story. The agreement was quite clear. No exclusives and you lot leave us alone.'

'A woman's come forward,' Tanya said, pausing for dramatic effect and staring straight ahead as if they were two strangers sharing a bench.

What woman? Damian's heart fluttered with a slight panic.

'She says you were in a relationship.'

Fuck.

Damian swallowed hard, a lump forming in his throat.

'By my calculations, it would have been around the time Lucia was pregnant with your daughter. April, isn't it? Such a pretty little girl.' She said it more like a threat than a compliment.

'I don't know what you're talking about,' Damian stammered.

'I'm surprised you've forgotten. Polly seems lovely, by the way. Attractive, if you like that kind of blonde-in-a-bottle look. She says she had no idea you were married until she read about you and Lucia in the papers.'

Polly? Damian wracked his brains. Polly Porter, the blonde intern at his old firm? It was hardly a relationship. At best it was a drunken fumble at a Christmas party. They may have had a couple of sordid afternoons at a cheap hotel off the A24, but it was never anything serious.

Even though they were sitting outside, Damian felt as though the air had been sucked out of his lungs. 'What do you want?' he hissed.

Tanya took a breath, about to answer, when Dylan came rushing up with his arm outstretched. 'Hey, Dad, look what I found.'

He opened his fist to reveal a shiny conker bigger than a golf ball.

'That's a beast,' Damian said, trying to summon some enthusiasm, but wishing Dylan would run off with his friends so he could settle things with Tanya. 'Why don't you see if you can find some more. I bet there's an even bigger one if you look carefully.'

'Ok, Dad,' Dylan said, running off.

Damian and Tanya sat in an uncomfortable silence watching him bound across the playground with the energy of a spring lamb.

'I didn't believe her at first. You didn't, I mean you don't seem the type. And yet, here we are.'

'What do you want?' Damian repeated.

'You're not even going to deny it? Poor Lucia, stuck with a toddler at home and a baby on the way while her husband's out shagging around. And I bet she still has no idea.'

'Fuck you.'

'The headline virtually writes itself: Sister of brave kidnap victim breaks down as husband is unmasked as love rat.'

'Print that and I'll sue your tawdry little paper for every penny it's worth.'

Tanya gave a hollow laugh. 'You're quite the stud by all accounts. Polly was most explicit with all the gory details,' she said. Damian felt sick. 'But I'm willing to make a deal with you.'

He breathed in slowly through his nose. 'Go on.'

'If you cooperate with me, I can spike the story like that.' She clicked her fingers.

'How?'

'I'd need to persuade my editor I have a better story, like if I had the exclusive on what really happened in that house between Mara and James Finch.'

Damian shook his head. 'Mara's already spoken about everything that happened to her. I don't know what more you want.'

'I'm not interested in what it was like living in a concrete cell or sleeping on a damp mattress on the floor. We've heard all that already. I want to know about Mara's relationship with Finch. I want the human interest angle.'

'He was her abductor. She can barely bring herself to speak his name.'

'Come on, you must know there's more to it than meets the eye? Why does she always refuse to talk about him? She never even condemned him for what he did.'

She was right, Mara had always been cagey about talking about

James Finch, and the snippets she did give away about him were hardly scathing.

'And there's something else about how she escaped that doesn't add up.'

'I don't know anything about it. You'd have to ask Mara.'

'That's precisely my problem. I can't get near her, can I?' Tanya raised a perfectly plucked eyebrow.

Damian shrugged. 'I can't help you.'

'What if she'd fallen in love with Finch and helped him plot his escape in return for her freedom?'

Damian laughed. 'That's ludicrous.'

'Is it?'

'Look, Tanya, she's never spoken to me about him. She clams up if I so much as mention his name.'

'That's a shame. I guess I'll have to go with the love rat story instead.' She gathered up her handbag at her feet.

'Hang on a minute,' Damian said, grabbing her arm. 'You can't run that story. It'll kill Lucia. And what about my kids?'

'Then help me out, Damian. You need to find a way of getting Mara to open up.'

'How?'

Mara was hardly speaking to him after he'd accused her of almost killing Dylan. It was unthinkable that she'd talk to him about James Finch. Tanya was putting him in an impossible situation.

'I'm sure you'll find a way. And of course, I'll need a recording. It's probably easiest if you use your phone.'

She said it so matter-of-factly as if it was something people did every day. 'I don't think I can.'

'Fine, we'll go with your grubby little affair with Polly Porter then.'

'No, wait!'

Tanya turned to him with wide eyes.

'I'll do it,' Damian said. 'But I'll need a few days.'

'You have one week.' Tanya tossed her long, blonde hair over her shoulder. 'Get Mara talking and find out everything about her and Finch. I'm sure whatever she has to say will make fascinating reading.'

34

Damian wondered if Tanya had been bluffing. Even if she had spoken with Polly, surely it was her word against his? Hearsay and gossip he could deny, the fantasies of an office junior spurned when she made an unwanted advance. Unless there was some supporting evidence. CCTV footage or a hotel receipt? Had Polly kept the incriminating text messages he'd sent? The thought of his ill-considered lustful declarations printed in a national newspaper made him shiver. There was no way he could take the risk. Tanya had him by the balls.

But seven days didn't give him much time.

For a brief moment, he considered throwing himself at Lucia's mercy. What if he explained that it had been a moment of weakness, that it had meant nothing? After she'd fallen pregnant with April, she'd lost interest in sex, but he still had needs. Surely she'd understand that he didn't do it to hurt her. The opportunity had arisen, and he'd been too weak to resist. It didn't mean he loved her any less. It was a silly fling, that's all. She'd be angry, but maybe they'd be able to work things out.

No, it was ridiculous. The risk was too high, and it wouldn't stop Tanya publishing the story to be read, not only by Lucia but by Damian's family, friends and business contacts. It would destroy his reputation.

There had to be another way, and so two days after their impromptu meeting in the park, Damian came to a decision. He spent the evening scouring the internet for some suitable equipment. If he was going to go through with Tanya's demands, he wasn't going to rely on his phone to record Mara's confessions. He would do things properly.

The following day, the parcel arrived by express delivery in the safe hands of a skinny courier with acne-scarred skin. Damian scurried into his study, locked the door and ripped it open with trembling fingers. The miniature video camera had set him back a couple of hundred pounds, but it was a small price to pay for the sake of his marriage.

It came out of the box ready to use, no bigger than the packets of raisins Damian sometimes popped into the kids' lunches, and it seemed simple enough to operate. A red button on the top to record and a touch screen monitor on the back to review the footage. He tested it by balancing it on a shelf above his desk and pointing it at the sofa behind his chair.

The images it captured were remarkably sharp, even in the gloom of his study, the camera's fish-eye lens capturing a wide arc of the room and bending the straight lines of the wall behind him out of perspective. The only issue was a flashing red light on the front of the camera when it was set to record, a problem he resolved with a narrow strip of black tape.

All he needed now was to encourage Mara into his study, then the challenge would begin, getting Mara to talk openly about what had really happened between her and James Finch.

35

Lucia and Mara returned home early on Sunday evening as Damian was about to run April's bath. Lucia looked more relaxed than he'd seen her for a long time. Her skin was glowing, and she'd lost the dark rings around her eyes. By contrast, Mara appeared tired and tense. Her left eye had almost entirely closed up, and the bruising had turned a rainbow shade of yellow, purple and red.

'You look amazing,' Damian said, wrapping his arms around Lucia's waist and welcoming her home with the sort of kiss which he hoped demonstrated how much he'd missed her. 'Did you have fun?'

'It was fantastic.'

Mara said nothing as she disappeared up to her room, dragging her overnight bag behind her.

'Mummy! Mummy! Mummy!' April came racing through from the kitchen.

Lucia swept her up and smothered her head in kisses. 'I've missed you so much. Have you been good for Daddy?'

'Yes!' April squirmed free and ran away, almost bowling over Dylan as he appeared in the kitchen doorway.

'Don't run off. I want to hear all about the things you've been up to.'

Lucia chased them into the kitchen, growling like a monster. When she caught them, she bundled them onto the rug in front of the woodburning stove, tickling their ribs until they could hardly breathe while Damian watched by the breakfast bar, his heart swelling.

He loved seeing Lucia play with the children. She was a great mum. But as Dylan jumped on her back, pulling her off balance with his arms around her neck, a pang of regret stabbed at his conscience. Their joyous laughter was a bitter reminder of everything he'd put in jeopardy when he'd been foolish enough to fall for Polly Porter's flattering advances. How could he have risked all this? Memories surfaced in his mind of Polly's tight, lean body. The taste of vanilla on her skin. He pushed them away. It had been a long time ago. A stupid mistake. He wasn't going to let Tanya Hayes dredge it all up for public consumption and destroy everything he held dear.

Dylan pulled away from Lucia's grasp, giggling, his sweaty face flushed red. 'I found this in the park,' he said, pulling a conker from his pocket.

'And I made you a card,' April said, not to be outdone. She picked herself up off the floor and ran to the kitchen table, pushing her hair off her forehead with pudgy fingers.

'She spent most of the morning on it,' Damian explained, as April presented Lucia with a folded piece of red cardboard she'd fashioned into a greetings card.

'Sweetheart, that's amazing.' Glitter showered Lucia's legs as she carefully peeled it open and read April's scrawling felt pen message out loud. 'To Mummy, you're the best mummy in the world. I missed you. Love, April.'

'She did it all herself,' Damian said.

'Let's put it on the shelf where I can always see it.'

Lucia took over bath and bedtime duties while Damian concentrated on cooking dinner. When she was done, he handed her a glass of wine, looking forward to spending the evening together after a weekend largely starved of adult company.

'What did Mara make of the hotel?' Damian asked, between mouthfuls as they sat eating on the sofa, watching TV.

'A bit overwhelming, I think. Maybe it wasn't such a good idea, after all. I booked a massage for us, but I hadn't appreciated quite how much she hates to be touched, especially by strangers, so in the end, we spent most of the time just wandering around the gardens, chatting.'

'What did you talk about?' Damian asked, wondering if Mara had revealed anything new about her time in captivity.

'You know, this and that.'

'Anything about Finch?'

Lucia shook her head. 'Not really. I don't like to bring his name up. I'm never sure how she's going to react. What about you? What did you do with the kids?'

'We went to the park yesterday,' Damian said, trying not to look and sound guilty. 'I took them for pizza afterwards as a treat.'

'Oh, Damian.' Lucia shot him a reproachful glance.

'It was only pizza. It's not going to kill them.'

'You know I don't like them eating junk all the time.' She sighed and rolled her eyes in mock exasperation. 'Anyway, did you miss me?'

'Of course. We all did.'

Lucia placed her tray on the floor. 'I had a chance to do some thinking while we were away,' she said, turning down the volume on the TV.

'Uh-oh,' Damian laughed, nervously. 'Sounds serious.'

'I'm worried I've been neglecting Mara. It's not fair leaving her home alone with you. I'm her sister. I should be here for her more. I was serious when I said I wanted to take a sabbatical, but I'd like to do it with your blessing.'

'I thought you'd already made up your mind?'

'I have, but I want this to be a joint decision.'

'It's hardly a joint decision then. And besides, you shouldn't feel guilty. You've done so much for her already.'

Lucia shook her head. 'She's not coping so well. I need to be here more.'

'We can't afford for you to take time off.' They struggled to make ends meet month to month on two salaries, let alone on Damian's income alone. The nature of his business meant the money he brought in was variable at best.

'We have enough in our savings to live off for at least six months, maybe more if we're careful. We might have to go without a holiday next year, but I think it's a price worth paying. And we'd be saving on my train fare too.'

No matter how she framed it, the thought of Lucia giving up work for several months terrified him. 'I don't know. It's a lot of money to lose every month.'

'It won't be forever,' Lucia said, scooting across the sofa to sit closer to Damian. 'We'll make it work, I promise.'

'Don't you think we should be encouraging Mara to become more independent, not less? If you give up work, she's going to become more and more reliant on you. Have you spoken to her psychologist? What does she think?'

'I don't need to speak to her. I know what's best for my sister.'

'You think you do, but you're still carrying the burden of guilt for what happened to Mara, and you think this will make amends for everything, but I'm not convinced it's the right thing to do. We should be helping her to move out, to start living her own life again.'

'Not this again, Damian. I've missed the last nineteen years of her life, so if you think I'm going to throw her out now, think again.'

'Nobody's going to throw her out. I'm talking about supporting her to find her own place, where she can make her own decisions and lead her life the way she wants to. We can set her up in her own flat. It doesn't have to be far away. We know she can cook, and you can visit any time you like.'

'She's not ready.'

'She's already told me she wants to go.'

Lucia raised an eyebrow. 'That's not what she said to me.'

'She has a short memory.'

'Why do you hate her being here so much anyway?'

'I don't.'

'Well, you've hardly gone out of your way to make her feel welcome.'

'You want the truth? She scares me. She's unpredictable and unstable. I don't trust her. Maybe it's not her fault. Being abducted has obviously had a big impact on her, but you're right, I don't want her here.'

Lucia's eyes narrowed. 'I knew it,' she said. 'You know she's terrified of you?

'Of me?' Damian laughed. 'You're kidding, right?'

'She didn't want to say anything, but I dragged it out of her while we were away.'

'Dragged what out of her?'

Lucia's steely gaze cut through him. 'Tell me what really happened to her eye.'

'How the hell should I know? She walked into a door or something, didn't she?'

Lucia crossed her arms and said nothing, waiting for him to elaborate.

'Oh, come on, you think I did it? Is that what she said?'

'Did you?'

'Are you serious?'

'Keep your voice down. You'll wake the kids. So you didn't touch her?'

'No!'

Sure, he'd come close to hitting Mara. She'd pushed all the right buttons and provoked him to the point he thought he *might* hit her. But he hadn't. He wasn't a violent man. He was no James Finch. But the fact Lucia could believe it made him realise he was losing her.

'Sorry, I didn't really believe it, but I had to ask,' Lucia said. 'I had to see the truth in your eyes.'

'Whatever,' Damian huffed.

'Don't be like that.'

'I'm tired,' he said. 'I'm going to bed.'

'Don't.'

'We'll talk about it in the morning.' He pulled himself off the sofa, the weeks of simmering resentment finally boiling to the surface. He knew if he stayed, he'd say something he regretted. Instead, he stormed out like a sulky teenager and slammed the door shut behind him.

36

It didn't take long to set up the camera among a stack of books on the shelf above the desk in Damian's study. He plumped up the cushions on the sofa, double-checked the camera was well concealed and headed up to Mara's room.

He knocked three times.

'What is it?' she answered, her voice thick with sleep.

'Can we talk?'

'About what?'

'I wanted to apologise.'

He'd spent another angst-filled, restless night and woken in a terrible mood. A grey cloud of worry lurked at the forefront of his mind as he contemplated Tanya Hayes' threats. Time was ticking. If he didn't deliver, he could kiss goodbye to his marriage, his kids and maybe even his business.

'I'd like to clear the air. Maybe we could make a new start,' he added.

The floorboards creaked. Damian heard the rustle of clothing and the bolt on the door snap open.

'Are you going to hit me again?' Mara stared at him through an inch-wide gap between the door and the frame.

'What?'

She opened the door wider and stood with her arms folded across her chest, one eye still graphically bruised. 'If you lay another finger on me, I'll scream,' she said.

'What are you talking about? I've never hit you.'

The rise of her eyebrow was so subtle he almost missed it. 'What do you want?'

'I never hit you,' Damian repeated. 'You said yourself you walked into a cupboard door.'

She continued to stare at him, not saying anything, so he carried on with the script he'd prepared. 'I'm sorry I lost my temper. I was worried about Dylan, but I shouldn't have taken it out on you. It wasn't your fault.'

'No,' she said. 'It wasn't.'

'I said things I should never have said. You know you're welcome to stay as long as you want.'

Her eyebrow twitched again.

'Then I realised over the weekend, while you were away, that we don't really know each other very well, do we? We should talk, you know, just you and me. Sort out our differences.'

Mara glanced down at her feet. He'd caught her off guard. It was probably the last thing she'd been expecting him to say. He could only hope he'd sounded genuine enough to convince her.

'Why don't you get dressed and come and have a coffee with me? Join me in the study.'

Mara stared at him blankly for a second or two, then nodded, pushing the door closed in his face.

Damian raced back down to the study and checked the camera again, hitting the record button and fine-tuning the angle of the lens, so he was absolutely sure it was covering the sofa and the far side of the room. He made coffee and carried the cafetiere through with two mugs and a jug of warm milk.

Mara sloped in precisely twelve minutes later, just as Damian was beginning to worry how much time was left on the camera's memory card. She'd thrown on a pair of slim-fit jeans and a hooded top, her cropped hair still damp from the shower. Damian pointed her to the sofa and handed her a mug of lukewarm coffee.

She sat stiffly on the edge of the couch, with her knees together and her back straight, looking nervous. Damian rocked back in his chair and threw his hands behind his head, trying to give off the appearance of someone settling in for a relaxed, friendly chat.

'The thing is, Dylan's allergy is so unpredictable,' he said. 'Even the smallest trace of sesame could bring on an attack.'

'I didn't realise,' she said, in a small voice. Damian suspected it was an act.

'Fortunately, he's okay now, so no harm done.'

Mara nodded, holding her mug in two hands.

'Let's put it behind us, shall we? Tell me, how was the weekend?'

'Not really my thing. Too many people.'

'But it must have been good to spend time with Lucia?'

'Of course,' she said. 'We have so much to catch up on, but when we're together, it's like we've never been apart.'

Damian's cheeks ached as he held his smile, ignoring the niggling irritation he always felt when Mara spoke about her relationship with Lucia.

'And how are things generally?'

'Okay. I meant what I said before. I'm grateful you've given up a room for me.'

'You're welcome,' Damian said, the words clawing in his throat.

'But I still have nightmares.'

'Really?'

'Every night. It's always the same. I feel like I'm suffocating and I can't move.' She stared into her coffee with a sadness behind her eyes. 'I'm worried I'll never get better.'

'You will, with time,' Damian said. 'Maybe it would help if, one day, you got a place of your own and started to live independently.'

She looked up at him sharply, regarding him with suspicion. 'I can't think that far ahead.'

'We'll help you, of course, then you can do whatever you want, in peace without us.'

'Maybe. One day.' She dabbed the corner of her black eye with the knuckle of her finger and winced.

'Does it hurt?'

'I'm used to it,' she said. 'At least when he hit me, he knew where the bruises wouldn't be seen. He didn't like to see them.'

Damian ignored the barbed comment. She wasn't going to get a rise out of him that easily. 'I can't imagine how much you must hate him after everything he did to you.'

Mara cocked her head to one side and frowned. 'No,' she said. 'I don't hate him. I pity him.'

'The psychologist said it's likely you formed a strong bond after all those years you spent together.'

'Not particularly.'

'It's only natural. It happens all the time in these sorts of cases,' Damian said, remembering what Helen Barrett had told them. 'It's nothing to be ashamed of.'

'I'm not ashamed. He abducted me when I was a child and kept me imprisoned for nearly twenty years. What kind of a person do you think is capable of doing that to a kid?'

'God only knows. A monster?'

'I wouldn't call him that.'

'So what would you call him?'

Mara shrugged.

'It must be strange that he's not in your life anymore?' Damian persisted.

'Strange?'

'You must miss him, I mean, at least a little bit?'

'No,' she said flatly. 'Not at all. I don't feel anything for him.'

Damian placed his empty mug on the tray on his desk, avoiding the temptation to glance at the camera. 'It's odd he vanished after you escaped.'

'Why?'

'I mean, where would he go?'

'I have no idea.'

'Didn't he ever give you any clues? He must have said something.'

'If I knew that I would have told the police. Why would I keep something like that secret?'

Because maybe you're harbouring him, Damian thought. Just maybe your relationship ran deeper than you're admitting and you helped him escape. How else had he managed to disappear with police forces across the country hunting for him?

There was a loud knock on the front door. 'Who the hell's that?' Damian muttered, jumping up. 'Stay here. I'll be right back.'

A courier was on the doorstep, balancing a large package in one hand.

'Can you take this in for number twelve?' he asked. 'There's no one in.'

'Yeah, sure,' Damian said, irritated at having been interrupted just as Mara had started talking about Finch. He made a ham-fisted attempt at signing his name on the man's hand-held computer and left the parcel on the floor in the hall.

When he returned to the study, Mara had relaxed a little. She was leaning back into the cushions examining her fingernails. 'Sorry about that,' he said. 'More coffee?'

'No. Thank you.'

'You were telling me about James Finch.'

'Was I?'

'It's amazing that after nineteen years you were able to walk out right under his nose,' Damian said. 'You said he never let you out of his sight.'

'I saw the opportunity, and I took it.'

'And he didn't chase after you or try to stop you?'

'I told you, the house was in the middle of woods. There were plenty of places to hide,' Mara said. 'I don't know if he tried to find me.'

'And in nineteen years you'd never had a chance to run away before?'

'He said if I ever tried to escape, he'd hunt me down and kill me. Why do you keep asking about it?'

Damian crossed his legs and folded his hands in his lap, trying not to look like he was interrogating her, hoping her words were being picked up clearly by the camera's microphone and that it would be enough to satisfy Tanya. 'I'm just trying to understand. Did you love him?'

'Stop it.'

'It would be understandable if you'd developed feelings for him.'

'Of course not. And I already told you, I didn't sleep with him.'

'Did he sexually abuse you?'

Mara's face darkened. 'I know what you are, Damian, and you might have fooled Lucia for all these years, but you don't fool me.'

'I'm only trying to understand what you went through, so I can help you,' Damian pleaded.

'It's none of your business. You couldn't even begin to understand what it was like.' She stood suddenly, knocking over the empty coffee mug by her feet. 'Don't you dare judge me.'

'I'm not judging... '

'You can never understand what I went through. Nobody can, and I really don't want to talk about it anymore. Why can't you accept that, Damian?'

'I'm trying to help.'

'No,' she shouted, 'you're not. You're like everyone else. You want everything to be black or white. You can't see some things are shades of grey. Thank you for the coffee. I'm going back to bed.'

She stormed out of the room and thudded up the stairs.

With his heart still pounding, Damian let out a deep breath. Now he was convinced she was hiding something.

He waited until he heard the dull thud of Mara's door slamming shut and reached up to the shelf, hoping he'd captured enough to keep Tanya off his back. It hadn't exactly been a full confession, but at least Mara had talked about Finch.

With shaking hands, he removed the books on the shelf, but the camera wasn't there.

With a swelling panic, he tugged the books down, letting them clatter onto his desk and the floor. But sure enough, the camera had vanished.

Damian slumped in his chair, his mind racing. He'd definitely checked it before Mara had come down, so where was it? He remembered the knock on the door, the courier handing him a parcel for number twelve. He'd only been out of the room for a minute, but in that short period, Mara must have noticed the camera and removed it. There was no other explanation. And now, not only did he have nothing for Tanya, he'd handed Mara one more nail for his coffin.

37

Lucia announced, on her return from work that evening, that she was taking Mara out for a drink before dinner. It was something she'd never done before, and so came as a surprise to Damian. He and Lucia had once been regulars at The Star, before they had kids, but he couldn't remember when they'd last popped in together, although he didn't care about missing out this time if it meant getting Mara out of the way long enough to poke around her room to look for his camera.

'You don't mind, do you?' Lucia asked.

'Of course not. I'll look after dinner. You girls have fun.'

Mara looked less than thrilled as she stood in the hall with a sulky pout.

'We'll only be an hour.'

'Take as long as you like. Call me when you're leaving, and I'll put the rice on,' Damian said.

Mara eyed him suspiciously as he ushered them out and waved them off from the doorstep. He noted the time and bounded up the stairs, taking them two at a time.

'Is it bath time yet, Daddy?' April called out as he shot past her room.

She was kneeling on the floor surrounded by her dolls.

'You can have five more minutes playing.'

'I'm tired,' she whined.

'Too tired for stories?'

'No!'

'Right, well I'll be down in five minutes.'

'Where are you going?'

'I need to look for something in Auntie Mara's room,' he said. She knew full well that Mara hated anyone going in her room. He only hoped she wouldn't call him out.

'What are you looking for?'

'She borrowed one of Daddy's pens earlier and forgot to bring it back.'

'Okay.'

Damian crept up the steep, narrow staircase to the attic room and flicked on the light. Mara's bed had been made, and her cosmetics lined up neatly on the dressing table. A small pile of clothes had been folded on a chair under one of the dormer windows, and a hint of citrus perfume lingered in the air, mingling with the familiar lavender scent of washing powder.

Where would she have hidden the camera? He began with the wardrobe they'd managed to squeeze in at the end of the bed. It was only a cheap, flat-pack unit, and not as tall as a normal wardrobe, which meant it fitted in neatly under the low, sloping ceiling.

Inside, a cluster of bare coat hangers was a testament to how few clothes Mara owned. A spare pair of jeans. A couple of blouses Lucia had donated, and a tight-knit beige sweater with a giant red love heart on the front. Lucia had tried taking her shopping, but Mara still struggled with the concept of owning anything other than the clothes she was wearing. She didn't see the point of them.

With a little sadness, Damian eased the wardrobe doors closed and turned his attention to the dressing table. Mara had folded her underwear into the top drawer, and as he picked through a pile of her cotton briefs, he felt a pang of embarrassment and shame. She'd put socks in the next drawer down and left the bottom drawer empty, but there was no sign of his camera.

Next, he checked the empty drawers in the bedside table and cast around in the built-in cupboards under the eaves where he'd shoved the boxes of Christmas decorations, the kids' old toys and stuff they no longer needed but couldn't bear to throw away when they'd cleared the room.

Nothing.

Damian slumped down on the bed to think. If he was Mara, where would he have hidden it? All the floorboards they'd had sanded and polished when the loft was converted were firmly nailed down, and being an attic room, there was no roof space. Which meant there was a possibility she'd hidden it elsewhere in the house.

He hauled himself to his feet and was about to admit defeat when it occurred to him to check under the bed. He lowered his face to the floor, placing his cheek on the stripped floorboards, but all he found was a ball of dust which made him sneeze.

Slowly, he stood up, smoothed out the unicorn duvet and backed out of the room checking he'd not left any evidence he'd been there. His hand reached for the light switch, but he hesitated as his eyes swept the room. Something looked off. The mattress wasn't sitting squarely on the bed frame, and as he looked more closely, he saw it was raised a fraction near the headboard. Mara had hidden something underneath it.

He crossed the room, threw the edge of the duvet back and, with one hand, lifted the mattress. A shiver travelled down his spine at what he found. What the hell was Mara playing at?

Carefully, he picked it up by its handle, holding it away from his body like it was a venomous snake that could strike at any second. If he'd thought Mara was a danger to him and his family before, this was the final confirmation he needed and hopefully the proof that would also open Lucia's eyes to the truth.

38

Lucia and Mara returned from the pub unsteady on their feet and giggling girlishly at each other's silly jokes. Damian had had a glass of wine while he was cooking, but his relative sobriety left him feeling excluded from their private party. He served up plates of chilli and rice as they stumbled into the kitchen and picked out an expensive bottle of Italian red from the wine rack.

Unusually, Mara decided she would eat with them, which gave Damian a rare opportunity to observe her as they sat around the table, warmed by the stove. It was the first time he'd seen Mara drunk. Her face flushed, laughing and talking too loudly, he could almost believe she'd grown up in normal circumstances. Of course, most of her scars were on the inside, unseen, but he didn't kid himself for a second they weren't there, poisonous and festering, which is why he watched her like a hawk. After everything that had happened in the last few days, he trusted her less than ever and his discovery in her room had left him scared of what she might be planning. He wanted to tell Lucia, but that would mean admitting he'd been snooping and there was no way to explain that away without telling her about the camera, Tanya Hayes and Polly Porter. God, what a mess.

Lucia drained her glass and, with a doe-eyed pout, tipped it up to show Damian it was empty. 'Is there any more?' she slurred.

'I think you've probably had enough,' he said, clearing away the plates.

'Don't be such a bore.' She stumbled across the room and selected a random bottle from the rack, then made a terrible mess of the cork as she tried to remove it.

'Let me,' Damian said, trying to take the bottle from her.

'I can do it!' she yelled as Mara burst into an uncontrollable peal of laughter.

'Fine, I'll leave you to it then.'

'I'll leave you to it then,' Lucia said, mimicking him, which irritated him more than it should, especially when Mara laughed even harder.

'You should go easy on the wine if you're not used to drinking, Mara,' Damian said. 'Maybe you should have a glass of water?'

'God, Damian, you're such a loser. She's fine. She's having fun,' Lucia said, almost missing her chair as she sat down.

'Don't say I didn't warn you.'

'Don't say I didn't warn you,' Lucia mimicked again, in a silly high-pitched whine.

'Fine. You know best, darling. Make sure you lock up before you come to bed. I'm going up.'

'Boring!'

'Yeah, whatever. Just remember you have work tomorrow.'

DAMIAN HAD to wake Lucia the next morning after she slept through her alarm, still half-dressed and with make-up smudged around her eyes. Her hair was a rat's nest, and you could have lit her stale alcohol breath with a match.

'I'm never drinking again,' she moaned as she tried to sit up, looking green.

He actually felt sorry for her. Although he was still cross at how she'd mocked him in front of Mara, he could see how hard it was for her adapting to having her sister back from the dead and making up for lost time. What he hated was that she continually put Mara before everyone else. Dylan and April were only young, and they needed their mother more than ever.

Damian brought Lucia breakfast in bed and sat with her while she nibbled dry toast.

'Why don't you call in sick this morning? I don't mind phoning Jennifer and telling her you've come down with a stomach bug.'

'I can't,' she said. 'I've too much on.'

'Then try to get away early.'

'I'll do my best.'

She finally managed to get herself up and out to work on time, but after she was gone, and Damian had dropped the kids at school, he couldn't face another day in the same house with Mara. Her presence was claustrophobic, pervading the house like a dense fog. He needed some space to clear his head, so he collected his laptop and headed for one of his favourite coffee shops in town. The Coffee Pot was a cross between a café and an antiques' shop, with an eclectic mash-up of furniture and quirky old watercolours for sale on the wall. It was one of those places you could fade away from the world unnoticed for an hour or two. And the coffee was great.

Damian sat in a beaten-up old leather chair in the corner by the window with a flat white in a chipped china cup and a mismatched saucer, taking solace in the chattering hubbub of strangers. He flipped open his computer, but couldn't concentrate. The same question kept bouncing around his head, taunting him. If Mara had found the camera and knew he'd been filming her, why hadn't she said something to Lucia, or at least confronted him?

All he could conclude was that she was messing with his head, trying to make him question his sanity. Like when she gave herself a black eye and accused him of hitting her. He knew she'd been through hell, and he'd really tried to make allowances, but she was twisted. It was as if, after sharing the same house for nineteen years, James Finch's depravity had rubbed off on her. They should never have taken her in. She needed professional counselling, but Lucia was having none of it.

It was hard not to conclude that Mara hated him. But he guessed she would have hated anybody who'd monopolised Lucia's time and love. It was apparent she wanted Damian and the kids out of the way at any cost. And that was truly terrifying.

'Is everything okay?' asked a waitress standing over Damian's table with a tray tottering with empty cups balanced on one hand. 'Can I get you anything else?'

He realised he'd been staring into space. She stood patiently waiting for his answer, the curl of her jet black hair scraped tightly back from her face looked like ripples in water. Damian glanced at his watch. It was later than he'd realised and the blank screen of his computer was blinking back at him as a reminder he'd achieved nothing that morning.

'No, I'm fine, thanks.'

'Sure?'

'Maybe a sandwich?' His stomach rumbled loudly.

'No problem,' the waitress said, jotting down his order.

When she returned with his food, his computer screen was still blank, his fingers poised over the keys.

'Are you sure everything's okay?' she asked, with genuine concern. 'You look like you're carrying the weight of the world.'

It was the first time anyone had asked how he was since they'd been reunited with Mara. They'd had the odd follow-up call from Mara's psychologist, but she seemed more concerned with Mara's mental state and how Lucia was coping. And despite all the promises, she'd never found the time for a house visit. They'd been left alone to work everything out for themselves.

The urge to off-load, to tell this stranger everything, what had happened and how he felt about Mara being in their lives, was overwhelming. He wanted to tell her he was angry and felt neglected, and terrified that they'd allowed someone with such deeply disturbing psychological issues into their home. He wanted to cry and scream and tell her his life was spinning out of control. That he was losing his wife and a journalist was threatening to publish scandalous details about his affair and that sometimes he wanted to crawl into a hole and forget about everything.

'Yeah, I'm fine, thanks,' he said, because who off-loads that kind of emotional baggage to a stranger?

He also carried the worry that whatever he told her could end up on the front page of a tabloid newspaper. The press were still clamouring for gossip about Mara, with fake news about her abduction appearing almost every day. The stories he could have told would have kept them going for months. He couldn't take the risk.

'All right, darling. Well, you look after yourself,' the waitress said and pottered off to wipe down the next table.

39

Damian sensed something was wrong the moment he slotted his key in the lock. Dylan and April crashed through the front door, shedding coats, bags and shoes before racing each other up the stairs to their rooms. Damian pushed the door closed and cocked his head to listen as their noise faded away. He heard voices, speaking quietly, not much more than a murmur, coming from the kitchen.

He was surprised to find Lucia and Mara sitting at the table, facing each other.

'What are you doing back so early?' he asked.

Lucia looked up, still in her work clothes, her eyes stony serious. She must have caught an early train.

'What is it? What's happened?' Damian feared the look in her eyes. All sorts of thoughts chased through his head. Had Mara told her about the camera in his study? Had Tanya Hayes been in touch? Did she know about Polly? He flushed hot and then cold.

'Mara called me at work.' Lucia cleared her throat, reached across the table and held up his missing camera. 'I thought I'd better come straight home.'

Damian swallowed hard and heard the blood rushing in his ears. 'Where did you find that? Is it the camera from my study?'

He'd already thought through this scenario and had planned his excuses. He was going to explain that he'd set it up as a test, and that he was planning to install more security cameras around the house, but that it had inexplicably disappeared and he suspected one of the children had taken it.

Mara turned slowly to face him. Her black eye had opened up a little, but the bruising was still colourful. She stared at him with a look of pure disdain.

'Mara found it in the bathroom this morning,' Lucia said. 'It was hidden behind the towels, pointing at the shower.'

Her words were like a body blow. What the fuck?

'Did you put it there?'

'No, of course I didn't,' Damian said. His cheeks flushed. He was being set up.

'But you don't deny it's your camera?'

'Yes, but I told you -'

'So can you explain what it was doing in the bathroom? Because it looks to me like you'd set it up to film Mara.'

'God, no. I'd never do that. What is this?'

'Don't lie to me, Damian!'

'I didn't put it there. Jesus, how could you believe that?' His mind was spinning so fast he could hardly think straight.

'It just magically found its own way into the bathroom, did it?'

'Yes. No. She must have put it there,' Damian said, jabbing his finger at Mara. 'She's trying to frame me.'

'Please, spare us the dramatics. Why would Mara try to frame you?'

'Because she hates me. You have to believe me, Lucia, I didn't do this.'

Lucia sighed and shook her head. She lowered her gaze. 'I'm honestly lost for words.'

'I'm not a pervert.'

'How long's this been going on? And I want the truth.'

'Nothing's been going on.'

'My own sister, for God's sake, and after everything she's been through.'

'I don't believe this.' How could he possibly prove his innocence? If Lucia was convinced he'd been spying on Mara in the bathroom, they were finished. There was no way back from something like that. 'Lucia, please.'

'Is this something you've done before?' Her face curled with disgust.

'Give me the camera,' he demanded, a thought suddenly occurring to him. He snatched it from Lucia's hand and switched it on.

He doubted Mara had actually gone through with filming herself. In which case, there would only be clips on the memory card of Mara in his study. He turned the camera over and swiped the touch screen until he found the playback mode. It should have shown all the footage that had been recorded, tiny thumbnails with timecodes and durations. But the folder was empty. There was no footage on the camera at all. Damian sighed with relief and handed the camera back to Lucia with what he hoped wouldn't look like a smug smile.

'There's nothing on here,' he said. 'Happy now?'

40

Lucia's brow furrowed. 'Give me your laptop,' she demanded, pointing at the bag slung over Damian's shoulder, 'if you've seriously got nothing to hide.'

'Fine.' He stood watching nervously as she slid his laptop out of his bag and flipped it open.

'Password?'

'I'll do it,' he said.

He spun the computer around and tapped in the password he'd used since the kids were small, an amalgamation of Dylan and April's names and the year he and Lucia were married. Nothing someone couldn't figure out if they knew enough about him.

'What are you hoping to find?' he asked.

'It's what I'm hoping I won't find,' Lucia said, snatching the computer back and hunching over the keyboard, her finger scrolling across the trackpad.

Damian watched as she located his media folders and searched for video files. She quickly found around a dozen with random numerical names, half of which he didn't recognise, but then he'd never been good at keeping an organised filing system.

She clicked on the first one. After a few seconds, a media player opened. A short film of Dylan holding April as a baby that Damian had shot on his phone began to play. April could only have been a few days old, her face angry and scrunched up, her skin a dark puce that contrasted with the creamy whiteness of Dylan's bare arm. Damian smiled at the memory, but Lucia immediately clicked away and returned to the list of other videos.

She scrolled down a dozen files with meaningless titles but stopped with her finger hovering over the trackpad when she found three files named 'Mara_1', 'Mara_2' and 'Mara_3'.

Damian's heart faltered. He'd never seen those files before in his life.

'What the hell?' he gasped.

Lucia glanced at Damian, an eyebrow raised. 'Anything to say before I open these?'

'I swear I didn't put those on there,' he pleaded.

Lucia double-clicked on the first of the files. The screen filled with a wide-angled view of Damian's study. His distorted face leered into the camera as he checked the angle of the lens before disappearing out of shot. Lucia scrubbed through the footage until he reappeared, carrying coffee and mugs on a tray.

She scrolled on until Mara emerged, looking sulky. The camera clearly showed Damian guiding her to the sofa where she sat, perfectly framed, looking anxious and uncomfortable.

'There you go,' he said. 'I told you I'd set it up in the study. I forgot I'd switched it on before Mara came down for a chat.' He laughed nervously.

Lucia closed the film without a word.

She navigated back to his folders and selected the file that had been named 'Mara_2'.

Damian sucked in a deep breath.

The first few frames were so overexposed and blurry he couldn't even tell what he was looking at. A second or two later, the camera made all the necessary adjustments, and the room came into focus. Damian already knew they were going to be seeing the inside of the family bathroom. The door to the shower cubicle was half open.

A figure emerged from the left. Mara in her pink, cotton pyjamas, her blonde hair sticking up wildly in all directions as if she'd just woken up. She moved to the centre of the screen and reached to peel off her top, turning her back to the camera.

Lucia slammed the laptop shut with such force the table shuddered, but not before Damian had caught a glimpse of Mara's pale skin, her ribs painfully visible.

'What the fuck, Damian?' Lucia screamed.

He scowled at Mara, unable to believe she had it in her to be so duplicitous. 'This has nothing to do with me,' he yelled back.

'Then what the hell is that footage doing on your computer?'

'Honestly, I don't know, but I've got a good idea.'

'Well, this should be good.'

Damian glowered at Mara, who'd lowered her head, playing the part of the unsuspecting victim beautifully. He had to hand it to her, it was an Oscar performance.

'Can't you see? This is all Mara's work,' he said. 'She's trying to poison you against me.'

'Let me get this right. You're saying Mara stole your camera, set it up in the bathroom, filmed herself getting undressed and then uploaded the footage onto your computer?'

'Yes!'

'You really do take the piss, Damian. You disgust me.'

Mara had frozen.

'Tell her!' Damian shouted, grabbing her arm and pulling her violently out of her chair.

'Ow, you're hurting me!' she squealed.

'Get your hands off her.'

'She's not so innocent, you know.' Damian sensed his world falling apart. 'You want to know what I found in her room yesterday?'

'What the hell were you doing in Mara's room?'

'Looking for my camera, obviously. But you know what I found instead? One of our kitchen knives stashed under her mattress.'

'So what?'

'A kitchen knife, Lucia. Under her bed. You want to ask her why?' Damian crossed his arms defiantly across his chest.

Mara had started to cry. 'I'm sorry,' she whimpered. 'I was scared. It made me feel safer. I know I shouldn't have taken it.'

Lucia looked stunned. 'Scared?' she asked. 'Look, even if James Finch was still alive, and that's highly unlikely, you're safe from him here.'

'I wasn't afraid of him.'

'Then, who?'

Mara pointed a bony finger at Damian. He took an involuntary step backwards, and the room fell silent.

'Damian?'

Mara nodded, bowing her head.

'Hang on a minute,' he said, just as he thought things couldn't get any worse. 'She had a knife under her bed. What if the kids had found it? What if she planned to use it on us?'

Lucia ignored him, her gaze fixed on her sister. 'Mara?'

She took a deep breath and let it out in a long sigh. 'I didn't walk into a door. He hit me,' she said. 'He punched me because of what happened to Dylan.'

'That's a lie! I never touched her.' Waves of panic washed over Damian with a dizzying ferocity, as he realised it was her word against his. He had no way of proving she was making it up.

Lucia reached for her sister's hand across the table. 'Why didn't you say anything before?'

'I didn't want to make a fuss. And I was worried you wouldn't believe me, that you'd think I'd made it up and you'd make me move out. I don't want to go.'

'Of course I would have believed you. You're my sister. You're not going anywhere.'

'Is this some kind of wind up, because it's not very funny,' Damian said. 'I didn't hit her, and I didn't set up a camera in the bathroom. What do I need to do to make you see that she's made all this up?'

'I'll make sure he never lays a finger on you again.' Lucia pulled herself slowly out of her chair and stood nose to nose with Damian, her movements so deliberate and considered it scared him.

'Lucia, please,' he begged.

'Did you hit Mara?'

'Lucia - '

'Answer me! Did you give her that black eye?'

'No, I didn't. Why would I?'

'Get out.'

'What?'

'You heard me. Get out of the house. I want you gone. I never want to see you again.'

'This is unbelievable,' Damian said, reeling. 'You're seriously going to take her word over mine?'

'She's my sister!'

'And I'm your husband.'

'Not for much longer.'

'What's that supposed to mean?'

'I want a divorce.'

A divorce? Damian thought for a moment his legs were going to buckle. He grabbed a chair to steady himself, trying to comprehend what had just happened.

'Let's all just calm down and talk about this for a minute.'

'I don't want to hear any more. I hate you,' Lucia yelled. 'Get out of the house and take your camera with you.'

She picked it up and threw it at him. It bounced off his arm and clattered to the floor.

'Please, don't do this.'

'If you don't get out, I'll call the police. Just go!'

41

Ben Collins wasn't exactly a close friend, but he lived nearby, which was the main reason Damian had ended up on his doorstep, swaying unsteadily with his finger aiming for the doorbell and an overnight bag slung over his shoulder.

He heard footsteps in the hall and a lock turning. Ben threw the door open and did a double-take. 'Damian?'

'Ben!' Damian said, a little too enthusiastically. He held out his arms as if he was greeting a long lost brother.

Damian had worked with Ben before turning freelance. They'd become friends after discovering a similar sense of humour and an appreciation of the same TV shows. They'd had a few nights out together and he and his girlfriend, Claire had even come for dinner. How long ago was that? Three years? Five? Damian tried to recall if they'd had Dylan at the time, but his alcohol-befuddled brain struggled. All he remembered was that they were a nice couple. Sincere. Unpretentious.

Ben glanced nervously over his shoulder, stepped outside and pulled the door to behind him. 'What are you doing here? I haven't seen you in ages.'

'Lucia's thrown me out.'

'Shit. Really?' Ben looked older, greyer around the temples, and his face was more lined than Damian remembered.

'Yeah.' Damian gave him his best hangdog look. 'I don't suppose there's any chance of a bed for the night, is there? I wouldn't ask if I wasn't desperate.'

God knows what sort of state he must have looked, with bloodshot eyes and reeking of beer. After Lucia had kicked him out, he'd spent the afternoon and early evening drowning his sorrows in The Star, trying to piece together how everything had gone so wrong so quickly. If he'd had his doubts before, he was convinced now that Mara was evil. She'd plotted to get him out of the way the moment she'd learnt Lucia was married, and now she'd finally got what she wanted. Damian had to make Lucia understand and stupidly thought the answer might lie in the bottom of a pint glass or six.

Now it was late, and he needed a bed for the night.

Running through the list of all the friends and acquaintances he could have turned to in his hour of need had proved a depressing experience as he realised the list was far shorter than he'd imagined. He'd lost touch with most of his mates from school and university, and although a few of them still exchanged the occasional disparaging remark on Facebook, the physical friendships had withered and died. They all had their own interests, jobs and families now. Many of them had moved away following careers and their love lives. The only other people they socialised with were Lucia's friends, and Damian wasn't going to humiliate himself turning up on any of their doorsteps begging for a bed.

'Oh, mate, I don't know.'

He could see Ben was struggling with his conscience. He wanted to help, but something was stopping him.

'You're married,' Damian said, spotting the silver band on his ring finger.

'Yeah, we finally got hitched last year,' he said.

'Congratulations. So, can you help an old mate out in his hour of need?'

'You're drunk.'

'Only a little.'

'Ben? Who's that?' Damian recognised Claire's voice calling from inside the house.

Before he could answer, she was at the door, drying her hands on a tea towel. She'd put on a bit of weight since he'd last seen her, and her shoulder-length hair was now cut into a short bob. 'Damian,' she said, not looking altogether pleased to see him.

'Surprise,' he said. It most definitely was.

'Lucia's chucked him out.' Ben rolled his eyes as if Damian's drunkenness had rendered him blind.

'Oh no, you poor thing. What happened? Do you want to talk about it?'

He was about to explain, but she grabbed his arm and coaxed him inside.

'Don't stand out in the cold. Come in. Tell us all about it,' she said. What was it about women like her who loved nothing more than someone else's crisis?

Of course, they'd heard all about Mara. It had been on the TV and in the papers and still continued to generate column inches. The poor little girl snatched from a tent in her garden, held against her will in a concrete cell under the floorboards and subjected to nineteen horrifying years of servitude and subjugation. Like everyone else, they were fascinated by every facet of her story, and couldn't help quizzing Damian all about it. How could he tell them what she was really like, that she'd turned Lucia against him, accusing him of hitting her and spying on her naked in the bathroom?

Instead, he told them Mara's arrival had put their marriage under enormous strain and that they'd agreed to separate for a short time while they sorted out their differences. He didn't go into specifics and to be fair to them, they didn't ask.

Claire instructed Ben to bring strong coffee and sat Damian down on the sofa, commiserating about his break-up, although he was less heartbroken and more angry that after nearly ten years of marriage, Lucia had taken Mara's word over his.

They made up a bed for him in a spare room at the back of the house, and he was grateful to finally crash out with his own company. It had been good to see Ben and Claire again, and he was grateful they'd taken pity on him, but he needed some headspace. He didn't need to talk it over or analyse it. He just needed to think through how he was going to rid Mara from their lives so they could get back to normality.

As he lay staring at the ceiling, Mara's leering face kept creeping into his mind, taunting him. But she was only part of his worry. There was still Tanya Hayes to deal with. If he didn't come up with the story on Mara for her, he'd never get Lucia back. His marriage would be finished, and his reputation destroyed. But how the hell was he going to get Mara talking now? They weren't even living in the same house.

He hardly slept a wink and, as the long hours of night turned into early morning, he was glad to hear movement in the house and the sound of a shower running. He rubbed his sore eyes and sat up, wishing he'd thought to bring a glass of water to bed as his mouth was as dry as the Sahara.

He checked his phone for messages from Lucia. Nothing. Not that he'd expected to hear from her. He had no doubt she was still furious, but in his heart, he'd hoped she'd have realised she'd made a mistake.

A notification on his home screen warned him he had twelve unread emails. He flopped back on his pillow and checked to see if there was anything important he'd missed. Four were from a difficult client, his tone increasingly irate, wanting to know why Damian still hadn't fixed his website. The last of his messages, sent late the previous afternoon when Damian had been drowning his sorrows, was notification he'd taken his business elsewhere. Another contract lost. Brilliant.

Damian threw the phone on the bed as the throbbing in his temples and behind his eyes induced a wave of nausea.

A knock on the door.

'Damian, are you awake?' Without waiting for a reply, Ben barged in, already dressed smartly for work, his hair slicked back and his face rosy and fresh, like he'd just stepped out of the shower. He handed Damian a mug of tea. 'How're you feeling this morning?'

'Like crap.'

'Right,' he said, standing at the end of the futon bed. He shoved his hands in his pockets.

The hot tea burned the taste buds on the tip of Damian's tongue. 'Thanks again for taking me in last night,' he said.

Ben smiled thinly. 'Did you want a shower? Only Claire and I have to leave for work in about fifteen minutes.'

Damn. They wanted him out of the house. He hadn't thought about that. 'Oh, no I'll be fine,' he said, waving Ben away. 'I'll just get dressed, and I'll be gone.'

'If you're sure? Claire can find you a towel.'

'No, really. I ought to be going anyway.'

'Right you are.'

Damian hadn't planned beyond finding somewhere to stay the night, so he ended up wandering into town and stumbling into the first café he came across, desperate for a shot of caffeine to ease the hangover which had now properly kicked in. As he sat at a table on his own, he was hit by the sudden realisation that he had nowhere to go. Nothing to do. He hadn't even thought to pick up his laptop when he left the house, so he couldn't work, even if he had been feeling up to it.

Staring out of the window, he watched legions of people hurrying for work, their faces set grim. It was another grey, dank day that sucked the colour out of the town. He closed his stinging eyes and felt his head grow heavy with sleep, but as his chin fell onto his chest, he woke with a start and noticed his phone buzzing on the table.

He snatched it up and pressed it to his ear. 'Lucia?'

'Damian, it's Tanya Hayes. Not caught you on the school run, have I?'

Damian swore silently under his breath and felt a wash of shame as he realised he'd not given Dylan or April a single thought since Lucia had thrown him out, caught up in his own self-pity. Then he wondered who'd taken them to school that morning, praying to God Lucia hadn't left it to Mara. 'What do you want?'

'Got anything juicy for me yet?'

'You said seven days.'

'I know, but I need to check you're making progress so we can plan some space in the paper.'

'Of course,' he lied. 'Mara's beginning to open up, but I'll need a few more days.'

'Good, because to be honest, I wasn't sure you had it in you.'

'You'll get the story.'

'Are you okay? You sound a little hoarse.'

'I'm fine. Was there anything else?' Damian ran a hand across his brow, wiping away a fine sheen of sweat.

'No, that's all. Oh, I almost forgot. I was going to let you know that I've found a great picture when I was doing some research.'

'What are you talking about, Tanya? I'm not in the mood for games.'

'Makes you look quite handsome. I can see why you chose it for your profile.'

Everything around him faded away, and Damian became aware of nothing other than Tanya Hayes' voice. His stomach tightened. 'What picture, Tanya?'

'Your Tinder picture, silly. What did you think?'

She let the words sink in. Damian could tell she was enjoying his discomfort. He opened his mouth to speak, but he had nothing to say. He'd completely forgotten his account was still active. He should have deleted it months ago. He'd only set it up for a laugh, to see what all the fuss was about, but had never used it seriously.

'I wonder,' Tanya said, her voice dripping with innocence, 'does your wife know?'

42

Damian wasn't sure what he'd hoped to achieve by returning to the house, but as he stood in the street, half-hidden behind a paint-chipped red letterbox with a chill wind cutting through his thin jacket, he knew he'd made a mistake. He had no evidence to disprove Mara's lies, and he doubted Lucia had changed her mind about him overnight, but he couldn't sit around doing nothing.

He and Lucia had fallen in love with the house from the moment they'd seen the estate agent's sign in the garden, but as he stared at its handsome proportions from a discreet distance, its charms that had once seductively attracted them both were lost on him. Its towering frontage, set behind a pretty garden, now looked more like a resolute fortress built to keep him out.

'Damian? What are you doing?'

The voice made him jump. 'Jesus, Rose, you scared the life out of me.'

She was standing with a shopping bag in each hand, and a knitted hat pulled down over her ears.

'I was just... ' He thought about lying, embarrassed to admit that he'd been thrown out of his own home, but instead found himself saying, 'Lucia and I had an argument. I've moved out.'

'I hope it's nothing serious?'

An uncomfortable lump formed in Damian's throat. 'I don't know.'

'Why don't you come in for a cup of tea. You can't hang around out here all day, and besides, it looks like you could do with a friendly ear.'

Rose's house was identical to theirs from the outside, and yet quite different in style inside. The basic layout was a mirror image of Damian and Lucia's. The hallway and stairs were in the same place, with the kitchen at the back overlooking a long garden. But where Lucia had insisted on knocking through to create an ample, open plan living space, Rose's house still had all its interior walls and original features intact, which gave it an old-fashioned, gloomy feel. It didn't help that dark, wooden antique furniture and the smell of dust and polish filled all the rooms. Over the silence, a ticking grandfather clock in the hall marked the slow passage of time. It was an old person's home, suspended in a bygone time that technology hadn't yet discovered.

Rose made tea in bone china cups, and they sat in the lounge at the front of the house facing the net-curtained window overlooking the street. There was an eerie silence about the place. No TV blaring. No kids bickering. No one thundering up and down the stairs. Just the metronomic beat of the clock. It was so much more peaceful than Damian's house, but he would have hated to live there.

'Why don't you tell me what's happened,' Rose said, sinking into a high-backed chair and balancing her cup and saucer on her knee.

'I don't know where to start.'

'Mara?'

'She hates me,' Damian said. 'I tried to make her feel welcome, but she treats me like I'm an intruder in my own home.' He sighed, wondering how much to confide in her. 'Mara told Lucia I'd given her a black eye, but I've never hit anyone, let alone a woman.'

'Why do you think she said it?'

'She resents my relationship with Lucia.'

'Can you blame her? She thought she was getting her sister back only to find she now has to share.'

'She's got a short memory. I was the one there for Lucia through all the bad times.'

'I'm not saying she's right. All I'm saying is think about it from Mara's perspective. The last time she saw Lucia, they were little girls. Now she's a married woman with two children and a wonderful husband. Mara must be wondering where that leaves her.'

'I've tried to make allowances, to make her feel part of the family. I don't know what else I could have done.' The strain behind Damian's eyes from his hangover and a lack of sleep left his skull feeling as though it was in a vice.

'Have you tried talking to Lucia about it?'

'I've not had a chance. It all came to a head yesterday when Lucia accused me of spying on Mara in the bathroom.'

If she was shocked, Rose didn't show it. An ambulance with flashing blue lights and an ear-piercing siren raced past the house. Damian finished his tea and placed his empty cup on the floor. It was good to talk. In fact, it felt better than he'd expected. He'd never been one to wear his heart on his sleeve, but talking with Rose felt good, so good he nearly confessed that a journalist was also threatening to publish a damning story in a national newspaper about his infidelity with an office junior, but stopped himself. The fewer people who knew about that, the better.

'Marriage isn't easy, Damian. You have to take the rough with the smooth.'

It was such a tired cliché, the sort of thing smug couples trotted out when asked how they'd survived seventy years of marriage without killing each other. That kind of sentiment didn't take account of evil sisters coming back from the dead and spouting their poison.

'Were you married?' Damian asked.

'A long time ago.'

'Happily?'

He followed Rose's glance to a sideboard overcrowded with photographs in dusty frames. Front and centre was a faded wedding picture, in which a dark-haired bride with a bouquet of white flowers smiled lovingly into the eyes of a sharp-suited man with a hooked nose and a mischievous grin.

'That's my Charlie,' she said. 'We were married for almost forty years. I loved him even when that terrible disease robbed him of his memories. If you love Lucia, you should fight for her.'

'It's too late. Mara's turned her against me.'

Rose sucked in her cheeks and sat up straight. 'That sounds like you're giving up. You can either go back and beg Lucia for forgiveness or try to patch things up with Mara and make her understand you're not in competition with her.'

Damian shuddered at the thought of making peace with his sister-in-law. 'I just want her gone,' he said. 'She needs psychological help. It's not something we can help her with, and it's not fair on any of us, least of all Dylan and April. I found a knife under her bed the other day, and now I keep thinking about her alone in the house with the kids and what she's capable of.'

'Then you have no choice. You have to persuade Lucia to forgive you.'

Rose pulled herself out of her chair and shuffled stiffly to the sideboard. She picked out the wedding photo with gnarled, arthritic fingers. 'We hardly had two pennies to rub together back then, but Charlie was a grafter, and he knew how to sell. He had this knack of persuading people to part with their money, even for old rubbish they didn't want or need.' She smiled fondly. 'He always said it didn't matter what he was selling. What was important was to understand your customer. And the only way to do that is by getting to know them.'

She carefully replaced the picture.

'Do you miss him?'

'Every single day.' Rose collapsed in her chair. 'But no one can take away the memories.'

'I wish I'd known him.'

'You'd have got on well. So, what are you going to do about Mara?'

Damian opened his mouth to tell her he still had no idea but then clamped it shut.

'I need to go,' he said, jumping out of his chair, inspired by Rose's words, suddenly realising what he needed to do.

He grabbed her by the shoulders and kissed her cold cheek. 'Thank you. I don't know what I would have done without you. I'll let myself out.'

43

Damian waited for the night's inky cloak to fall before driving to the house in the woods. Everything looked the same as he remembered, except now there were no police cars, forensics teams or TV news crews. No brilliant lights illuminating the tumbledown building with its rotting window frames, mossy roof and overgrown garden, only a thick, heavy silence broken by the occasional squawk of an owl.

When he'd visited before, he'd had to park a little way up the narrow lane. Now he was able to pull up right outside the house, close to where he'd first encountered Tanya Hayes and regurgitated half-remembered anecdotes about Mara from her school days. How he wished he could have turned back the clock and never gone there in the first place. If only he'd not spoken with her, he may never have needed to have come back.

It was a dark and foreboding place. Damian shivered as he locked the car and tentatively climbed a short flight of stone steps up to the house. The windows had all been boarded up, presumably to keep out the mawkish curiosity tourists looking for a glimpse inside at its now-famous underground cell, while the tattered remains of plastic police tape caught in a spiky bush fluttered in the wind.

Damian crept around to the rear of the building, lighting his way with a cheap torch he kept in the car for emergencies. Thick cloud rolled past the moon, and as it briefly thinned, a silvery light revealed a scrubby garden overgrown with tall grass and thick weeds. Beyond it, a dense forest of trees stood like an ominous wall.

He paused to shine the torch around the garden and picked out a rickety old wooden shed, the remains of a greenhouse that had lost most of its panes of glass and a rectangular vegetable patch in a state of neglect. A wigwam of bamboo canes tangled with the shrivelled vines of runner beans stood tall among dying and shrivelled tomato plants and curly-leafed lettuce that had run to seed.

Damian tried the back door, weather-worn and cracked, but it was locked and didn't even budge when he tried to force it open with his shoulder. He had better luck with one of the windows, its frame rotten and twisted under the protective board nailed to it. It was ridiculously easy to prise off using a spade he found in the dilapidated shed.

Cupping his hand to his brow, he peered through the glass and with the faint light of his torch saw a kitchen with dark brown work surfaces, beige cupboard doors, and a red linoleum floor.

He shuddered. Finally, he was looking into James Finch's lair, the place he'd brought Mara all those years ago and kept her in servitude. The window frame, rotten with damp and old age, didn't so much split as crumble when he used the spade to force it open. He hauled himself up and clambered awkwardly inside, over a sink and a stainless steel faucet which caught his foot and sent him sprawling.

He fell to the floor with a thud and lay motionless in the dark listening to the sound of his heart pounding in his chest, telling himself to man up. The house was empty. Just him and the memories of all the horrifying abuse that had taken place under its roof.

He wrinkled his nose at the smell of damp and pulled himself to his feet, shining the torch around to get his bearings. He'd imagined the house would be a festering dive, but the kitchen was spotless, even though the house had been boarded up for the last few months. Then he remembered Mara's stories of how fastidious Finch had been about cleanliness and how he'd forced her to work like a slave to keep it to his exacting standards.

Damian threw open a cupboard. Then a few more. They were all bare, apart from a few crumbs, the odd mouse dropping and at the back of one of them, over the oven, he found a key for the back door. He shoved it in his pocket and, brightened by his good luck, continued his search.

A door at the back of the kitchen swung open with the lightest of touches. Damian aimed his torch into the dark and took a step into the unknown.

In contrast to the immaculately tidy kitchen, he found a scene of chaos. Dining room chairs had been knocked over, a table pushed up against a wall, and a rug rucked up and crumpled. In the middle of the floor, no more than a metre square, he saw a gaping hole. Damian knew immediately he'd found the entrance to Mara's cell. The hole was smaller than he'd imagined. A wooden hatch had been cast to one side next to a metal bar and two brackets screwed into the floor which he guessed was how Finch had secured the hatch closed and sealed Mara inside.

A prickle of sweat ran down his back as he edged closer, his feet as hesitant as if he was approaching a cliff edge. He switched his torch from one sweaty hand to the other and pointed it into the blackness below. A set of wooden steps led down into a rectangular room, about twice the width of the hole itself and lined with breeze blocks. The floor was formed of smooth, grey concrete. On one side of the room, a steel toilet and basin had been plumbed in, the pipework concealed behind the walls. But the most unsettling sight was a mattress, stained with dark, muddy-coloured patches, pushed into the corner next to an industrial-looking chain hanging from a metal loop attached to the wall.

A wave of nausea swelled in Damian's stomach as he pictured Mara as a terrified eleven-year-old, disorientated and confused, thrown into the pit, chained to the wall by her wrists and left cold and alone in the dark.

He stepped back from the edge, his head dizzy. Some of the newspapers had named it the House of Horrors. They weren't far wrong. The place was as eerie as hell. Staring down into that pit, because you could hardly describe it as a room, he had to fight the urge to get far away. But he still needed answers, to get closer to understanding

Mara, and this was the only place he stood any chance of finding them.

The rest of the dining room, apart from the overturned furniture, was unremarkable, if not a little old-fashioned. It probably looked a lot like a million other dining rooms across the country. The ordinariness of it was the most horrific part.

The light from Damian's torch bounced off the walls and illuminated a mantelpiece above a tiled fireplace crowded with an assortment of trinkets and tacky ornaments, like Damian's gran used to bring back from holidays to Scarborough and Margate.

But he wasn't interested in any of that. What caught his eye was something else. He stared at it, squinting.

He knocked a chair out of the way and grabbed the framed photograph he'd spotted from across the room, realising his suspicions had been confirmed. But he felt no satisfaction. He held the picture up to the torchlight and studied it carefully before letting out an anguished laugh, not sure whether he should feel vindicated or sad.

'So Mara,' he whispered to himself. 'You were lying all along.'

44

Like the room, the photo frame was unremarkable. The picture, however, was fascinating. There were two figures, both smiling, arms wrapped around each other's shoulders. Relaxed. Happy. A casual observer might have concluded it was a father and daughter enjoying time together. The blur of trees in the background gave no clues as to where it had been taken, but it could well have been the back garden of the house where Damian was standing. He was surprised it hadn't been seized by the police. Maybe Finch had returned to the house and put it there after they'd left? The thought made him shudder.

Damian brought the photograph closer to his face. James Finch looked younger than in the artist's impression the police had issued through the media after Mara's escape, but he instantly recognised the shock of curly black hair. Finch was tall and crookedly thin, almost undernourished, the collar of his shirt gaping around his scrawny neck.

At his side, Mara stood smiling brightly. At a guess, she was about eighteen or nineteen. Her hair was cropped so short she looked almost bald, and her legs were dangerously thin, poking out from under a pair of over-sized shorts and bowing at the knees.

Damian wondered who'd taken the photo. Was it proof Finch had an accomplice? And if so, were they hiding him now? It hardly mattered. Damian was more interested in their body language and what the picture told him about their relationship. Mara hardly looked like a woman cowed and subjugated as she'd led everyone to believe.

Damian ripped the photo out of the frame and stuffed it into his back pocket. It wasn't exactly a smoking gun, but he hoped it would go some way to satisfying Tanya's hunger for evidence about Mara and Finch's relationship. Not quite enough to get her off his back, but a good start.

There was only one more room on the ground floor, a lounge with a worn, brown carpet, a threadbare sofa and a TV set that looked like a relic from the last century, a big boxy thing like Damian's family had owned when he was a kid. No pictures on the walls. No books on the shelves. Not even a coffee table. He pictured Mara and Finch cosying up in the room together, curled up on the sofa, and wondered what they watched.

Upstairs, he discovered two bedrooms and an avocado green bathroom. Over the bath, a shower head was hooked to the wall and connected to the taps with a rusting silver hose. The smaller of the two bedrooms was full of cardboard boxes filled with paperbacks. Crime thrillers mostly, their covers dog-eared and creased.

A double bed and a cheap white wardrobe dominated the main bedroom. As Damian stood in the doorway clinging to the frame, he wondered whether Finch slept there alone. He swung the torch into the darkest corners but found no evidence of a companion; no female cosmetics, clothes or womanly touches. Certainly, nothing to suggest Mara shared the room.

After exploring the entire house and finding nothing more of interest, Damian was left with the unenviable prospect of investigating the one place he didn't want to go but knew he had no choice.

He shuffled back down the stairs like a man condemned, into the dining room and approached the entrance to Mara's old cell. The staircase creaked and groaned as it took his weight. He descended slowly, feeling his way with his feet.

The smell hit him first. Sweat and blood and despair seemed to ooze from the walls. It was cold too. A degree or two cooler than the rest of the house. Damian zipped up his jacket as suffocating claustrophobia surfaced within him. At just under six foot tall, he had to stoop to stand up, and if he spread his arms, he could touch opposite walls at the same time.

He glanced up through the narrow entrance hole and tried to imagine what it must have been like for Mara watching Finch's leering face silhouetted as he sealed her inside the tiny, airless dungeon.

A single light fitting had been recessed behind a metal cage in the ceiling, but there was no switch; a reminder of how Finch had controlled everything about Mara's life, how he'd deprived her of light for days on end, and let her suffer alone in the dark.

On an initial glance, there were none of Mara's belongings, even though she'd said Finch had given her books, crayons, colouring books and even an old CD player and headphones. Damian guessed the police had boxed them up and either dumped them or put them somewhere safe in case she ever wanted them back. The only evidence anyone had lived there was the crumpled up, dirty bed sheet on the filthy mattress.

Damian dropped to his knees, hoping to find something, anything, that had been missed. He lifted the mattress, ignoring the smell, and found the end of a stubby yellow pencil with one end crushed and chewed. Further towards the wall, his fingers found a crinkle of paper. A ragged edge. He teased it out and held it up to his light. A child's drawing on a single sheet ripped from a notebook. The picture was faded, but the house with its classic pitched roof, smoking chimney, four windows and door was clear enough. Standing in the garden were four figures; a man and a woman with smiling faces and holding hands with a young girl in a blue dress. Another girl, slightly shorter than the first, was standing apart from the other three with tears like giant raindrops falling from her eyes. It was enough to break Damian's heart.

He folded the drawing and slid it into his back pocket with the photograph of Mara and Finch. Something else for Tanya, but he knew an old photograph and a faded child's drawing weren't enough if he couldn't get Mara talking.

He slumped on his haunches with a sinking feeling. He'd taken a massive risk coming to the house. And for what?

There had to be something else.

He took a breath and put himself in Mara's shoes. Abused, neglected, told when to eat and sleep, and forced into slave labour, what would he have done to wrestle back some control, to gain some independence?

He'd have looked for someplace to hide his drawings where Finch couldn't find them. Maybe Mara had had the same idea.

Filled with renewed hope, Damian scooted around on his knees, turning in a circle, wondering whether she'd managed to loosen any of the bricks in the walls. She could have used a pencil to scrape out the mortar. It wouldn't have been easy, but over time it's something she could have worked on.

With mounting excitement, Damian scrambled around the tight space, testing each brick, pushing them with his free hand until his jeans were covered in dirt.

'Come on, come on,' he muttered to himself, determined he couldn't be wrong.

He pulled himself over to the sink on his backside and held his breath against the stench of sewage and stale urine, probing around the toilet bowl.

Finally, reaching into the corner where it was damp and cold, one of the bricks shifted a fraction. Laying on his side, and with the torch resting on the floor, Damian wriggled his shoulders so he could get both hands in the small gap between the back wall and the toilet bowl, then used his fingers to pull the loose brick free, edging it out inch by inch.

When the brick came away from the wall, it left a hole no bigger than a shoebox.

Giddy with excitement, Damian reached inside. His fingers wrapped around a wad of papers and a notebook. He pulled them out and sat with them on his lap, the torch between his teeth.

The notebook's cardboard cover had gone limp with damp, and the pages were stuck together. Carefully, he peeled them apart and ran his eyes over tiny, scrawling handwriting. Every page was covered in densely packed words and scribbled drawings. A lot of it was gibberish, Mara's random thoughts and feelings. A diary of sorts, but more than that. It felt like peeling open her brain and staring into her mind.

Damian read a couple of lines about a brutal assault she'd suffered, how she'd hardly been able to walk the next day and how the blood had clotted on her legs and on her sheets, and how she planned to take her revenge on him with unspeakably cruel violence.

Damian closed the book and put it to one side, unable and unwilling to read any more. These were words Mara had no doubt intended for no one else to read, and as much as he hated her, it felt like he was violating her all over again.

Among the wad of papers were more drawings, far more disturbing than the picture under the mattress. Dark and moody, they mostly all featured a tall man with curly black hair having his eyes plucked out, his legs snapped or grotesquely penetrated by arrows and spears. In one of the pictures, he was being torn limb from limb by a pack of dogs, heavy red pencil swirls denoting pools of blood.

At the bottom of the wad of pictures was something that surprised Damian more than the brutality of the drawings. A pile of old birthday cards. One for almost every year Mara had been held in captivity. The first had the number twelve in large, pink numbers on the front, popping out from an explosion of vivid flowers and stars. Inside, a handwritten note.

To my beautiful girl, Mara. Hope you have a wonderful birthday. All my love forever, James xxx

Damian wasn't sure if he was more surprised Finch had sent her a card or that Mara had chosen to keep it.

He counted them. Eighteen in total. Those for her teenage years, up to when she turned twenty-one, had her age in numbers on the front. Inside, the handwritten message was almost always the same, apart from the landmark birthdays, when she'd turned eighteen and twenty-one. Then Finch had added saccharine words about how she was now a woman and ironically had her whole life to look forward to. Nothing overtly sexual. More like a father's words to his daughter.

Damian laid them on the floor next to the drawings and the notebook, imagining the field day Tanya Hayes would have if she ever laid her hands on them. They were gold dust. Everything that had happened to Mara handwritten in her own words. Which is precisely why Damian was determined she'd never know they existed. For everything Mara had done to bring him down, he wouldn't stoop to that level. They were too personal. Too raw.

But as he stared at the cards spread out before him, he had a niggling feeling something wasn't right. Eighteen cards over the nineteen years she'd been in captivity seemed about right. So what was it?

And then it struck him like a thunderbolt. Mara's birthday was in July. Three weeks before she'd escaped, but there was no card for her thirtieth birthday.

45

Damian woke with a crick in his neck and shivering with cold. With nowhere else to go, he'd slept in the car, parked up in a layby on the dual carriageway behind a Polish articulated lorry, with the doors locked and sprawled out on the back seat with a picnic rug for a blanket.

He sat up and stretched, his tongue furry, his mouth sour and his head throbbing. He checked his watch. Just after half five. Still early. He had so much buzzing around his head, but at least he'd woken with a clarity of understanding. Everything was starting to fit together. The fact that James Finch had disappeared without trace. The missing birthday card. Mara's miraculous escape after nineteen years. It all pointed to one thing, although he couldn't prove it yet.

He climbed into the front seat, turned on the engine and sat on his freezing hands while he waited for the heat to blow through.

He needed to speak to Lucia, to make her understand, to warn her about the danger she and the children were in. But she was still refusing to answer his calls, and he didn't want to cause a scene by turning up on the doorstep. That left him with only one realistic option to get her to listen to him.

He pulled on his seatbelt and was about to drive back to town when his phone buzzed with a message from Tanya Hayes.

Tick tock, Damian. Time's running out.

He grabbed the phone and dialled her number. It rang twice before she answered.

'Damian, good morning,' she said, with a brightness that irritated him. 'You're up early. Do you have news for me?'

'Lucia's thrown me out,' he said. 'I'm going to need some more time.'

'Oh, you poor thing.'

'And if you publish that story about Polly, it'll be the end of my marriage.'

'Sounds like it's falling apart without me.'

Damian bit his tongue as his anger simmered. 'I'll get you what you want, but stop hassling me.'

'Yes, I know you will, Damian. But I can't wait forever. I've promised a story I intend to deliver, with or without your help.'

'Don't push me, Tanya.'

'Calm down, Damian. Look, there's something interesting I've been puzzling over about Mara's supposed escape.'

'What do you mean "supposed" escape?'

'Have a guess how many days she was held by Finch.'

'I've no idea.' His mind was too foggy to even contemplate the maths.

'Seven thousand. I've checked and double-checked, and it's exactly seven thousand days from when Mara was abducted to when she was found in the woods. Doesn't that strike you as a bit of a coincidence?'

'*Exactly* seven thousand days?'

'Almost to the hour.'

'It's a coincidence,' Damian said, wondering what she was driving at, his mind pondering the missing birthday card.

'Is it? And of course, still no sign of James Finch. Do you want to know what I think?'

But he already knew what she thought. He suspected it was the same conclusion he'd been moving towards. 'Go on.'

'I think they planned Mara's escape together. I think James Finch was in on it all along.'

46

Business people, office workers and schoolchildren thronged through the concourse with their heads down, earphones in, and phones in hand. Not that Damian cared. The crowds would make it far less likely Lucia would spot him on the platform.

He made sure he was early for the 8:07, Lucia's usual train, and took a seat in one of the front carriages ten minutes before it was due to depart. By the time they pulled away, it was standing room only, and he could only hope Lucia had made it on board. He waited until they'd picked up speed and left the sprawling outskirts of town before squeezing out of his seat with an apology to all the cross-looking commuters packed into the aisle around him.

He didn't know how they did it every day, crammed onto muggy carriages, shoulder to shoulder with strangers, breathing in the same fetid air and with no guarantee of a seat.

He found Lucia five coaches back. She was sitting at a table with a woman and two men, one hand propping up her head, the other flicking through her phone.

'Lucia,' Damian said, squeezing past a tall man with a hipster beard nodding his head in time to the silent beat on his wireless headphones.

'Damian? What the hell are you doing here?' Lucia glanced up from her phone and glowered at him.

'We need to talk.'

'I'm on my way to work.'

'You didn't return any of my calls.'

'Because I don't want to talk to you right now,' she growled.

'But I need to tell you something about Mara.'

It was hardly the most private location to hold a conversation, especially about such delicate matters, but Damian couldn't think what else to do. Lucia hadn't been picking up his calls, and he knew if he'd turned up at the house, she would have slammed the door in his face. At least on the train she couldn't run away. She'd have to listen.

'Where've you been staying? You look bloody awful.'

Damian ran a hand over his stubble and brushed his fingers through his hair. He hadn't given any thought to how he might look, or that he'd not had a chance to wash that morning. 'Since you kicked me out, sleeping in the car.'

He noticed a few curious glances from some of the other passengers. But screw them. He didn't care who heard what he had to say. This was important.

'You couldn't afford a hotel for a couple of nights?'

'It's about how Mara got away.'

'Not now, Damian, for God's sake.' Lucia looked around to see if anyone was listening. Damian was sure they all were, but he couldn't worry about that. 'I'll call you later. We can talk tonight.'

'No,' he said, shaking his head. 'We need to talk now. It can't wait.'

A businessman sitting opposite Lucia looked up. 'Would you like my seat?' he offered, already starting to stand and reaching for a leather briefcase in the overhead rack. He probably didn't fancy being stuck between them, or maybe he was being polite, but Damian gratefully accepted his seat and leaned across the table.

'The thing is,' he said, choosing his words carefully, 'I don't think Mara's escape was a coincidence. I think she planned it with Finch.'

'Seriously?'

'There was always something about how she managed to get away from that house that bothered me. It didn't add up. What if she was in love with Finch, that they'd planned a future together and then something happened? What if they thought the net was closing in on them? She wouldn't have wanted Finch to have been caught by the police, so I think she helped him escape.'

Lucia's eyes opened wide. 'Jeez, Damian, would you listen to yourself.'

'I know it's hard to believe, but think it through for a minute. What if I'm right? It means Mara could still be protecting him.'

'You're insane.'

'No, I'm not.' He reached for her hand across the table, but she pulled it away and dropped it in her lap.

'Is that why you hit her? Is that why you thought you'd film her in the shower?'

'I didn't do any of those things, and you know it. It's Mara. She wants you to believe that all happened.' Damian hung his head and took a breath. 'Okay, look, I'll admit I came close to hitting her once. I raised my hand to her because she'd wound me up. But I stopped myself, okay? I would never hit anyone. You know that.'

'And the camera in the bathroom?'

'It's complicated,' he said, with a sigh. 'Yes, it was my camera, but I swear to you I never left it in the bathroom or downloaded those clips onto my laptop.'

'Why do you hate her so much?' Lucia stared at Damian like she no longer recognised him, as if their marriage had been based on a lie. 'Is it jealousy? Or are you really that uncaring you can't see she needs our help? She told me you'd tried to talk her into moving out, by the way. Why couldn't you just cut her some slack? Not everything in the world revolves around you.'

'Because she's dangerous,' Damian hissed. 'How many times do I need to spell it out? I don't trust her, especially around Dylan and April. She needs help. I get it; anyone would be fucked up after what Finch put her through, but we can't fix her. You've done your best, and you want to take care of her. That's fine. But not in our house, and not around our kids.'

'Don't bring Dylan and April into this. Mara loves them.'

'She's got a funny way of showing it.' Damian had a sudden,

disturbing thought. 'Who's taking them to school this morning? Please tell me Rose is helping out.'

'Why would I need Rose when Mara is perfectly capable?'

Damian's stomach turned over. 'You've left them with Mara? Jesus Christ, Lucia. Are you mad?'

'She managed perfectly well yesterday in your absence. She's my sister. I trust her.'

'Well, I'll pick them up tonight,' he insisted.

'It's fine. Mara can do it.'

'I said, I'll pick them up. I'll take them out for tea, and maybe we'll go bowling. I'll bring them back later.'

'They've got school tomorrow.'

'You can't stop me seeing them, no matter what's going on between us. That's not fair.'

He thought Lucia was going to protest, but the fight seemed to evaporate from her. 'Fine,' she said. 'But make sure they're home by seven.'

Lucia crossed her arms and stared out of the window at the blur of hedges, fields and sheep. 'Was there anything else?'

'Look, I just want you to open your mind to the possibility, at least, that Mara has been lying to us.'

'Change the record, Damian.'

'There's one more thing.'

Lucia glanced briefly at him. 'What?'

'It's about how long Mara was held by Finch. I've worked it out,' he lied. He'd taken Tanya's word for it and hadn't bothered to try the calculation for himself. 'From the day she went missing to the day she was found was exactly seven thousand days.'

Lucia shook her head as if she didn't understand his point. 'So what?'

'Exactly seven thousand days, almost to the hour. Don't you think that's odd?'

'Not particularly.'

'It's almost as if she planned it that way. And what about Finch? Every force in the country's been looking for him, but he's managed to vanish. How do you think that's possible without help?'

‘I don’t know, but it's a long stretch of the imagination to suggest Mara is involved.'

'Is it?'

'I know what's going on here, Damian.'

'You do?' he asked, puzzled.

'You've hated the attention I've given Mara since the day she was found. That's what this is really all about. Why do you have to be so needy all the time? It's worse than living with a child. You're jealous and this is your way of getting back at her.'

'Jealous of Mara? Don't be ridiculous,' Damian huffed.

'Then what exactly is your problem?'

'I went to the house in the woods.'

Lucia stared at him in disbelief, her mouth hanging open.

'I had to see it for myself,' he continued. 'So I broke in, and I found the cell Finch had dug out under the floor.'

'Why?'

'To understand,' Damian said. 'I found some of Mara's old things. Some drawings and a diary, but there was also a stack of birthday cards, one for every year she'd been in the house, starting on her twelfth birthday. They were all from Finch, but there was a card missing.'

Lucia looked at him blankly.

'Remind me, when's Mara's birthday?'

'July. You know that,' Lucia said.

'And when did she escape?'

'August.'

'A few weeks after her thirtieth birthday, right? And yet there was no card.'

'That's it? Finch forgot to send her a birthday card on her thirtieth birthday, and you think that proves some great conspiracy?'

'But he'd never missed a birthday in the previous eighteen years. I think it proves he'd already left.'

Lucia frowned. Damian could almost hear the cogs turning in her mind.

'And if that's true, Mara was living there alone for at least a month before she ran away.'

Lucia continued to stare at him and then laughed. 'Honest to God, Damian. Your imagination's going to get you into serious trouble one of these days. That's the most ridiculous thing I've ever heard.'

'Do you have any other explanation?'

'There are a million other explanations,' she said, but as she lowered her gaze, he could see he'd finally lit the fuse of doubt in her mind.

47

MARA

A LOUD BANGING, urgent and insistent, echoed through the empty house.

Someone at the front door.

I froze with my heart pounding in my chest, terrified and unsure. I tried to ignore it, hoping that whoever it was would go away. I wasn't expecting anyone and Lucia wouldn't be home for several hours.

Bang. Bang. Bang.

I closed my book and sat up, swinging my legs off the bed and grasping thick handfuls of my duvet. I listened hard, hoping to hear the sound of footsteps drifting away from the house.

Go away.

A few seconds of silence and then the banging resumed, so loud I thought someone was trying to break down the door.

I crept across the room, unlocked my bedroom door and padded down the first flight of stairs. I hesitated outside April's room and jumped when the banging started again, even louder.

'Open the door!' A man's muffled voice shouted.

'Who is it?' I called out, my voice trembling, but he can't have heard me.

Bang. Bang. Bang.

Please make it stop.

I tiptoed down to the hall, clinging to the bannister and cringing when the knocker struck the plate with such force I could see the door shake in its frame.

'Please go away. There's nobody in. Lucia won't be back until later,' I shouted, edging along the wall, fearing the door was about to burst open.

'Mara?' It's me.'

'Damian?'

'Let me in.'

'What do you want?'

'Something terrible's happened. I need to talk to you.'

I immediately thought about Dylan and April. Damian was supposed to have picked them up from school and taken them out bowling.

'What is it?'

'Lucia's been in an accident. Please, open the door.'

Lucia? An accident? Oh my God. I had the sensation of the ground opening up and swallowing me whole.

When I unbolted the door and threw it open, Damian was standing on the step, hopping from one foot to the other with his phone in his right hand and clutching a carrier bag in the other. 'What's happened? Is she all right?'

He pushed past me into the house. 'She was hit by a taxi,' he said breathlessly. His face was flushed, and his eyes were darting furtively left and right. 'Her office called me. They've taken her to hospital.'

My legs felt almost too weak to support my body. 'When?'

'About an hour ago. I came straight here when I heard the news. Get your shoes and coat. I'll drive. She'll want you to be there.'

'What about Dylan and April?'

'I've dropped them off with Rose. She'll look after them while we're gone. Come on, hurry.'

I shook my head in disbelief, paralysed with shock. 'Is she badly hurt?'

'I don't know. Come on, I've parked around the back.'

'I'll just grab a jumper,' I said, bolting for the stairs and racing up to my room, imagining the worst. The thought of losing Lucia again was unbearable, but I fought back my tears. No point crying until I knew the facts.

Being reunited with Lucia had been the happiest day of my life. I'd spent hours dreaming about it, picturing how it would be, imagining her face as it turned from shock to disbelief and finally overwhelming joy. I hung onto that vision through the years, even when James had tried to tell me my family had forgotten about me. Sometimes, he would let me watch the news to prove no one was looking anymore. It was cruel of him, but I never gave up believing. I knew my sister would never forsake me, and the day she came back into my life was better than I'd dreamt. Until she'd introduced me to Damian.

I'd never imagined Lucia's life would have moved on while I was gone. Learning that Mum and Dad had died had been a shock, but not entirely unexpected, but finding out Lucia was married with kids had been a blow I'd not foreseen. Maybe it was because I'd spent so many hours thinking about how her wedding would be, me as a bridesmaid in a pretty, silk gown, beaming with pride as Lucia glided down the aisle to marry a dashing rugby player called Steve or Brett or Ethan. I never once contemplated she'd go ahead and get married without me to someone like Damian. I'm not sure he even loved her.

I snatched a grey cardigan off the end of the bed and tugged it on, not stopping to wonder why Damian would have parked around the back of the house. He hardly ever did, unless he was loading up the car with rubbish or garden waste. Nor did I hesitate to think why he'd come by to pick me up. If I'd thought about it for a second, I'd have realised he wouldn't have thought about me before rushing to the hospital to be with Lucia.

But I wasn't thinking. That was the problem. My mind was on my sister.

I hurried down the stairs and was slipping on my shoes in the hall when I heard breaking glass. Sharp and sudden, coming from the kitchen.

'Damian?'

I tip-toed through with a sense of unease, a coat I'd grabbed from the hook in the hall draped over my arm. Damian was standing by the door with his back to me, and the hood of his top pulled up over his head. At his feet were a thousand crystal shards of glass, glistening in the late afternoon light.

'What happened?' I asked, wondering if he'd hurt himself.

I gasped with fright as Damian whirled around.

'Time to go,' he said, with an evil smile. 'Are you ready?'

I opened my mouth to speak but the words stuck in my throat, my gaze fixed on his head and the thick, black curly wig under his hood.

48

Damian lunged at me, fast and unpredictably like a cobra striking a mouse. I squealed as he snatched my wrist, his face hardening into a contemptuous snarl.

'Shut up!' he snapped.

He pulled me close, and I didn't have the strength to fight him off. I'd gained some weight after years of surviving on the scraps James had fed me, but I was so much weaker than Damian.

'You're hurting me,' I cried, but instead of loosening his grip, he wrapped an arm around my throat and clamped a latex-gloved hand over my mouth.

I should have put up a struggle, but instead, I gave in. You'd have thought I'd have learnt my lesson, that I would have kicked and punched and wriggled like my life depended on it. But I didn't. I submitted to him, suddenly an eleven-year-old girl again, frightened and helpless, too terrified to do anything but acquiesce. He produced a roll of black tape from his pocket, tore off a strip with his teeth and pulled it tightly across my mouth, forcing me to breathe through my nose. Then he yanked my arms roughly behind my back and bound my wrists together.

In an instant, he'd rendered me completely helpless and totally at his mercy. It was history repeating itself and just like before I couldn't comprehend what was going on. I know Damian thought I'd driven a wedge between him and Lucia, but when had he become the kind of monster who was capable of this? Besides, it wasn't true. The cracks in their relationship had been clear to me from the day I'd first met him. My arrival in their lives had merely hastened their inevitable break-up. There was no way he could blame me.

As we shuffled out of the door, our feet crunching over the smashed glass, I noticed a rock lying on the kitchen floor amongst the shards. Several chairs around the kitchen table had been knocked over as if someone had broken in, and I realised Damian had staged it to make it appear as if there had been a struggle. What the hell was he playing at?

He dragged me through the garden and into the lane behind the house where a van was parked outside the back gate. A white van, unremarkable and spotted with mud. Not dissimilar to the vehicle James had bundled me into nineteen years ago. All the bad memories came flooding back, searing through my mind. At least before I had no idea what was happening or what would become of me. I thought then it had been a mistake or a joke. This time I knew the horrors and suffering that might well lay ahead, and for the first time in my life, I wished I was dead. I'd survived once. I wasn't sure I had the strength to face it again.

My feet scuffed through the dirt as I desperately tried to dig my toes into the ground, but it was hopeless. I was powerless against Damian. He threw open the back doors of the van and shoved me inside. I fell on my front and, with my arms tied behind my back and unable to break my fall, struck my face on the cold metal floor.

I grunted in pain, but he didn't care, plucking the phone Lucia had given me out of the pocket of my jeans. He slammed the doors shut, and although I managed to roll over onto my side, my shoulders screamed in pain at the unnatural rotation of my arms.

Damian jumped in the front and started the engine. The van rattled and growled, and as we pulled away heading for God knows where, I managed to sit up, struggling to breathe through the snot and blood caking my nose.

At the end of the lane, we turned left, picking up speed. With the afternoon sun low in the sky, Damian's head was silhouetted against the windscreen, wisps of hair from his wig catching in the weak rays and for a moment he looked just like James. A whole host of different emotions surged through my body, and I found my lips trembling, unable to believe the nightmare I'd been caught up in again.

'Why are you doing this?' I wanted to yell at him. 'I'm sorry if I've upset you. I'll try to be a good girl in the future. You can trust me, I'll behave.'

But all that came out of my mouth was a muffled noise that was drowned out by the sound of the engine.

We stopped at a set of lights, and when they turned green, Damian accelerated away. Soon we were on the fast road out of town. I closed my eyes and tried to relax, saving my strength and fearing what Damian had in mind. Were we heading for a quiet spot in the woods? A clifftop? A bridge? I had no idea. I could only imagine he was planning to kill me, but if he wanted me dead, then maybe it would be a relief, an easy escape from the pain and suffering.

But no. I refused to succumb just like that. It would mean all those years I'd fought to survive would be for nothing. I thought about Lucia and her anguish if I gave up. She deserved better. And in that instant, I resolved things would be different this time. I owed it to myself and to Lucia to fight back. This time, things would be different.

49

The warning signs had been there all along, but I'd failed to see them. I'd been blind and stupid, imagining that all the bad things that could possibly happen in my life were far behind me. I thought I'd left the violence as a distant memory.

That was until Damian punched me; an unexpected blow that took my breath away and sent me flying across the bed. I'd lain motionless for a moment, shocked and scared, until April had appeared at the door. A second or two earlier and she'd have seen her father strike me. I didn't warm to the girl, but it would have been devastating for her to witness that. It was something no daughter should ever see.

I could see she knew something was wrong. Maybe she'd heard the crack of her father's fist connecting with my face, or caught my shocked gasp, or just guessed from the terrified look in my eyes. Whatever it was, she recognised in that instant what her father was capable of, and her rejection of him when she ran off, ignoring his pleas, was at least some consolation to me.

It had all happened so quickly. Damian had barged into my room, screaming and yelling like a madman, claiming it was my fault Dylan had ended up in hospital and nearly died.

Me? Was he serious? I couldn't believe it.

He was the one who'd made Dylan's sandwiches. It was Damian who'd used the wrong bread because he was too tired, or too drunk, or in too much of a hurry, I don't know. But I certainly didn't go near the boy's lunch. Why would I?

I suppose my mistake was in raising my voice to him. I should have learnt my lesson from James, who hated it when I argued back. At least he'd never left a visible bruise, especially on my face. That would have reminded him of what he'd done and how he'd damaged me.

When I'd first met him, Damian had seemed welcoming enough. Easy going. Kind even. He was intrigued by my abduction, sympathetic to the hurt I'd suffered, and curious to find out more. But then there had been that weird incident at the hospital. Lucia had only left us alone for a minute, and without any warning, he'd picked up a jug full of water, lifted it above his head and hurled it across the room. I was so shocked I screamed, terrified and confused until Lucia had come running. And then he lied to her. He stood in front of her, and as bold as you like, he blamed me.

It was only later that I realised he was sowing the seeds of doubt in Lucia's mind about my mental and emotional state. He wanted her to believe I was unstable, that my mind was fragile, that I was maybe even dangerous.

I'd hoped it had been an isolated event and I put it out of my mind, especially when Lucia announced she wanted me to move in with them, and I started to look forward to rebuilding my life as part of a real family. They gave me my own room, let me choose how it was decorated and for a short while I was happy in the sanctuary of my attic space. I loved sleeping between clean sheets and listening to the rain on the roof tiles above my head.

That's not to say I wasn't still haunted by nightmares, waking most nights with my body dripping with sweat. The psychologist from the hospital had said that the bad dreams were a symptom of the trauma I'd suffered, but she expected me to get better in time and the dreams to become less frequent. I'd have settled for the nightmares every time over waking to find Damian standing at the end of my bed, staring at me with cold, dead eyes.

It only happened once, but it left me paralysed with terror, unable to move or scream, wondering whether he was going to hurt me. I'd pulled the covers up to my chin and watched as he continued to stare, his gaze boring through me. Eventually, without speaking a word, he'd turned and walked out, leaving me shaken and afraid. It was the creepiest thing. For all his faults, I'd never had to worry about James molesting me in the night.

I thought that was freaky enough until I found out Damian had made up a story about discovering me in April's room that night, sitting in her chair in the corner, watching the girl sleep. It was a complete fantasy, another of his attempts to make out I was the crazy one, and worse, I was a threat to the children.

I made him fit a lock on my bedroom door, and as an extra precaution, hid a kitchen knife under the bed. It was the only way I could guarantee getting any sleep. I hated being left alone in the house with him, which frequently happened when Lucia returned to work. I didn't trust him, and Damian's mere presence under the same roof left me on edge. So I spent my days locked in my room, waiting for Lucia to return home.

Even now, I don't know why I didn't tell her that Damian had hit me. I suppose I was afraid of making a fuss, and part of me couldn't shake the feeling I'd asked for it. James had always made me believe I was to blame for his savage beatings, and it was hard not to think I deserved it when Damian punched me. After all, I'd argued with him and made him angry. So I lied and told Lucia I'd walked into a cupboard door when the bruise around my eye had come up in a hideous riot of colours, and I could barely see through the swelling.

I suppose I was also trying to protect Lucia. In the same way, I was glad April hadn't witnessed her father hit me, I didn't want Lucia to know she'd married a monster. But they say the truth will always out. In the end, I suppose I was partly responsible for Damian and Lucia's break-up. I wasn't sad because it was apparent they weren't right for each other. They were mismatched in so many ways. Surely, everyone could see that? I think Lucia genuinely loved him, but it wasn't reciprocated. Not in the same way, at least. My sister was beautiful, intelligent and caring. Damian was a user who thrived on the control he asserted over her. In fact, I couldn't really see what she saw in him.

In the end, Damian made my decision to confide in Lucia easy. He'd called me into his study on the pretence of a friendly chat over coffee, luring me with the lie that he wanted to apologise for his behaviour in recent weeks. But it was so out of character, especially when he turned on the charm, that I knew instantly something was wrong and looked for a trap. I found it poorly concealed on the shelf above his desk, in the shape of a camera poking through a pile of books.

I don't know what he was planning or what he thought I might say to incriminate myself because that's all his motive could be. I acted without thinking, seizing the opportunity when his attention was distracted by a knock at the door. While he was briefly out of the room, I took his camera and hid it in the pocket of my jeans, hoping he wouldn't spot the bulge.

The next day, I wasted no time in setting it up in the bathroom behind a stack of towels. I positioned it facing the shower and put on a little show. Nothing too gratuitous. Just enough skin to convince Lucia that Damian had been spying on me for his own gratification.

The hardest part was hacking into his computer to download the files. It took me the best part of an hour, that night when they'd gone to bed, to work out how his computer worked and to crack his password. A combination of his kids' names and the year he and Lucia were married. Then I renamed the files and dumped them in a folder where they'd easily be found.

A few days later, I set everything in motion. Damian was working away from the house for the day, so I phoned Lucia at work and burst into tears. I let her drag it out of me that I'd found a camera and could only think Damian was to blame. I thought she'd stew over it all day and by the time she returned home might have worked herself into a frenzy. But instead, she dropped everything and caught the next train home.

We sat at the kitchen table, and I showed her the camera. We both cried, and although at first Lucia wouldn't entertain the idea that

Damian was responsible, I guided her towards the idea of checking his laptop.

When Damian returned home with the kids, he had no idea of the shit storm he was walking into. Lucia went berserk. Honestly, I had no idea she was going to throw him out, but it was nothing more than he deserved. I certainly didn't lose any sleep over it. I'd always thought Lucia could have done so much better than Damian, and that I'd done her a massive favour.

I was foolish to think that would be the end of it, that he'd walk away without a fight, but I never imagined the lengths he would go to in retaliation.

50

With a little effort and some discomfort, I sat up and blinked the tears of self-pity from my eyes, forcing myself to calm down. I'd been in this situation once before, with James, and never fought back. I was too afraid, too helpless to do anything but submit to his will. But I wasn't that little girl anymore. My destiny was in my own hands.

I shuffled up against the rear doors, never taking my eyes off Damian in the driver's seat, and with a vague plan forming in my head. My fingers explored blindly along the smooth, cold metal, tracing the lines of the aluminium panels, rivets and mouldings until I found a sharp edge where two pieces of metal had been badly welded together. A centimetre of ragged, serrated metal.

Angling my body and ignoring the protestation in my shoulder sockets, I ran the tape binding my wrists over the metal burr, back and forth, sawing with short, sharp movements. Sweat poured from my brow, and the top of my arms screamed in agony, but finally, I felt the tape give a little. With renewed hope, I increased my effort until I was able to tear the tape and pull my hands apart.

I ripped off the strip over my mouth and gulped in large lungfuls of air, relieved to be able to breathe properly again. I rubbed the feeling back into my arms. We were travelling too fast to even contemplate jumping out of the van without causing myself serious injury or even death, which meant the only choice I had was to get Damian to stop.

Slowly, I crept forwards, remaining low to the ground as I shuffled towards him on my hands and knees, watching his head rocking gently with the sway of the road, his eyes fixed ahead, the grotesque sight of his black, curly wig a sickening reminder of the last time I'd been bundled into the back of a darkened vehicle.

Inch by agonising inch I closed the distance between us until I was right behind his seat, close enough to hear his breath over the hum of the tyres. I rose up and wrapped my hands around his face, pressing my fingers into his eyes and squeezing with all my strength.

Damian screamed in panic, and as he hit the brakes, we slewed across the road, tyres screeching. Another vehicle flashed past, its horn sounding a discordant note of alarm, its headlights momentarily dazzling me. But I held on and kept pressing. Harder and harder, until I thought I'd burst his eyeballs. Time seemed to slow down, and as the van rocked heavily on its axles and Damian let go of the steering wheel to snatch my hands away from his face, I was thrown heavily against the side of the vehicle. My head collided painfully with the metal framework, and I crumpled to the floor. Then, as suddenly as the chaos inside the van had unfolded, it stopped.

We came to a grinding, jarring halt, the engine silent. I lay unmoving on my side. My head, shoulders, neck and back were all tender, but nothing seemed to be broken.

Damian moaned, and I heard him move. A rustle of clothing. A door being opened and slammed closed. The sound of his heavy footsteps on the ground outside. I tried to pick myself up off the floor, but my mind was foggy, and I couldn't co-ordinate my limbs. Nothing wanted to work properly. Panic built in my chest as the rear doors opened with a clunk and a blast of cold air hit me.

'You stupid cow,' Damian hissed, reaching for my leg and dragging me on my back towards him. 'You could have killed us both.'

'I'm sorry,' I whimpered, anticipating the violence I was sure was coming. I winced and tried to curl into a ball as he reached into his pocket.

Sometimes, when James was particularly cross, he'd put keys between his fingers before punching me in the stomach or on my arms or legs. I wondered if Damian was planning some similar kind of brutality.

I screwed my eyes shut and tensed every muscle, praying the beating would be brief. It was the drawn-out punishments I hated the most. The prolonged ones James stretched out over hours, sometimes taking me to the dark edge of consciousness before bringing me back again. He'd been a master at it.

But rather than hitting me, Damian pushed my feet together and tied my ankles with more tape until I was left with hardly any movement in my legs. Then he rolled me over, yanked my arms behind my back and applied more tape around my wrists and hands.

'What are you doing? Where are you taking me?' I cried, but my questions fell on deaf ears.

'Shut up. Try a stupid move like that again, and I'll kill you.'

Damian grabbed a handful of my hair and pulled my head up roughly before shoving a dirty rag into my open mouth. As it hit the back of my throat, it made me gag. I thought I was going to suffocate. He let go of my hair, and as my face hit the floor with a thud, I sucked in a deep breath through my nose, my body rigid with terror.

The doors slammed closed, and Damian jumped back behind the wheel. He fired up the engine, reversed and pulled away with a squeal of burning rubber as I heard the low rumble of a passing vehicle heading in the opposite direction.

I groaned as the sound faded away. A couple of seconds earlier and everything might have been so different. Whoever was passing might have noticed the van stopped at an awkward angle at the side of the road, seen the skid marks and been intrigued enough to investigate. Someone might have peered into the back and seen me trussed up like a turkey. They might even have confronted Damian and demanded to know what he was doing, or called the police. But luck wasn't on my side that evening. The sound of the vehicle faded into the distance, carrying with it my hopes of escaping from Damian alive.

I estimated we drove on for another fifteen minutes, and when we finally stopped, my shoulders and hips were aching and the side of my face numb. Without the hum of the engine, we were enveloped by the sound of silence. No passing cars, just the occasional screech of buzzards somewhere high above. My heart pounded. Where the hell were we? Was he going to kill me now? The panic snowballed inside my chest, but there was nothing I could do. I was completely immobile, hardly able to breathe, let alone scream for help. Perhaps I could reason with him? Talk him around? Damian wasn't an unreasonable man, at least I hadn't thought so until this. I'd tell him I'd happily move out, and I'd never breathe a word of what happened if he would just let me go.

His feet crunched on the road, and then he flung open the doors, letting in cold air, washing away the fetid stink of my fear. He dragged me onto the soft ground by the side of the road, and I stood unsteadily, my body stooped as I cowered from him. A liverish crescent moon hung in the dusky sky, high above the tips of the bare branches of the trees surrounding us.

We were in woodland, surrounded on all sides by towering sycamores, ash and sweet chestnuts, the ground covered in an autumnal carpet of fallen leaves. Damian reached behind his back and pulled out a knife, its blade curving into a vicious point and dangerously sharp. I was sure it was the same carving knife I'd hidden under my bed. The irony of it would have made me smile if I'd not been so terrified.

Was this where he planned to dump my body? I prayed he would at least make my death quick and painless.

He dug his fingers into my mouth and pulled out the dirty rag. I coughed and spluttered, but was grateful to be able to breathe freely again.

'Are you going to kill me?' I asked, swallowing hard, my throat sore. In all my years living with James, during all my suffering and sorrow, I'd never actually thought he would kill me. Confronting death now felt hollow and empty.

'No,' he said, frowning as if the thought had never entered his mind.

'So, what then?'

'Don't you recognise where I've brought you?' he said, crouching to slice through the tape around my ankles.

I caught my balance and looked around. There, half-hidden between the trees, was a building I knew very well, its grey slate roof shadowed by moss, a crooked chimney stack on the verge of collapse. My stomach lurched, and my heart sank.

'I've brought you home, Mara,' Damian said.

51

The sight of the house sent a shudder through my aching body as the bad memories surfaced from the deep crevices of my mind; flashes of the pain and hurt I'd suffered behind its thick walls. But something else caught me by surprise. Nostalgia? Happy memories of cutting flowers from the garden, of being allowed to watch TV curled up on the sofa, and the warmth of early morning sunlight on my skin as it spilt through the kitchen window. The house was where I'd experienced so much emotional and physical torture, but it was also where I'd grown up. It was the only home I could really remember, the house where I'd arrived as a girl and left as a woman. I only ever retained vague memories of my life before; brief recollections of sharing lunch around an oval table while I bickered with Lucia; a day trip to the beach in my father's old car, and my mother in the kitchen up to her elbows in flour. Hazy snatches of the times I'd lost that could have been dreamt or belonged to someone else. Unexpected tears blurred my vision.

'Why would you bring me back here?'

'Because it's where you belong.' Damian shoved me in the back and forced me to start walking, up the mossy steps from the lane towards the house.

Everything looked so familiar even though I'd forced myself to forget. I'd tried to bury the memories, but now they came flooding back with every sight, smell and sound. The broken flagstones under my feet, the earthy smell of mulching autumnal leaves and the creak of the garden gate. Damian was right. This was where I belonged.

Night was already chasing away the dusk, and when the sliver of moon illuminated our vegetable patch at the back of the house, my heart skipped a beat. Bean vines hung dead on their canes, and the lettuces had run to seed, half-covered by fallen leaves. I tried not to let my gaze linger on the plot where I'd once sown succulent smelling sweet peas and towering sunflowers in the summer. Instead, I let Damian lead me towards the back door.

To my surprise, it wasn't locked. He pushed it open and invited me to step inside, smiling as he saw the confusion on my face.

'You've been here before?' I gasped, noticing a wooden board had been forced off the kitchen window.

'I needed to see it with my own eyes after everything you told me,' he said.

'Why?' I couldn't understand. Was it some kind of morbid fascination with witnessing the scene of a crime? Or had he not believed anything I'd told him? How many times had he been here? I wondered if Lucia knew.

'Doesn't it feel good to be home?'

I shook my head, resisting his hand between my shoulder blades as he forced me inside. How could I tell him that secretly I was pleased to be back, even after all the terrible things that had happened here?

'Get in,' he hissed, raising his knife to my throat.

As I stumbled into the kitchen, Damian slammed the door shut and turned the key in the lock, sealing us inside.

Everything smelled damp and musty, and when he switched on the lights, I noticed with disgust that a film of dust had settled across the kitchen worktops. James would have hated to have seen the place looking so dirty. I had an urge to grab a bucket and cloth and give everything a thorough wipe down.

Damian shoved me into the dining room where the light switch crackled and fizzed. A dodgy wire James somehow never found the time to fix despite his constant promises. It had become a running joke, and I almost smiled at the memory, until I saw the gaping hole in the floorboards and the dark pit where I'd spent so many nights scared, shivering and alone.

'Give me your hands,' Damian demanded, grabbing my wrists and slicing through the tape with his knife.

'What do you want, Damian?' I asked. 'Why are we here?'

'Isn't it obvious?' he said, frowning as if he couldn't understand my confusion. 'You don't belong with us. I don't want you in my house, around Dylan and April. You're poisonous, Mara. Damaged. I told Lucia you needed professional help, but she wouldn't listen. But then, I wonder if you're beyond help after all these years? No, the best place for you is here, where you belong. Your home.'

'My home? Are you insane? Did you ever listen when I told you what he used to do to me here?'

'I'm sorry. I truly am. But I'm doing this for my family, don't you understand?'

'I am family.'

He shook his head, sadly. 'No, Mara, you're not. You're deranged, poisoned by that man who took you.'

'James,' I said, raising my voice as my anger bubbled. 'His name is James.'

Damian stared at me. 'Yes,' he said. 'I know his name.'

'Whatever I've done wrong, however I've upset you, I'm sorry,' I pleaded. 'I'll try harder in future.'

'You're evil,' he hissed, his face so close to mine I could smell his dog breath.

'I'll find a place of my own like you said. I'll stay away from you and the children, I promise.' My mind raced as fast as my heart as it dawned on me that he intended to leave me here.

'It's too late. You can't be trusted. You taint everything you touch. You've ruined it all, and I despise you for it.'

'What are you going to do to me?' I hated how pathetic my voice sounded.

Damian glanced at the hole in the floor. 'Get in,' he said. 'Get back in the hole you crawled out of.'

'No,' I mumbled, staggering backwards. 'I can't. Please don't make me.'

But he snatched my wrist and flashed the knife in front of my eyes.

'Do it!' he yelled. 'I won't tell you again.'

My legs gave way, and I collapsed into a sobbing ball on the floor, shaking uncontrollably and covering my head with my hands as I'd done so many times before as James loomed over me, eyes burning with rage and the veins on his forehead throbbing. 'I'll do anything, but please, not that.'

Damian grasped the collar of my t-shirt and pulled me up, dragging me across the floor towards the hole.

'No!' I screamed hysterically, my tears burning my cheeks. It was literally the stuff of my nightmares. I couldn't breathe. My lungs constricted, every muscle wound tight. But I was helpless to resist. Too weak. Too pathetic to fight back.

The ground disappeared beneath me, and I tumbled down the rough steps, my head and shoulders bearing the brunt of my fall.

As I hit the dirty, concrete floor, I jumped straight up, scrambling on my hands and knees back up the steps towards the artificial light from the bulb swinging from the ceiling, my fingers clawing for freedom.

But there was no way out.

Damian was already lifting the hatch into place, shutting out the light and trapping me in the airless hole. It fell into place with a deadening thud. As I was plunged into darkness, an all too familiar panic rose like bile from the pit of my stomach.

With a final effort, I threw myself at the hatch, hoping Damian hadn't locked it yet, ramming my neck and shoulders against its underside, driving through my thighs, ignoring the pain in my upper body.

But it didn't budge an inch.

I heard a scrape of metal from above. Followed by two dull thuds. The sound of my incarceration. I looked up at the thin streams of light needling through the cracks in the wood. And then they were gone as Damian threw the rug back in place.

I fell on my haunches with my chest rising and falling, trying to catch my breath.

'Damian! Please!' I screamed, tasting concrete dust at the back of my throat. 'Let me out! For God's sake, don't leave me here.'

I reached up to hammer with my fists, banging so hard I made them bleed.

'Goodbye, Mara.' Damian's muffled voice sounded so dispassionate.

I clung to the hope he was only trying to scare me, that in a moment he'd let me out, that he was trying to teach me a lesson, and I made a promise to God that, if he did, I'd never be any trouble to him again.

Another thud and a scrape, and I knew he was pulling the furniture back into place. The table over the hatch. Four chairs around the outside. Not only was he making my escape impossible, he was covering up the evidence of my underground cell. Just as James had done before him.

I listened to his footsteps, and a moment later, the back door opened and shut. I strained to hear the lock turning and listened for the sound of his feet crunching along the path around the outside of the house. But I heard only the sound of empty silence and my heart pounding in my chest. And then faintly, in the distance, the van starting up and the hum of tyres as it pulled away.

52

The mattress, stained with my sweat, blood, tears and worse, was thinner than I remembered, and as I curled up with my knees tucked under my chin, my bones dug into the floor. I wrapped my arms around my shoulders and rocked gently, both to comfort myself and to fend off the bone-chilling cold. How quickly I'd forgotten the frigid squalor I'd lived in, pushed it so far back in my mind it had become a speck on my memory. The urge to cry was overwhelming, but what use were my tears now? My only hope was that Damian would return to free me, that he was only trying to scare me. I tried not to think about the alternative, of the long, lingering death that lay ahead if he'd left me here to rot.

Hope had once kept me going through the long, dark nights of misery, when I was bruised and beaten, chained and imprisoned, because despite everything James had told me, that my family had forsaken me, I held onto the belief they were still looking, and that one day they would find me. Hope nourished my will to survive. And in the end, it had saved me.

Finding myself here again, thrown back into misery after the briefest taste of freedom, was like the worst kind of recurring nightmare. I desperately wanted to hope again. I wanted to hope Lucia had discovered what Damian had done. I wanted to hope that she was already on her way at the vanguard of a police convoy. I wanted to hope that this was all a terrible dream and that any minute I would wake up, sweat-drenched and with the sheets twisted around my legs. But instead of sustaining me, my hope trickled away like grains of sand through my fingers.

At least before I was never really on my own. Even when James had left me chained up in my cell for days on end, I was comforted by hearing him around the house. I listened to his footsteps on the floorboards, the sound of knives chopping onions in the kitchen and the songs he hummed in the shower. And when he did occasionally have to go away for a day or two, I always knew he'd be back. He'd promised never to leave me. When Damian walked out of the house, I felt totally alone. Helpless and bereft.

I stared into the darkness, despondent and numb. I knew there was no point wasting energy feeling around the damp, dank space looking for an escape. I'd had nineteen years to accept it was impossible. The walls, floor and ceiling, were impenetrable. When James had finally trusted me enough to stop chaining me up at night, I'd explored every single inch, night after night. Eventually, I'd managed to scrape out the mortar around a brick behind the toilet to create somewhere to hide things I wanted to keep from him. Personal things. Drawings and a diary of my thoughts and feelings. He'd taken everything else from me; my freedom, my dignity, and my self-respect. It felt as though I'd finally gained back some control, and it gave me a huge psychological boost.

I rolled onto my back with fear gripping me like a frozen hand. What would it be like to starve to death? I'd known hunger for most of my life. James limited my food to keep me weak. He was bigger and stronger than me, but he worried I might try to fight back, although I would never have done that. A restricted diet left me emaciated and low on energy. My skin grew parchment-thin, grey and lined, my bones stuck out at odd angles and my stomach bloated like I'd swallowed a balloon. I'd been hungry for nineteen years, hunting for scraps whenever he allowed me in the kitchen, but I'd never come close to starving to death. Not really. He would never have allowed that. I was his prize. His treasure. And what kind of man would willingly destroy the thing he loved above everything else?

Dehydration could kill you in hours, but I knew you could survive for days without food, slowly wasting away. I wondered if it would be painful. Was this really how it was going to end, sprawled out on my mattress, too weak to stand, blind and helpless? It was an ignominious death, and that's what upset me the most.

I'd tried my best to give James dignity in his death, and I thought it was the least I deserved in return. I took a deep breath and closed my eyes, accepting my fate, realising I'd been doomed from the moment I was born. I'd never been destined to lead a normal life. It was stupid to imagine anything different. I didn't even have the luxury of determining when or how I would die. If Damian didn't return, all I could do was lie and wait. How long would it take? A few days? A week? A month? I shuddered at the thought and tried to put it to the back of my mind.

I pictured my happy place; a desert island with soft, golden sand. A cloudless azure sky. The sun warming my skin and the sound of waves rushing up the shore. It was a place where I was free and happy, unencumbered from misery. It gave me peace when I'd been so severely beaten that pain wracked my body, and in my dark moments, it helped me to sleep.

Listening to my heart throbbing in my chest, I slowed my breathing, imagining the heat of the tropical sun on my face. My muscles relaxed, and the strangle of anxiety loosened its tight grip.

I'd almost drifted off when I heard a door slam. Voices, muffled but urgent, coming from above.

I sat bolt upright and listened.

Damian! He'd come back! My heart soared, my spirits lifting. I vowed I'd do whatever he asked of me in future and never cross him again if he would only let me out of this cell.

A loud thud against the floorboards above my head made me jump. Then a woman's pitiful squeal. Terror in her voice.

Lucia?

And then I heard the scraping of furniture. The dining room table being moved, and the hatch being opened.

53

Bright light blinded me. I raised a hand to shield my eyes and squinted to see a silhouette of a figure staring down. I was right. Damian had only been trying to frighten me. Now he was back to take me home.

But as my eyes adjusted to the light, I saw the angry scowl on his face, and suddenly I wasn't so sure.

'Here, see for yourself,' he said, glancing over his shoulder.

'Thank God,' I said. 'You came back. I couldn't have stood another second down here.'

But before I made it to my feet, a woman edged into view, her beautiful face ghostly pale. She flinched when she saw me, a flash of recognition and horror in her eyes.

'Oh my God,' she gasped.

'So now you can ask her yourself,' Damian said. They stood shoulder to shoulder, staring down at me like I was an animal in a zoo.

I wrapped my arms around my body, as self-conscious as if they'd caught me naked.

The woman seemed to be struck dumb.

'Come on, you wanted a scoop. I'm giving it to you on a plate. You can take some photos too if you like. The first pictures of Mara

Sitwell in her cell. Who knows, you might even get a promotion off the back of it.' Damian's tone was laced with sarcasm.

'What's going on?' I stammered, frozen like a fawn in the headlights.

'Did you put her in there?' the woman asked. Her skin was so perfectly smooth that even when she frowned a crease barely rippled her brow.

'I got you what you wanted, didn't I?'

The woman couldn't take her eyes off me, even as she started to shake her head in disbelief.

'Mara, meet Tanya Hayes,' Damian said, suddenly turning his attention to me as I shuffled towards the bottom of the steps, drawn to the light. 'She's a reporter who'd like to know a bit more about your relationship with James Finch. But then, wouldn't we all?' He grabbed my arm as I emerged through the hatch, and pulled me up onto my feet.

Tanya Hayes backed away. 'I'm so sorry,' she said to me. 'I didn't know anything about this, I swear.'

'Sit down!' Damian ordered, pushing me towards James' armchair by the window. I sank into the soft cushions, my mind racing, with no idea what was going on.

'You're insane.' Tanya backed away from Damian as he turned on her.

He snatched a dining chair with one hand and banged it down on the floor directly in front of me. 'Sit!' he ordered.

Tanya fumbled in her handbag. She pulled out a phone and with shaking hands prodded at the screen. 'I'm calling the police,' she said.

Damian put his hands on his hips and laughed. 'You'll be lucky to get a signal out here.'

Tanya continued to prod at her phone and with wide-eyed terror put it to her ear, watching Damian cautiously. A second or two later, she glanced at the screen again and let out a roar of frustration.

Damian lunged, swiping the phone from her hand with such violence I cringed. He threw it across the room. It bounced off the wall with an sickening crack. 'Now, do you want this story or not?'

'No,' Tanya said, drawing back her shoulders. 'Not like this.'

She was trying to make it look as though she'd regained her composure, trying to make Damian understand she wasn't afraid of him, but her eyes gave her away. I saw the fear and uncertainty. She didn't know what to do.

The words had hardly fallen from her lips before Damian had grabbed a handful of her lustrous, shiny hair and marched her across the room to the dining room chair. Tanya screamed, and suddenly we were sitting face to face, so close I could count the freckles on her nose. Her eyes were red and puffy, and her mascara had run. I slunk deeper into the armchair, making myself small, just like I had when James lost his temper.

'What is it with you women?' Damian raged. 'Lucia and I used to be happy, but between you, you've ruined everything. And you,' he said, directing his ire at Tanya, 'are nothing but a leech feeding off other people's misery. Does it make you happy, destroying people's lives? Do you get a kick out of it?'

Tanya sobbed, her head falling onto her chest. 'Let me go,' she whispered.

'Why do you do it?' Damian persisted.

'I don't know.'

'Not good enough,' he said. 'Try again.'

'Please, stop.'

'Not so funny now the boot's on the other foot, is it?'

'Just let me go.'

'But you don't have your story yet.'

'You're crazy,' Tanya said, sniffing. She didn't look so beautiful now. The elegance and poise I'd seen when she'd appeared at the hatch above me had vanished.

'So why don't you start asking questions?'

Tanya swallowed, wiped her nose with the back of her hand and composed herself. She looked directly at me, like she was peering into my soul, and tilted her head to one side. She smiled, like we were in it together, two sisters sharing a taste of hell. But she had no idea. How could she possibly think we were anything alike?

'Mara, it's nice to meet you at last,' she said, swallowing hard. She cleared her throat and sat up straighter. 'I've read so much about you.'

'Enough with the pleasantries,' Damian barked. 'Get on with it. Ask her about Finch.'

Tanya dragged her chair closer until our knees were touching. I pulled away. I hated anyone but Lucia touching me.

'I wondered if you could tell me some more about the man who abducted you,' Tanya said.

I shrugged, glancing nervously at Damian. 'What do you want to know?'

'What was your relationship with him?'

I bit my lip, controlling my irritation. 'He abducted me and abused me for nineteen years. There was no relationship,' I said, delivering my words deliberately like a schoolmistress talking to a five-year-old.

'Really?' Tanya said, frowning. 'You don't really expect anyone to believe that, do you?'

'I don't care what people believe.' I hated how meek I sounded, like a church mouse. It was pathetic. I didn't feel in control and hated answering her questions, but I knew if I didn't, Damian would almost certainly throw me back into the cell.

'How long did he make you stay down there?' she asked, nodding towards the hole in the floor.

'For the first six months, I spent most of my time in there, chained up to the wall,' I said, the memory painfully sharp even after all these years.

'And afterwards?'

'He'd let me out during the day if I was good.'

'To do what?'

'Keep the house clean. Cook. Sometimes to watch TV.'

Tanya glanced at Damian who was leaning against a wall, toying with the kitchen knife he'd threatened me with earlier, turning it over menacingly in his hand and running a thumb over the sharp edge of the blade. 'How cosy,' he said.

'He starved me and beat me, and if I didn't do what he asked, he'd shut me in the dark down there for hours.'

'I'm sure it was awful,' Tanya said, without sounding remotely sympathetic. But how could she begin to empathise? She, with her perfect hair, polished nails, flawless skin and beautiful clothes, couldn't possibly have any idea. 'But you and James Finch were together for nineteen years. You must have built some sort of attachment to him?'

'No more lies, Mara,' Damian said, pointing the knife at me. 'It's time for the truth.'

I hesitated before answering, rolling Tanya's question over in my mind, feeling the weight of my lies heavy on my shoulders. 'Yes, I liked him,' I said, holding her intense gaze. 'But he was the only person I ever knew in all that time.'

Tanya nodded with encouragement, her expression softening. 'I spoke to a psychologist. She said it would have been highly unusual if you'd not formed an attachment to him.'

'Is that a question?'

'Did you love him?'

The directness of her question startled me, and I felt a warm flush rise from my neck to my cheeks. How was I supposed to answer that truthfully? As my eyes darted around the room, avoiding Tanya's gaze, I caught sight of the empty frame on the mantelpiece and wondered where the photo had gone. It used to contain a picture James had taken of us in the garden. He'd set up a camera on a tripod and jogged in a mild panic across the lawn towards me. I remembered how we'd both giggled waiting for the timer to take the shot. He'd kept the picture in pride of place above the fireplace. He said it was his favourite picture of me because it reminded him of happy times. I tried to hide the smile that threatened to curl across my lips.

James had made my life a misery. He'd reduced me to skin and bones, made me feel beneath contempt, a worthless worm not worthy of love. And yet I was embarrassed to admit I had feelings for him. Powerful feelings I couldn't explain.

'Yes,' I said, my voice catching in my throat.

Tanya nodded. 'And did you sleep with him?'

The harder I tried to hold my emotions in check, the harder they fought to be free. A solitary tear ran down my cheek. 'Yes.'

Tanya took a deep breath, in through her nose and out through her mouth. It was a confession I'd never expected to make, to anyone.

'Did he rape you?' I was surprised by the tender way she asked the question. It was disarming and made me feel as though she might actually be on my side after all.

'No,' I said, quietly. It would have been easy to have slipped in another lie, to paint James as a sexual predator who'd forced me against my will. But it hadn't happened like that. If anything, I'd come on to him, desperate for his love and attention. At least when he was screwing me, he wasn't beating me.

'No?' Tanya looked surprised.

'No,' I reiterated, more forcefully.

Damian pushed himself off the wall, his eyes narrowing. 'The truth, Mara,' he said.

'I'm telling the truth!' I snapped back. 'He didn't rape me. I wanted to sleep with him, and I enjoyed it, okay? Is that what you wanted to hear?'

'I want to hear the truth.'

I shook my head. 'James Finch abducted me. I hated him for it, but after that, for nineteen years, he was the only person in my life. Our relationship was... ' I searched for the right word. But how could I sum up how I felt about him? Love and hate are supposed to be at the opposite ends of the spectrum, never sharing the same space. And yet the feelings I had for James crossed both boundaries. 'It was complicated,' I said, knowing I couldn't even get close to explaining it. Who could possibly understand if they'd not experienced what I'd been through?

'Do you know where he is now?'

The change of tack threw me momentarily. I picked at my fingers while I gathered my thoughts.

'Mara, what happened to James Finch?' Tanya asked again.

I thought about the last days we'd spent together. How we'd laughed and how we'd cried, how he'd sobbed when he told me he was so sorry for what he'd done but that he didn't regret it for a second. And I remembered how he'd taken my hands in his and told me I was his soul mate and we'd never be apart. My tears came hot and heavy, blurring my vision.

'The police haven't been able to find him,' Tanya said, leaning forwards. 'But you know where he is, don't you?'

I bit my bottom lip so hard I tasted blood. I nodded.

'Tell me, Mara.'

I took a deep breath. I didn't care anymore. It was finally time for the whole truth.

'He's in the garden,' I said, 'buried under the vegetable patch.'

54

Even when the headaches had left him screaming in agony, and debilitating sickness meant he was barely able to drag himself out of the bathroom, James had refused to see a doctor. We both knew something was seriously wrong, but there was nothing he could do about it because he resolutely refused to leave me, despite my feeble appeals. I tried to talk him around, but he wouldn't listen. James always knew best. I was never allowed an opinion. To seek help would have meant leaving me to starve to death, or releasing me and the world finding out what he'd done. So he chose to do neither, letting his health deteriorate to the point where it had been a blessing to put him out of his misery.

We'd planned it over several weeks as James finally lost his sight and his speech became almost indecipherable. I hated to see him wither and wane, the person I once loved and hated with equal passion rotting before me like a piece of overripe fruit left in the sun. His skin turned grey as the disease ate away muscle and fat, leaving only a shell of the man who'd controlled me, terrorised me and cherished me for all of my adult life.

When the day came, I propped him up on the bed with as many pillows and cushions as I could find. I kissed him goodbye and with tears coursing down my face fed him a handful of white pills between sips from a glass of water. Only when he drifted towards sleep did I slip the bag over his head and twist it tightly around his neck. With laboured breaths, he gulped down a small pocket of air, sucking the plastic into his mouth as it moulded around his face like a mask. The sound had stayed with me ever since, preying on my dreams. When his body began to convulse as the panic of suffocation set in, I couldn't watch anymore. I wanted to stay with him to the end, but it was too much to bear.

With my heart tearing in two, I'm ashamed to say that I slunk away, down the stairs and willingly into my concrete prison, where I curled up into a tight ball on my mattress and let the tears flow.

It was dark when I finally found the courage to return to his room, by which time I was cold and numb. James' wizened body was laid out across the bed, his head, still wrapped in plastic, fallen to one side, his arms outstretched.

Carefully, I removed the bag and took one last look into his sunken, staring eyes. His skin was cold to the touch, and his ghostly pallor gave him an inhuman appearance. I sat on the edge of the bed, shivering, wondering why I felt nothing. It was almost as if my sadness at his death had been cancelled out by my joy at being free at last. Two polar emotions suppressing each other so that all I felt was an emptiness. I'd longed for freedom for so long, but now I had it, I wasn't sure what to do with it. Where was I going to go? What was I going to do?

I pushed the thoughts from my mind. Plenty of time to work that out later. For now, I still had a commitment to James to fulfil. It took all my energy to drag him from his bed and down the stairs. His muscles were stiff and unyielding, and I was weak and undernourished. Even now, I wonder how I managed it. I sweated and toiled for what felt like hours until I finally bundled his body into the kitchen where I collapsed in an exhausted heap.

There was no nobility in his final journey to the grave, but I'd made a promise to him I was determined to keep. I sat on the floor with my back against a cupboard door, every muscle in my body aching, and studied the cadaver of the only man I'd ever known in my adult life. Once his mere presence had terrified me, even when he'd taken me to his bed. But now his limbs were scrawny and wasted away, his chest concave and even his hair had receded and become tinged with grey. An ugly, purple bruise had appeared around his neck where I guess I'd twisted the bag too tightly. A scarlet ribbon of blood ran from his nose.

With one final effort, I hauled his body into the garden and rolled him into the shallow grave I'd dug in advance, next to the shrivelled tomato plants and beans. I'd laid him on his back and arranged his arms across his chest as the tightness in his limbs softened. Then I stood at his graveside and wondered if I should say a prayer. But as I'd long since given up on God, I thought better of it. So with a final whispered goodbye, I grabbed the spade and shovelled freshly-dug earth over his body.

When I was done, I returned to the house, took a long, hot shower and slunk back to the sanctuary of my cell, comforted by the familiarity of its terrible smell.

'You killed him?' said Damian, who'd been listening open-mouthed.

'He was already dying,' I said. 'I helped him out of his pain.'

'You poor thing,' Tanya said. I saw the pity in her eyes I didn't want nor deserve.

'I'd dreamt for so long about what it would be like to kill him, but in the end... ' I shook my head, unable to find the words to finish my sentence. 'I just didn't expect it to be like that.'

Tanya's brow furrowed. 'Why did you tell the police you'd escaped when Finch had turned his back?' she asked, looking puzzled.

'Does it matter?'

'I suppose not.'

Damian moved closer, waving the knife around. 'What happened after you buried him?' he asked.

'I already told you.' I couldn't take my eyes off the knife, the light glinting off its deadly blade.

'No, I still don't understand. James Finch was dead, and you were finally free, but you didn't leave straight away, did you? You stayed here when you could have run for help. Why?'

I hung my head with shame. He was right, although I had no idea how he knew. 'I don't know,' I said, almost to myself.

The truth is James had ruled my life for so long, dictated when I ate, when I slept, when I worked, when I watched TV, even when I could have light in my cell, that I'd forgotten how to make decisions for myself. I didn't know what to do. Although I was finally free, it was easier to stay. The house was what I knew. Everything beyond it scared me. There were some tins of food in the kitchen that lasted me for a few weeks, and in the end, it was only when those supplies ran out that I plucked up the courage to leave.

'I didn't know where to go,' I explained.

Tanya nodded, silently, but Damian continued to stare at me as though he was weighing up whether to believe me.

'And you're sure James Finch is dead? Because if you were in love with him and you helped him get away, that would be a convenient story,' he said.

I shrugged, the melancholy I'd suffered in the days after James' death consuming me again. 'I don't really care if you believe me or not. It's the truth.'

'We'll see.'

I don't know what he meant by that, but I was beyond caring what he thought.

'What now?' Tanya asked. 'What are you going to do with her?'

'You two deserve each other,' Damian sneered. 'Maybe I'll leave you here together.'

Tanya jumped out of her chair and knocked it to the floor. 'This has gone far enough, Damian. Put the knife down before you do someone an injury. You've had your fun.' Her voice wavered.

'Sit down!' Damian snarled.

Tanya hesitated, then reluctantly picked up her chair and sat back down, chastened.

'Why did you help him die, after everything he'd done?' Damian asked. 'If it had been me, I'd have watched the bastard suffer.'

I shook my head. 'I couldn't stand to see him in pain. It was horrible.'

'But he'd made you suffer.'

'I'm not the same as him.'

'But you happily suffocated him with a plastic bag.'

'It was his idea. It's what he wanted.'

Damian sighed and fell quiet before the hint of a smile appeared across his face. 'I saw some plastic bags in one of the cupboards. Thank you, you've given me an idea,' he said, turning on his heel and disappearing into the kitchen.

A moment later, I heard cupboard doors banging open and slamming shut.

'What the fuck is he doing?' Tanya hissed at me, panic written across her face.

'Looking for a bag, I guess,' I said. 'I think he intends to kill us both.' My voice was calm, even though I felt anything but calm inside.

Tanya's eyes opened wide. 'We have to stop him.' She pulled me up and scoured the room frantically. 'Grab a chair,' she hissed. 'Use it as a weapon.' She directed me to stand on one side of the door while she took up a position on the other.

I shot her a despairing look. What was I supposed to do with a chair?

But before either of us could do anything, the door crashed open. Damian bowled back into the room and lashed out when he saw Tanya on her feet. He struck her across the side of the head, and she fell to the floor with a scream.

'You!' he said, turning to me.

I lunged for one of the dining chairs, but it was heavier than I imagined and totally unwieldy. Before I could lift it, Damian threw me to the floor, his hands around my throat, squeezing.

I grabbed his wrists, panicking as my lungs felt as though they were about to burst.

'Is this what you like?' he said, gritting his teeth and glaring at me with hatred in his eyes. 'Is this what James Finch used to do to you?'

I wanted to yell at him to stop, to tell him I couldn't breathe, that I was suffocating. But I couldn't. I hammered his chest with my fists as darkness closed around my vision. But he wouldn't stop.

'Does it turn you on?' he continued. 'Do you like it a bit rough?'

I let my arms fall loose, forcing my brain to overcome the panic.

My eyes fluttered closed, and I relaxed every muscle in my body, feigning the unconsciousness that was stalking up on me. It was a trick I'd learnt when James sometimes went too far. Sure enough, Damian released his grip.

I let my head fall away from him so I could draw in a gentle breath without being seen.

'Stupid bitch,' he seethed, kicking me in the kidneys for good measure as he stood up. I took the blow without wincing, internalising the pain like I'd learnt from years of practice.

It bought me some time, but I wasn't out of danger yet. If I could make it out of the house and into the woods, I was confident I could lose Damian in the trees, especially as it was dark. But I had no idea if he'd even locked the back door this time, let alone how I'd reach it without him seeing.

He moved away, his feet scuffing the carpet, his breathing laboured and shallow. And then I heard a noise that filled me with dread; the distinctive and sickening crackle of a plastic bag.

55

If this was the end, I guess I had it coming. No matter what James had done to me, I was wrong to have killed him. It made me nothing better than a murderer, although I'd always thought of it as a mercy killing. In the first few days after his death, wracked with misery and alone in the house, I'd wallowed in self-pity, imagining what it had been like for him in those last few moments as he exhausted the oxygen in the bag I'd pulled over his head. Did he panic as he slowly suffocated? Did he change his mind after I'd left the room but lack the strength to save himself? It was supposed to be an easy death, dignified, but now I couldn't think of a more horrific way to die. It wasn't quick or easy. A solitary tear rolled down my cheek. I never thought I'd end up going the same way. I suppose it was poetic justice.

There was no point fighting it. I couldn't get away, and Damian was just too strong. So I lay still and tried to calm my emotions, knowing it would be over soon.

I closed my eyes and waited for the inevitable.

But nothing happened. I heard Tanya's whimper and the sound of her shoes scratching the carpet.

'What are you doing?' Her voice trembled with fear.

I lifted my head and turned to see what was going on. Tanya was shuffling into a corner, sliding on her backside across the floor with Damian looming above her, a plastic bag dangling from one hand, his knife in the other.

'I'm sorry, Tanya, you've left me no choice,' he said, kneeling at her feet. 'Don't struggle and I'll make it painless for you.'

'Get away from me,' she yelled, her eyes wide and dark, her beautiful face scarred with mascara and her hair tangled and messy. Her cheek was flushed where Damian had hit her. 'Please, I'll do anything you want. I'll spike the story. No one ever needs to know I was here.'

I recognised the desperation in her voice, bargaining to save herself from pain and suffering. I'd grown up with the same desperation, but my pleas had rarely done me any good. Men like James and Damian were beyond negotiating with. Their souls had hardened and become impervious to anything apart from their own narcissism.

Damian sighed and shook his head as if her words had disappointed him. 'You expect me to trust you of all people? You're a parasite, Tanya, feeding off everyone else's misery. I actually feel sorry for you, because you can't help yourself. Why did it have to be my family? Why couldn't you just leave us alone?'

'I'm sorry,' Tanya cried. 'It was a mistake. I can see that now, but let me go, and I promise you'll never hear from me again.'

'That's right, Tanya. *No one* will ever hear from you again.' As he reached to stroke her hair, she flinched.

'You're serious, aren't you?'

'Deadly, and sadly for you, no one knows you're here. They'll probably never find your body.'

Tanya's silence and the pained expression on her face were enough to confirm Damian was right.

'Hey, don't cry,' he said when Tanya began to sob.

'You're insane.'

'No, you've driven me to this.'

'And when the police find out what you've done? What then?'

Damian's hollow laugh echoed off the walls. 'Who's going to know I had anything to do with this when it all points to James Finch? The police don't know he's dead. As far as they're concerned he's still on the loose. They'll assume he tracked Mara down and brought her back here.'

I remembered the wig Damian had been wearing when he took me from the house and finally realised why. If any of the neighbours had seen him dragging me into his van, their descriptions would have led the police to believe it was James.

'As for you, the police will assume you were so desperate for a story that you couldn't resist responding to Finch's invite to the house after he'd returned here with Mara, offering his exclusive version of events.'

'Which is why you called me from an unknown number.' Tanya lowered her head in defeat.

'Actually, Mara's number,' Damian said. He pulled my phone from his pocket and tossed it on the table.

'And what are you going to do about her?' Tanya asked.

I noticed an unusual smell. A hint of something unpleasant in the air. At first, I thought I'd imagined it, but when I inhaled more deeply, I caught it again. Stronger.

'Her?' Damian said, glancing over his shoulder.

I snapped my eyes shut.

'I'm going to kill her too.' He said it without any emotion as though he was talking about stamping on a spider or swatting a fly.

Gas. That was it. Like when the flame on the hob blew out if James left the window in the kitchen ajar. It was filling the house, turning the building into a giant tinderbox, the slightest spark liable to cause a massive explosion. I thought about the dodgy wiring in the light switch and shuddered. Was this Damian's doing as well?

It didn't matter. All I knew was that I had to get out and fast. I gauged the distance to the kitchen door. If I was quick on my feet, it might take only a second or two to reach the kitchen. Another second to fumble with the key in the back door. I could be out in the garden in no time at all, maybe even before Damian noticed I was gone. If I skirted past the vegetable patch and vaulted the low, stone wall where a bed of roses had grown tall and spindly through the warm summer, I might even make it into the woods.

Tanya's scream cut through me like a blade through flesh. I tensed my muscles, getting ready to move. I wasn't proud of myself, but all I could think about was getting out of the house and away from danger. I didn't give Tanya a second thought other than that she was providing a distraction for me to get away. With Damian's back turned, I rose onto my haunches, praying the movement wouldn't catch his attention.

At the kitchen door, I checked over my shoulder. Damian had pulled the bag over Tanya's head, and it had moulded to her face like a grotesque death mask, her mouth open wide as she sucked the plastic into her throat, her fingers clawing at her neck. I remembered the same open-mouthed silent scream when I returned to James' body and discovered the plastic shrink-wrapped around his eyes, nose and cheeks. It was an image that had haunted me in my nightmares and one I knew I would never shake off.

The acid burn of bile rose from my stomach. I should run. Get out of the house as fast as my legs would carry me. But I couldn't leave Tanya to die. Not like that. Not when I had the power to stop him.

I turned back, the floorboards creaking beneath my shoes. My foot struck something hard and metallic. The bolt James used to seal the hatch to my cell was lying on the floor, partly hidden under the folds of the rucked-up rug. When I picked it up, it felt reassuringly weighty.

By now, Tanya was making a terrible gasping sound, her legs thrashing wildly as the panic of suffocation took hold. Damian crouched by her side, holding the bag tightly around her neck.

I took a step closer and swung the metal bolt behind my head like a golfer as I sized up the patch of bare skin at the base of Damian's neck. With a scream of rage, I brought it crashing down across his shoulders, sending him spilling across the floor. When he groaned and tried to get up, I hit him again with all my strength, catching him across the side of his face and tearing an ugly strip of skin off his cheek. His body went limp.

I dropped the bolt and snatched the bag from Tanya's head. Her eyes were already closed, and her skin tinged blue.

'Tanya, wake up!' I yelled, slapping her across the face. 'Don't die on me. Come on, open your eyes.'

I hit her again, harder and shook her shoulders.

She coughed. Then spluttered. And her eyes sprang open as she took a huge gasp of air.

'We've got to get out of here.'

As I pulled her to her feet and helped her step over Damian's prostrate body, I hoped she wouldn't notice the gash across his face. She leaned heavily against me and clutching each other for support we staggered across the room.

'Did you kill him?' she coughed.

By now the smell of gas was so overpowering it was making my temples throb. 'He's just unconscious,' I said, unsure whether I'd killed him or not. I certainly didn't want another death on my conscience.

We stumbled into the kitchen where a wall of gas hit me like a punch in the face.

'Gas?' Tanya said, frowning.

'It's the oven.' I recognised the telltale hiss from the gas rings on the hob, fed from the tank in the garden.

I left Tanya swaying unsteadily on her feet while I went to investigate. I was right. Damian had turned on all four rings. They were all belching out bitter-tasting gas, but he'd snapped off the knobs so I couldn't switch them off. 'I can't turn them off,' I said, nausea rising from my stomach and my head swimming.

I rushed for the back door, desperate for fresh air, but when I wrapped my fingers around the handle, it wouldn't budge. 'It's locked,' I said.

'Damian must have the key.'

My heart thumped in my chest as I tried to think straight. 'I'll go back and check his pockets,' I said. 'Stay here.'

My limbs were heavy as I trudged back into the dining room where the light switch was sizzling ominously. One small spark was all it was going to take to blow us to kingdom come. Damian was out of his mind. All I could think was that he'd planned to destroy the evidence of what he'd done, making the explosion look like an accident.

I staggered around the table, knocking a chair over and fighting the urge to be sick. Spittle flew from my mouth as I began to cough violently. I put out a hand to stop myself falling, looking for Damian's body, hoping the key would be easy to locate. But instead of finding him crumpled and bleeding on the floor, there was only the metal bolt I'd used to hit him.

I couldn't understand it. I'd only left him there a few seconds before. And now he was gone.

56

Tanya's eyes were glassy and vacant. 'Did you find the key?' she slurred.

I scanned the room with a growing sense of panic until my gaze fell on the window above the kitchen sink. The frame was splintered. I remembered noticing the damage from the outside when Damian had dragged me into the house. I leaned over the sink and gave it a sharp shove. It flew open, and I sucked in a deep lungful of cold air.

'I can't find it. We'll have to climb out,' I said, snatching Tanya's arm and pushing her towards the sink.

Without any hesitation, she kicked off her high heels and hitched up her skirt to clamber over the basin. She ducked through the window and inelegantly stumbled out into the garden.

I wasted no time following her, grateful to be out of the house and having fresh, clean air to breathe. I allowed myself a second to get my breath back and stood with my hands on my hips, panting as if I'd just run a mile.

'We can't stay here. It's not safe. We have to move,' I said, grabbing Tanya's hand and pulling her along behind me, towards the protection of the trees.

We ran hand in hand, through the garden and over the wall by the rose beds, tumbling into a tangle of brambles and nettles which scratched and stung our skin, but we kept running. We had to. Above us, the wind rustled the leaves in the treetops. We crashed through the undergrowth, barely able to see the ground beneath our feet in the dark, and didn't stop until we reached a small clearing, the house a short distance behind us, our chests heaving and our lungs fit to burst.

I grabbed the thick trunk of a tall tree for support and noticed that somewhere along the way I'd lost a shoe. Tanya's tights were ripped and laddered and her dress shredded and dirty. We looked at each other and laughed, relief washing over us.

The house was no more than an indistinct shape at the edge of the tree line, caught in the silver glimmer of the moon. I stared at it like an old friend who'd betrayed me while Tanya collapsed to her knees and wept.

'It's okay, we're safe now,' I said, running a hand across her shoulders. 'It's over.'

She buried her head in her hands and let her hair fall over her face. I didn't know what to say, so I just stood staring at the house with my hand on her back and my mind a fog of confusion.

We must have stayed like that for several minutes, neither of us moving, both lost in our own thoughts.

'He was going to kill us,' Tanya sobbed. 'I thought I was going to die.'

'But he didn't. You're fine. Everything's going to be okay.'

'Is it?'

'Yeah,' I said. 'He can't touch us now.'

'Is he dead?'

My mind flashed back to the scene in the dining room, the spot where Damian had fallen and where his body should have been when I went back for the key. 'I don't know.' If he was still in the house, it was only a matter of time before he was overcome by the fumes. He wouldn't have been able to survive in there for long, I told myself.

Tanya pushed her hair back and wiped her eyes with the hem of her skirt. 'Crazy bastard,' she said. 'I always knew there was something odd about him. So what do we do now?'

'We find our way out of here, I guess,' I said, peering through the towering fortress of trees surrounding us. Although the sky was clear and the bright glow of the moon cut through the darkness, there was little light in the middle of the wood. The chances of us getting lost were worryingly high, and neither of us was dressed for the cold. There was every likelihood we could die of exposure before we found our way to safety. 'I'm sure there's a village nearby where we can raise the alarm,' I said.

'You don't know? After all the time you lived here?'

I didn't like her snide tone but didn't rise to it. 'I wasn't exactly given free rein to go exploring.'

'So which way?' Tanya peeled away from me and turned through a full circle, peering into the darkness. I sensed her despondency. I admit it seemed hopeless.

And then I had an idea. It was so obvious, I don't know why it didn't occur to me before. I put it down to the shock. 'We should follow the road. That's bound to take us -'

But my words were cut short.

A blast of hot air knocked us from our feet a moment before an ear-bursting roar of noise thundered through the trees. I landed flat on my face with the wind knocked out of my lungs, and my ears ringing. A roost of rooks squawked out of the treetops, scattering into the sky in a panic of flapping feathers.

I lay still on the damp ground for a moment, confused and disorientated. Slowly, I picked myself up, pulling leaves and twigs off my clothes, a high-pitched whining in my ears. I turned to look back at where the house had been but saw only a pile of smoking rubble.

Tanya stirred and groaned.

'Are you okay?' I asked, my words sounding woolly and indistinct to my own ears.

She rose slowly, her face streaked with mud, and spotted the house had gone. 'What the hell?'

I stared at the carnage with conflicting emotions. The house had been my home. But it was also where I'd been treated to the most inhumane cruelty. Now it was gone, I didn't know what to think. It was the same when James had died. I loved him and hated him. It was too much for my brain to process.

'Do you think Damian was still inside?' Tanya asked.

The thought hadn't even occurred to me. 'Maybe,' I said, the first simmering of guilt beginning to boil deep within my gut. If he'd died in the blast, I was to blame. I was the one who'd knocked him unconscious and left him there to die.

'We need to get help. Damian's car was at the front of the house. He might have left his keys in it,' Tanya said, hopefully.

I shook my head. I couldn't face going anywhere near what was left of the house. 'Go if you like. I'm staying here. There might be more explosions. It could be dangerous,' I said.

'I'll go on my own. You stay here.'

I should have tried harder to stop her. We should have stayed together, but instead, I stood watching her pick her way through the trees, treading a careful path through the brambles and bushes. I started to shiver, noticing for the first time how cold it was. Whether it was because of the shock or the chill air, my teeth chattered. I wrapped my arms around my shoulders, hugging myself tightly, and dropped to the floor with my back against the trunk of an oak tree.

As I closed my eyes, I reminded myself the nightmare was finally over. No more James Finch. No more Damian Caslocke. Just me and Lucia and our whole lives ahead of us. I smiled at the thought of all the adventures we had ahead of us, all the shared experiences waiting around the corner. At last, we would be properly reunited to pick up our lives where they had been cruelly disrupted.

The sudden grip on my wrist, so hard I thought it would crush my bones, jolted me from my daydream. When my eyes sprang open, Damian's grizzled and bloody face was right in front of mine.

'You stupid bitch,' he hissed at me, hauling me to my feet and pulling me so close our noses were barely inches apart. 'You could have fucking killed me.'

57

I glanced in the direction of the smouldering ruins, hoping to see Tanya on her way back.

'You're the one who left the gas on,' I replied, straightening my back and staring Damian down.

'Why can't you just die and leave us all alone?' His hands flew to my throat and gripped my neck, threatening to throttle the life out of me.

'If you kill me out here,' I wheezed, 'you won't be able to cover it up. They'll know it was you.'

'I'll take that risk,' he snarled in my face, rage burning in his eyes.

'And what about Lucia?'

He loosened his grip a fraction.

'What about her?'

'What's she going to think when she finds out what you've done? What you've become? You'll lose her forever.'

'I lost her the day you came back into her life.'

'Don't blame this on me.'

'I hate you, Mara. I hate that you've destroyed my family. Why couldn't you stay away? We were happy before.'

'I don't think Lucia was ever happy. She didn't love you, not really.

And you never loved her. You were thrown together because of me. You needed each other. But that's not love.'

He slapped me so hard across my face, it took my breath away. I tasted blood in my mouth and the sting of tears, burning my eyes.

'What do you know about love?' he hissed. 'You were screwing the man who abducted you. So don't preach to me.'

'I never said it was right, Damian, but he was the only man I ever knew. What choice did I have?'

'You're sick.'

'I guess it takes one to know one.'

The look in his eyes was pure hatred. James had never looked at me like that, even when I'd fuelled his anger to boiling point.

'I'm nothing like you,' he said.

'I love Lucia in a way you never could. She's my sister. We belong together, with or without you.'

Damian snorted a derisive laugh. 'She doesn't love you, she feels guilty about what happened, that's all. She thought she was the one Finch should have taken, and it's been eating her up for years.'

'I used to think the same way. I wondered why he chose me over Lucia. I didn't understand, and I resented her for it. But that's in the past. I've made my peace with her,' I said, my eyes glancing over Damian's shoulder, hoping to see Tanya creeping back.

'And I'm sure she'll shed a few crocodile tears at your funeral,' Damian said.

'So this is it? You're going to kill me?'

He stared at me with emotionless eyes. 'Yes.'

'And what about Tanya?'

'What about her?'

'She's gone to raise the alarm. The police are going to be crawling all over these woods at any moment.' A flicker of worry flitted across his face. 'Why did you bring her here anyway?'

'What does it matter?' he said, lowering his gaze.

'Because I want to understand what she has to do with any of this.'

'If you really want to know, she was blackmailing me, and the only way to get her off my back was an interview with you. She jumped at the chance. She never even questioned it when I told her I could bring her here to meet you.'

'Seriously?'

'She knew something was going on between you and Finch.'

'Jesus, Damian.' A realisation hit me like a slap around the head. 'That's why you tried to film me in your study, isn't it? You were trying to get me to confess about James.'

'She gave me no choice.'

I looked him straight in the eye. 'What did she have over you?'

'It doesn't matter.'

'It must have been something significant for you to go to these extremes.'

'I said, it's not important,' he snapped.

'Well, whatever. You might have got away with killing me, but bringing Tanya here was a mistake. She's a witness to everything. You've fucked up, Damian.'

'Which way did she go?'

'It's too late. She's gone.'

'I don't believe you.'

I shrugged. 'Believe what you want. You're pathetic. I'm done with this, Damian. I'm not playing your games anymore.'

A sudden sadness washed over his expression, and he removed his hands from around my neck, letting his arms drop to his sides, the anger evaporating.

'I can't let you go,' he said. 'Not after this.'

'Goodbye, Damian.' I turned my back on him. I started to walk towards the road with my pulse racing, but I'd barely taken a few steps before he snatched my arm and pulled me back.

As I whirled around, I aimed a kick at his groin with as much power as I could muster. His eyes bulged in surprise, and he yelped in pain as he collapsed to the ground clutching between his legs.

'Bitch!' he screamed.

I acted entirely on instinct, pressing home my advantage. I'd spent too many years passively accepting my fate when I should have, or could have, fought back. I grabbed a length of deadwood hanging off a nearby tree, a branch that had fallen from above. It was about a metre long and jagged at both ends where it had snapped, but solid enough to act as an improvised spear.

I aimed it at Damian's throat and pressed one end into the fleshy part beneath his Adam's apple, standing over him like an Amazonian huntress with her captured prey. My skin tingled as a surge of adrenaline coursed through my veins.

The urge to finish him off was intoxicating. With a little more pressure, I could drive my makeshift spear through his neck, ridding him from my life once and for all. But I resisted. One death on my hands was enough, no matter how much I hated him.

He held his hands up in submission. 'Don't do something you'll regret,' he said, the rage that had flashed across his face moments earlier now replaced by fear.

Then he smiled at me, like the first time we'd met. I didn't buy it then, and I certainly didn't buy it now. He looked so pathetic lying on the ground at my feet. 'Who says I'd regret it?'

'Come on, Mara, please.'

'Fuck you, Damian.'

From somewhere behind, I heard the sound of branches snapping and leaves rustling. Tanya burst out of the tree line and froze when she saw Damian lying at my feet.

'Did you find his car?' I asked.

'It's locked,' she said, staring at Damian, her jaw tight. 'Where did he come from? I thought he was dead?'

Damian smirked and tried to sit up, but I jabbed him with the branch, and he laid back down.

'I guess he managed to get out before the blast,' I said. 'Go and raise the alarm. I'll stay here with him.'

'You tried to kill me, you bastard.'

Damian watched Tanya warily as she edged closer.

'Why did you come to the house?' I asked.

'What do you mean?'

'Damian called you, didn't he? He said there was an opportunity for you to talk to me about James.'

'So what?'

'Why would he do that? Why was he so keen to give you that story?'

Tanya glanced briefly at me as she continued to circle Damian, keeping just out of his reach. 'I don't know.'

'He said you were blackmailing him. Is it true?'

'Blackmail's a strong word, Mara.'

'But you had something on him? Something he was prepared to kill for to keep quiet.'

Tanya stopped and looked me in the eye. Her lips curled into a cruel smile. 'If you really must know, Damian has a problem keeping it in his pants. A wandering eye. Did you know he was screwing an office intern while his wife was pregnant? No, I didn't think so. I merely mentioned I had all the unsavoury details, and he jumped at the chance to provide me with all the dirt on your relationship with James Finch instead, in return for spiking the story.'

I gasped. An affair. 'Is it true?' I asked, jabbing at Damian's throat.

His eyes opened wide, but he pursed his lips tightly shut.

'Is it true?' I asked again.

'It meant nothing. It was a long time ago.'

'Bastard. How could you do that to Lucia?'

'I didn't mean to hurt her. It was a silly mistake.'

'A mistake? Lucia was pregnant with your child. I should kill you right now.'

Tanya resumed walking in a slow circle around us both. 'Do it,' she hissed. 'He deserves everything coming to him. I'll tell the police it was self-defence. He came at you, and you had no choice.'

Fury raged in my chest. How could he do something like that to my sister? He'd called me unstable. Dangerous. A threat to his family. But it wasn't me who was the threat. Maybe Tanya was right. Perhaps he did deserve to die. I was pretty sure I'd get away with it.

I clenched the broken branch so tightly, my knuckles turned white. Every fibre of my being was screaming at me to do it, to plunge the narrow point of the branch through his throat, to finish it here and now.

But I couldn't. I wasn't that person. I'd killed James Finch, and even though it had been his final wish, the decision to go through with it haunted me.

'I can't,' I said, relaxing my grip.

I've run through in my head a thousand times what happened next, but I still struggle to understand. It's a cliché, but it all happened so fast, and in the dark, confusion reigned.

I remember Tanya rushing towards me, stumbling on the uneven ground, and Damian grabbing her ankle. And then she was falling and twisting, trying to catch her balance. She squealed, a girlish cry of surprise, and I can still recall the sickening squelch of flesh.

Damian's eyes opened wide with shock and rolled back in his head as a hideous gurgling wheeze emanated from a gaping wound in his throat where the branch had punctured the skin and been pushed through cartilage by the weight of Tanya's body.

I stepped away with my back pressed against a tree, unable to take my eyes off the appalling scene, of Tanya's lifeless body slumped above Damian, the upper end of the branch protruding through her shoulder blade, her head hanging forwards and her long hair almost brushing the ground.

It was apparent Damian had died almost instantly, but Tanya was moaning pitifully. I should have helped her. Maybe I could have saved her, but I was frozen, barely able to breathe.

She lifted an arm vaguely in my direction as if trying to summon my help, but all I could do was clamp a hand across my mouth to silence my scream.

A single pearl of blood dripped from her shoulder and landed on Damian's shirt, spreading and staining it scarlet. Another followed. And another. Until his clothing was drenched and finally Tanya stopped moving.

I turned my head away and threw up in a patch of nettles. I'd seen some brutality in my life, but the sight of Tanya and Damian impaled together was the most awful thing I'd ever witnessed. I slumped to my knees with the vomit burning the back of my throat and nose and cried bitter tears.

In the distance, I heard the wail of sirens and moments later, the trees were awash with the pulse of blue lights. The wood came alive with the sound of shouting and voices, legs brushing through the undergrowth. And then someone was at my side, a comforting arm around my shoulder.

I let them lead me away, my mind numb. And I never once looked back.

58

Everything was a blur. Nothing seemed real. I was aware of sitting in the back of a police car with a blanket draped over my shoulders, and that Lucia was at my side, clutching my cold hands. But I felt nothing, my mind dull as though it was swaddled in cotton wool. I stared through the windscreen into the darkness, not thinking about anything at all. I guess I was in shock. Too numb and exhausted to think or feel.

'Are you okay?' Lucia's voice was soft and tender, laced with concern.

'What?'

'I'm so, so sorry.'

I looked at her blankly.

'I called the police as soon as I got home and found someone had broken in and that you were gone,' Lucia continued.

My memory transported me back to the house. Damian snatching my wrist. The smell of his aftershave as he clamped a hand over my mouth, dragging me through the garden, and into the back of a van. 'How did you know where to find me?'

'I tracked your phone.'

'You can do that?'

'There's an app,' she explained. 'I couldn't understand why your phone was showing up here with Damian's.'

I glanced out of the window at the pile of rubble. Fire crews had erected an array of powerful lamps to light it up, and firefighters in breathing apparatus were combing across the smoking ruins.

'This is all my fault,' I said. 'Everything that's happened, it's all because of me.'

'Don't say that.'

'It's true.'

I could see Lucia was fighting back tears, trying to keep it together.

'I didn't want him to get hurt, but he was so angry with me,' I said, willing her to understand.

'It's okay, you don't need to explain.' She gripped my hands tighter.

'I think I probably do.'

Lucia chewed her lip as her face crumpled, and tears finally flowed down her cheeks. She tried to speak, but no words came out of her mouth.

'He wanted you to believe that James had returned and abducted me,' I said. 'I thought he was going to leave me here to die.'

'Damian wouldn't do that.'

'But he came back with Tanya.'

'The woman who died? Who was she?' Lucia frowned.

'A journalist. She wanted to know all about James and me, although there wasn't anything to tell,' I lied. Maybe I'd explain to her one day but now wasn't the time.

Lucia looked deep into my eyes, trying to read me. 'I don't understand why he would be talking with a journalist.'

I took a deep breath, contemplating how much I should tell her. About Tanya blackmailing Damian? About his affair while Lucia was pregnant? About his fascination with my relationship with James? 'No, you're right, it doesn't make any sense,' I said. 'I guess we'll never know for sure.'

What was the point of adding to her misery? It was bad enough that her husband had abducted me and that he'd died a horrible death as I stood by and watched. The least I could do was leave her with the good memories without tainting them with the truth of who Damian really was.

'I guess not,' Lucia said, dabbing her cheek with the corner of a tissue.

'What did the police say about what happened?'

'Not much, only that there was an explosion at the house. They said you and that other woman had managed to escape with Damian, and that there was some kind of accident in the woods.'

I closed my eyes as the vivid memory of Damian and Tanya's deaths flashed across my mind.

'He left the gas on to destroy the house,' I said. I didn't add that it was to cover up evidence of two murders. How could I tell her Damian had planned on killing us?

'The police said Damian had been impaled on a branch.'

'It was an accident like they said.' Lucia would find out the details soon enough. She didn't need to hear them from me.

'I just can't get my head around it. Why would he bring you back here and put you through it all again? It's insane.'

I wanted to tell her that Damian felt threatened by me, that he saw his relationship with her disintegrating with every day I was in their house and the only way he could end it was by getting rid of me. 'He wanted me to move out and thought he could frighten me into agreeing,' I said. 'He thought I was a threat to your marriage.'

Lucia nodded as if to indicate she understood.

'But I wasn't the threat. Damian never loved you in the way you deserved.'

'What do you know about it?' Lucia's sharp tone startled me.

'Only what I saw,' I said.

'Stop.'

I shrugged. What was I supposed to say?

The passenger door opened, sucking in the chill air. A policeman with a weather-beaten face leaned in and smiled. 'How are you both doing?'

Neither of us replied.

'Let's get you out of here,' he said. 'We'll need to get you to the station to make a statement. Is there anybody you'd like us to contact to let them know what's going on?'

There was no one other than my sister, and she was right here next to me.

I shook my head. 'No,' I said. 'There's no one to contact.'

59

EIGHT MONTHS LATER

THERE WAS A TIME, not so long ago, when I wouldn't have been able to cope in a public space surrounded by people and the sound of children's excited laughter ringing in my ears. But with the sun beating down on my face, prickling my skin, I was at peace with the world for once in my life.

Sitting on a wooden bench at the edge of the playground, I watched April, so full of childhood innocence, clamber up the ladder and throw herself down the slide entirely without fear. She picked herself up at the bottom, ran around and climbed up again, lost in her own world of uncomplicated glee and happiness.

'I miss Dad.' Dylan was sitting next to me, playing a game on his phone.

'I know,' I said. He'd taken his father's death much harder than his sister. 'But you know he's always with you, don't you?'

'How?' he asked without looking up from his screen.

'In all the good memories you have of him, and he'll always be watching out for you, Dylan, because he loves you very much. You know that.'

'So why did he have to die? Why did he leave us?'

'Everybody dies sooner or later.'

'It's not fair.'

'No, it's not,' I said.

My phone chirruped in my hand. I glanced at the screen before answering. 'Hey, Sis,' I said, the anticipation of speaking with Lucia bringing an instant smile to my face.

'I was just... '

'Checking up on the kids? They're fine,' I said, glancing at Dylan with his floppy fringe hanging over his face. I hadn't really warmed to either of Lucia's children when I'd first moved in, but following Damian's death, we'd grown closer as we all learnt to cope. Now I thought of myself as a surrogate mum, filling the vacuum Damian had left. Dylan could be spiky with me sometimes, but I put that down to his age. April, on the other hand, was a bundle of joy who appreciated the female company.

'Yeah, sorry,' Lucia said. She sounded breathless as if she was out and in a hurry. I could hear traffic in the background and the bustle of people. 'I used to hate it when Damian called me all the time.'

I detected the slight catch in her voice when she mentioned Damian's name.

'It's fine,' I reassured her. Besides, I was getting used to the regular calls, especially as I was looking after the kids during the summer holidays. Lucia said Damian used to call her five or six times a day to check up on her. How could anyone not think that was weird?

'I do trust you, it's just that. . . Anyway, where are you?'

'We're at the park having a lovely time.' I looked up, expecting to see April on the slide.

'Mara?'

My blood ran cold as I scanned the playground left to right, and back again. I couldn't see April anywhere. I jumped up, standing on tiptoes, craning my neck.

Shit.

I tried to push my fears away as their dark fingers reached inside my head. I didn't want to think about her being bundled into the back of a van, so terrified she couldn't even scream.

'Mara?' Lucia's voice sounded more urgent. But I didn't know what to say.

'Boo!' Thin arms wrapped around my legs and April nearly bowled me over as she jumped at me from behind.

My heart almost thumped out of my chest. 'April, you little monkey,' I screamed, grabbing her with my free hand and tickling her ribs.

She collapsed in a heap of giggles and wriggled away.

'Is everything okay?' Lucia asked.

'Yeah, it's fine,' I laughed. 'Just your daughter giving me the run-around as usual.'

'Oh.' Lucia sounded worried.

'It's okay. I'm going to let them have five more minutes, and we'll make our way back. What time are you home?'

'I'll try to get the earlier train,' Lucia said.

'That would be nice.'

'I'll see you later then.'

April skipped most of the way home, her sweaty hand in mine, chattering incessantly while Dylan moped along ten metres behind, his head down and his attention totally focused on his phone. The poor boy was still hurting, but I was confident he'd adapt in time and eventually accept his father was gone. If I'd learnt anything at all, it was that kids are resilient like that.

That afternoon I cooked bolognese while Dylan and April played upstairs. I chopped onions and mushrooms in Lucia's kitchen picturing myself as a dutiful housewife. I'd been thrilled when Lucia had asked me if I would look after the children during the long summer holidays. It was a sign she trusted me, and I even began to imagine what it might be like to have children of my own one day. Although maybe not for a few years yet. There was still so much I wanted to see and do.

When I heard the front door open and bang closed, I turned on a pan of water for the pasta and went to greet Lucia in the hallway.

'How was your day?' I asked, kissing her lightly on the cheek as she kicked off her shoes.

'You know, the usual,' she replied with a sigh.

She'd been seeing a bereavement counsellor since Damian's death and the difference in her mood in the last few months was marked. The dark depression that had clouded her days in the first weeks had gradually lifted. She was learning to live again, rebuilding her life on her own with the children.

She'd found it hard to come to terms, not only with Damian's death but with accepting what he'd done, snatching me from the house and making me relive the horrors of my first abduction. I guess it's hard when the person you thought you knew turns out to be hiding behind a veneer of normality. I don't think he was evil, any more than I thought James Finch was evil. They were flawed, without doubt, and victims of their need to control and coerce others, but it's oversimplifying it to call them monsters. There were reasons for their actions, and in Damian's case, I just happened to be the catalyst that pushed him over the edge when he thought I was threatening to destroy his family and the dominion he held over Lucia.

Nobody really had an answer for James Finch's behaviour or an explanation for why he chose to abduct me that night in the summer of 2000. All I know is that he wanted someone to love and to possess, and I fitted his ideal. Before he found me, he was described by the few people who knew him as a loner and an oddball, a man with an unhealthily close relationship with his mother, with whom he'd lived until her death shortly before my abduction. I rarely thought about him now. He'd become a footnote in a period of my life I'd mothballed as I looked to the future.

'Dinner won't be long.'

'Great, what are we having?' Lucia breezed into the kitchen, lifted the lid on the pan of bolognese and sniffed.

'It's nothing special,' I said.

'It smells delicious.'

We ate like a real family sitting around the kitchen table, the kids squabbling while Lucia filled me in on a problematic account she'd been trying to manage. I didn't follow most of what she was telling me, but I smiled and nodded in all the right places, just happy to be in her company and making up for lost time.

'But enough about me. How was your day?'

'Great,' I said, with a genuine smile. 'I love hanging out with the children.'

Dylan flicked his sister's earlobe, sparking April into a rage of tears and anger. She dropped her fork and punched him on the arm.

'Owwwwww!' he yelled, totally overreacting.

'Stop it! Both of you!' Lucia shouted at them. 'God, I hope they weren't like this the whole day.'

'No, they've been perfectly good for me.'

When we'd all finished eating, I loaded the dishwasher.

'Let me help,' Lucia said, scooping a dirty pan off the hob.

'Don't be silly. You've been at work all day.'

'Are you sure?'

'Of course. Go and sit down. Take the weight off.'

'You really are an angel. How did I ever cope without you?' Lucia said, wrapping her arms around my shoulder and planting a kiss on my head.

'You never had a choice.'

I set the dishwasher to run on an eco wash, while Lucia retired to the lounge with a glass of wine. Then I grabbed my jacket from the hall and slipped on my sandals.

'Right, I'll be off,' I said, poking my head around the lounge door.

Lucia stuck out her bottom lip. 'Do you really have to go? I hate you not being here.'

'Yes, you know I do,' I said, rolling my eyes. 'We've been through this. I'll be here first thing for the kids.'

'The bed in your room's still made up. You could stay the night.'

The offer was tempting, just like it was every time she suggested it. But I'd made the break, and we'd both agreed it was for the best that I moved out.

'I can't. I have plans,' I said.

Lucia sat up, suddenly interested. 'What plans?'

'I have a date if you must know.'

Lucia's eyes opened as wide as saucers. 'A date? With who?'

'Nobody you know,' I said, my cheeks flushing.

'Mara,' she said, in a stern voice that reminded me of Mum. 'Spill.'

'He's just some guy who moved into the flat downstairs. He's asked me to go for a drink with him. That's all.'

'Do you know anything about him?' Lucia frowned.

'It's only a date.'

'Well, be careful. And text me when you get in.'

'Yes, Mum,' I shouted over my shoulder as I walked out and pulled the front door closed behind me.

It was still light outside, and the air remained thick with the warmth of the setting sun. I slung my jacket over my shoulder and turned out of the garden gate, heading towards my flat.

It was only a simple place. No more than a bedroom with a small kitchen and bathroom in a recently converted block. But it already felt like home and the first step towards a new life. I had so many things I wanted to experience, but living on my own and learning how to stand on my own two feet was an absolute priority, especially after the police had concluded their investigation into the deaths of James, Damian and Tanya.

They'd exhumed James' body from the spot where our vegetable patch used to be before the explosion. I told the police everything, about helping him take an overdose and slipping a plastic bag over his head to end his life as he'd asked me to do. A post mortem confirmed everything I'd told them about the cancer that had ravaged his body and his brain, and after a few anxious weeks, they decided it wouldn't be in the public interest to pursue charges against me.

They also accepted my account of how Damian and Tanya had died, that it had been a tragic accident while Tanya and I were trying to defend ourselves. A death by misadventure, a coroner concluded.

I never told Lucia about Damian's affair. What was the point? She'd suffered enough already without reopening wounds. He'd paid the ultimate price, and as far as I was concerned, he could take his secrets with him to the grave.

Tanya's paper ran her obituary on their front page, describing her as a hero who'd died in the pursuit of the highest journalistic values, probing for the truth, which brought a wry smile to my face. She'd been probing for tittle-tattle, a salacious story about my sexual relationship with James. It hardly put her in line for a Pulitzer Prize.

I'd almost made it to the end of the road, happier than I could ever remember feeling, when I saw him, on the opposite side of the street, loitering behind a couple of parked cars, watching me.

I froze with my heart pounding and my legs weak, panic tightening my chest.

But it wasn't him. Just some guy with a shock of black, curly hair. The same loping gait. Except he was several pounds heavier than James and broader across the shoulders. I breathed in through my nose and exhaled for ten seconds, following the exercises my therapist had given me to control my anxiety. I used to see James Finch in every passing stranger, but slowly, with time, I'd noticed him less and less. I considered it a sign that I was beginning to heal. It gave me hope for the future. I was done with living in his shadow. It was time to start living for me.

I took a tentative step forwards, concentrating on putting one foot in front of the other, picking up speed, my good mood ruined. I wondered about changing my name, letting my hair grow long, dying it black. Erasing all memories of the person I used to be. A totally new beginning.

But that would be like admitting James had won, and I was stronger than that.

No, it was time to spread my wings, feel the wind in my hair and finally learn to fly.

ACKNOWLEDGMENTS

The inspiration for His Wife's Sister came after reading the horrific, truth life stories of kidnap and abduction that have happened all around the world. Stories like those of Natascha Kampusch, the Austrian woman who was abducted in Austria on her way to school and held captive in a cellar for more than 3,000 days.

Natascha's story is well-documented, but what fascinated me was what happens to these girls (and it is usually girls and young women) when they are freed and returned home. I could only imagine their experiences must impact on their lives and their families for years to come.

But those stories are rarely, if ever told.

And so an idea formed in my head, and Mara and Lucia were born. Two women, separated as young girls, when the younger sister is abducted and held captive against her will, and reunited after nineteen years.

How would they cope with being reunited? What impact would it have on their family? And would it really be possible to return to any kind of normality in the aftermath of a crime so despicable?

The result is His Wife's Sister, my second psychological thriller.

www.ingramcontent.com/pod-product-compliance
Lightning Source LLC
Chambersburg PA
CBHW021623030826
48979CB00036B/1916/J

* 9 7 8 1 9 1 6 1 2 9 9 7 9 *